MEL BEEBY
AGENT ANGEL

the
heavenly
collection

THREE AMAZING
MISSIONS
IN ONE BOOK!

Look out for more missions from

MEL BEEBY
AGENT ANGEL

Winging It

Losing the Plot

Flying High

Calling the Shots

Fogging Over

Fighting Fit

Making Waves

Budding Star

Keeping it Real

www.agentangel.co.uk

MEL BEEBY
AGENT ANGEL

the heavenly collection

winging
it

losing
the plot

flying
high

ANNIE DALTON

HarperCollins *Children's Books*

Winging It first published in Great Britain by Collins 2001
Losing the Plot first published in Great Britain by Collins 2001
Flying High first published in Great Britain by Collins 2001

First published in this three-in-one edition by Collins 2002
This edition published by HarperCollins *Children's Books* in 2006

HarperCollins *Children's Books* is a division of HarperCollins*Publishers* Ltd
77-85 Fulham Palace Road, Hammersmith
London W6 8JB

The HarperCollins website address is
www.harpercollinschildrensbooks.co.uk

1

Text copyright © Annie Dalton 2001

ISBN-13   978 0 00 723307 6
ISBN-10   0 00 723307 8

The author asserts the moral right to be
identified as the author of the work.

Printed and bound in England by
Clays Ltd, St Ives plc

winging
it

*With love to my three favourite angels, Anna, Reuben
(the original DJ Sweetpea) and Maria, whose
sparklingly fresh ideas and stern criticism brought Mel
and her angel mates to life*

CHAPTER ONE

I hadn't exactly planned on becoming an angel. But then I hadn't planned on dying young either. Well, you don't, do you?

If I'd thought about it, I'd have said *that* kind of thing was strictly for Venetia Rossetti. Venetia was a big hit with all the teachers at my school and WAY more suitable angel material than yours truly.

But there you go. Venetia's still on Planet Earth, writing her little poems about rain and violets. And I'm, well – not!

Know what I thought, when I got knocked down?

Now I'll never get the chance to prove Miss Rowntree wrong!

See what I mean? My last moments on Earth and that's all I could come up with. I am SO not poetic.

I wouldn't want you to get the idea I was a totally bad person. I didn't torture small animals, or go raving about our estate, scaring old ladies. I just couldn't get psyched up about school stuff, like exams or team games, or figuring out what I was going to do when I grew up (though as it turns out, I didn't really need to worry about that).

Shortly before I died, Miss Rowntree caught me flipping through a magazine in class. Honestly, you'd think I'd committed a major crime! "When will you realise there is more to life than makeovers, Melanie?" she yelled.

But I do, Miss Rowntree, I do, I thought. There's watching MTV. Hanging out with my mates. Ooh, and flirting with boys. And most sacred of all, yahoo! SHOPPING!

But I didn't share these thoughts with my teacher. I might be a bimbo but I'm a very *polite* bimbo. Whereas Miss Rowntree showed me no respect whatsoever. "Melanie Beeby, you are just an airhead with attitude," she snapped at me another time.

But on the last day of term, she said something so sarcastic, I get the chills just thinking of it.

"School is irrelevant to you, isn't it, Melanie?" she said in a scornful voice. "You're just killing time until you're spotted by a talent scout and get signed up as a TV presenter."

I nearly fell off my chair. Did Miss Rowntree have some creepy teacher's ESP? Not even my best friends knew my secret fantasy! It was like she'd deliberately set out to humiliate me, basically telling me in front of the whole class that my sad little daydream would never come true.

I didn't let her see she'd got to me, obviously. I just did my bored shrug, and spent the rest of her lesson peeling varnish off my nails.

But the minute I got home, I bawled my eyes out. First I cried all over Mum. Then Des, my step-dad, came in and I had to choke out my story all over again.

"Silly old battle-axe," Des said. "What does she know!"

"Yeah, she's a ole battle-axe," said my five-year-old sister fiercely.

Actually my teacher is depressingly glamorous. But if my family wanted to picture her as a bitter old bat with bristles on her chin, who was I to disagree?

As it happened, Miss Rowntree's spiteful put-down was the very last thing she said to me, because next day it was the start of the summer holidays.

I'd got an incredibly significant birthday coming up, my thirteenth, so I had some *serious* celebrating to do. My star sign is Cancer and if I say so myself, it fits me like a glove. Shy on the outside, with a squishy caramel centre, that's me.

Sometimes I wonder what I'd have done, if I'd genuinely understood I only had a few precious days left on Earth. Would I have appeared on TV, pleading with world leaders to throw down their weapons and stop all those stupid wars?

But as it turned out, my last days were just enjoyably average. And to be completely honest with you, all I cared about was that I was finally becoming a big bad teenager at last.

The day before my birthday, Des drove me and my two best mates to the local multiplex, to see a cool film with Will Smith in it, followed by a complete pig-out at Macdonalds. My actual birthday was purely family, which was nice but slightly boring – you know how it is. Secretly I'd have preferred to fast-forward to the *next* day, when I was meeting up with my mates for a major shopping spree. But finally it was all over for another year.

When I came to bed, my little sister Jade did something really sweet. She sat up in her sleep and said, "You're my best sister in the whole universe."

I said, "I'm your only sister, you nutcase." And without ever dreaming this was my last night on Earth, I fell into a deep peaceful sleep.

And all the time, like summer birds collecting on telephone wires, angels were gathering around me.

I didn't realise this then, but no-one is allowed to die alone. Ever. Some people see their guardian angels, just before they leave their bodies. I didn't. I didn't see much actually. My last few seconds on Earth went something like this.

One minute I'm crossing the road, humming a tune from a Jewel CD, totally fixated on the stuff I'm going to buy with my birthday money, then – BAM – it's over! Some sad kid in a stolen car snuffed me out. Just like that.

No, I didn't look down and see myself nee-nawing along in the ambulance. And as far as I remember, I didn't whoosh down a long bright tunnel and have a meaningful chat with some guy in robes either. I was just – GONE.

Don't get me wrong. That tunnel stuff could have happened. I could have blanked it out. But here's what I do remember, OK?

I remember a hush which might have gone on for days or hours. I went extremely vague about time at that point. This hush wasn't like normal silence, by the way. You could hear music in it. Far-off music, which throbbed on and on without stopping, like a beautiful humming-top. It was the most blissful sound I'd ever heard.

I totally had to know where it was coming from, so I floated out past glittering stars and planets, passing so close it took my breath away.

Then without any warning, my personal soundtrack was switched back on and – BANG! I was in brilliant sunlight, walking towards a pair of swanky gates with a cool little angel logo on them.

And there, in letters so large and round that even my little sister couldn't mistake them, was the most surprising sign I'd ever seen in my life.

The Angel Academy

CHAPTER TWO

Apparently, when some people arrive on The Other Side, as my Great Nan used to call it, they take one look and go, "Oh, hello, I must have died and gone to heaven!"

But I was only thirteen. It didn't occur to me I was dead.

What's going on? I panicked. Why am I hanging around outside this snobby school? Big snobby school, to be strictly accurate. Kids of all ages were crowding through the gates.

Hang on, Mel, I thought. This can't be right. It's the summer holidays.

But it didn't *feel* like the holidays. There was a

definite first-day-of-term zing in the air. All the kids had that "Yippee! Can't wait to see my mates!" look about them.

It was like being in a dream. The kind where you forget really vital personal info. For instance, I totally couldn't remember what I'd been doing just before my little trip around the galaxy (which I was rather carefully trying not to think about).

I *could* remember the Jewel song. Also an alarmingly big bang. Perhaps I'd been in some kind of accident, and I was concussed? That would explain why I felt so out of it.

I hung about uneasily as kids streamed past me in their gorgeous designer colours. For some reason, my eyes kept going back to that little logo on the gate. At first it struck me as just your basic logo. Like that Puma symbol, or whatever. Then I realised it was incredibly beautiful. And it wasn't that I *couldn't* stop looking – more like I didn't *want* to.

As I stared, hypnotised, at this dazzling thing, the little angel figure began to grow sharper and brighter… and suddenly it was shooting out huge starry rays like a Roman Candle.

I shut my eyes *fast*, telling myself it was purely an optical illusion. And when I opened them again, the logo was safely back to normal. Boy, Melanie, that must have been some bang on the head, I told myself.

I still didn't have a clue what to do. But I was starting to feel pretty stupid, hanging around like a spare part. It can't hurt to have a little peek, I thought. I'll just see what's on the other side of these gates, and if I don't like it, I can come straight back out.

I began to drift casually towards the gates with the others, hoping I didn't look as lost and panicky as I felt.

All the other kids seemed really chilled, kidding about and flirting, which I found quite reassuring. I remember thinking that if I HAD been worried about it being a school for actual angels (which obviously I wasn't), the flirting would definitely have put my mind at rest. Also their clothes, which were totally up to the minute. There wasn't a long white nightie in sight.

I *did* notice that everyone's cool fleeces and other stuff had that same little angel logo. Imagine that, Mel, I thought. A designer tag you don't know about!

One of the girls had this big throaty laugh, which started down in her boots. She was a real daddy-long-legs, like me. Everything about her zinged with energy: her springy black hair, her tough-girl walk.

I sneakily attached myself to her, trying to act like I just happened to be going the same way. But on the other side of the gates, I nearly blew my street cred once and for all.

I ought to explain that my old school was pretty much your standard comprehensive hell-hole. But this was practically a *palace*, with gorgeous gardens and domes and spires.

Yeah, but it's still school, I thought darkly.

We were hurrying along a shady walkway. You could see it was really ancient. The stone slabs had actual hollows worn into them by centuries of passing feet. One of my shoes accidentally slipped into a shiny long-ago footprint, and a shiver went through me. It fitted *exactly*.

The girl gave me a funny look. "Angel vibes," she said. "You get used to them."

But I didn't really register what she said because suddenly I'd got the strangest feeling.

"Do I know you, or something?" I blurted.

The girl froze in her tracks.

Now look what you've done, I scolded myself. She's going to have you down as some needy little groupie.

But she was staring at me with a stunned expression. "Weird," she whispered. "I was just thinking the same thing." She took a big breath. "I'm Lola."

"I'm Melanie," I whispered back.

Our eyes met for about a split second, and it was like a total replay of my shivery footprint moment. We both quickly looked away again and walked on, side by side.

This is going to sound bizarre, so please don't ask me to explain it. But somewhere inside, I just knew Lola was the friend I'd waited for my whole life.

It wasn't how she looked (although her clothes were lush). It was more like I already knew her really well. And I got the definite feeling she felt the same way. We kept giving each other startled little glances as we hurried along. Like, what is going on?

Melanie, get a grip, I told myself. Do you seriously imagine a girl this cool will want to hang out with you?

By this time, there was so much happening inside my head that I'd split into at least three or four Mels. First, I'm trying not to dwell too closely on what I'm doing here. Second, I've just run into a total stranger who seems like she's my all-time best buddy. Third, we are speeding through these school grounds which are getting more amazing by the minute. And I mean AMAZING! It was all I could do not to squeal like a little kid.

Obviously I still wasn't too impressed to find myself hanging around some strange school in the holidays. But I was starting to see how the right person just might get something out of a set-up like this.

At first, I thought I'd gate-crashed one of those really fogey institutions. The ones that call homework "prep" and have their own weird little school song on speech days. But parts of the Academy were incredibly futuristic. Plus they had all this water everywhere – trickling along little channels and into pools, bubbling out of fountains. It sounded wonderful, like some kind of dreamy, delicate music.

We even passed a spiral staircase which wound around a real waterfall. I'd never seen anything so lovely as those shining stairs, twisting and turning through crowds of tiny glowing rainbows. It was magic.

But there was no time to admire the scenery. The kids were practically running by this time. We seemed to be heading rapidly for some impressive wooden doors. Carved into them was the same little angel logo I kept seeing everywhere.

And at that point I went into a full-scale panic attack.

If I go in there, something's going to happen, I thought. Something which will change me for ever.

But before I could make a run for it, I was swept helplessly through the doors into a vast sunlit hall.

Inside, the hall was more like a huge theatre, with tiers and tiers of seats. High over our heads was a dome of stained glass. Sunlight poured through the glass, spilling extraordinary colours everywhere.

There was a stage, a very grand one. Right across the back wall was an outsized TV screen, the kind you get at pop concerts, with the words WELCOME BACK in glowing letters.

Teachers roamed up and down the aisles. Their fluttering, deep-dyed robes made them look more like birds than people. This place got more unbelievable every minute! But I couldn't think about that right now, because I'd just registered an extremely unpleasant fact.

There wasn't an empty seat anywhere.

Oh, great start, Melanie, I thought. Trust you to be the one person left standing in this weird scary hall.

Then I saw Lola waving frantically. She'd actually saved me a place! I squeezed on to the bench beside her. A split second later, a honey-coloured boy in cut-offs slid into the non-existent space beside me. "You think I'm late," he whispered, "but five minutes ago I was surfing."

Liar, I thought. It was true drops of water were running off his tiny dreads, but he'd probably just washed his hair or something.

Suddenly someone strode to the front of the stage. And without him yelling at us or anything, everyone went quiet.

"Good morning, school," said the headmaster. "First, a special welcome to those of you who have just arrived. If you have any problems, don't hesitate to come and talk to me."

Lola rolled her eyes. "Yeah, like he's ever here." Then I think she was worried she'd given me the wrong impression, because she hissed, "It's not his fault. The Agency takes up practically all Michael's time these days."

She calls the headmaster Michael! I thought. How hippie-dippie is that!

Michael was nowhere near as imposing as the

teachers in their robes. He wore a suit he had apparently slept in, giving the impression he'd just flown in on some long-haul flight. You could tell he was completely shattered.

Then I saw him in close-up, on the TV screen, and had another fit of my mysterious shivers. Michael had the loveliest face I'd ever seen.

It was also totally terrifying.

Of course, it should have been obvious to anyone with a functioning brain cell that this was NOT your average headmaster. But I'd never met an archangel before.

Plus, I can't STAND school assemblies. They make me feel as if I can't breathe. I have to tune them out or I'd scream with boredom.

I caught major yawn-words like "team work", and even (yikes!) "responsibility", and carried on scrutinising my split ends. But now and then, a more worrying word caught my attention. Michael used it more than any person I'd ever known. After a while it started getting to me like a dripping tap. Angel tradition. Angel skills. Angel Handbook. Angel angel angel.

Something deeply weird is going on here, Melanie, I told myself. Better check it out. I sneaked a look at Lola. She immediately pulled a silly face.

No way, I thought. Far too normal.

I cautiously scanned the hall. It was true all these kids had an unusual *glow*. But that didn't mean it was a *supernatural*-type glow. Probably their parents made them eat their greens and run around out of doors, you know, constantly.

Just one final itty bitty check. Twisting round in my seat, I gave the kids at the back of the hall a nervous once-over.

Melanie, I know this feels scary, I said to myself, but try to answer truthfully. Do any of these kids look like, erm, angels to you?

I had no idea. What did angels look like, assuming they didn't come with wings and halos like the one on our Christmas tree?

Oh-oh, I thought in a sudden panic. *They'd look like her!*

Behind me was the most angelic-looking being I'd seen since Venetia Rossetti. She had pale, almost silver-blonde hair, with cute little flowery slides fastened in it, and skin so pure and peachy, it looked totally unused.

The girl caught me staring and nudged the spookily identical boy beside her.

I quickly turned round.

It is! It's an angel school, I thought. That rosy glow isn't vitamins and fresh air. It's heavenly *radiance*!

A terrifying question slid into my head. Why was I hanging out with some bunch of angels? Unless...

Somewhere far away, I heard myself squeak with alarm.

100% brain freeze! Did that mean I was an angel too?

Like, did that mean I was...

CHAPTER THREE

At this point I had two major headaches.

Headache number 1: I am unexpectedly dead.

Headache number 2: I have accidentally infiltrated an angel school.

There was also a potential third headache which I refused to think about. The idea of me being an actual angel was just a *joke*!

Relax, Mel, I told myself. They mixed you up with one of the real angels on the way over. You'd better tell somebody.

But what will I say? I panicked. I couldn't exactly waltz up to someone and say, "Erm – anyone reported a missing angel?" I mean, suppose I'd broken some really heavy cosmic law just by being here?

I was in such a state, I completely didn't notice Michael's pep-talk finishing. A woman in purple had started calling out names from a sheet. The hall emptied around me, as kids jumped out of their seats and went to join their teachers.

"Reuben Bird," said the woman. The skinny boy beside me sprang off the bench and ran down to the front. "Lola Sanchez."

"That's me!" cried Lola. A ripple of laughter went through the hall, but Lola didn't seem a bit embarrassed. She went to stand beside Reuben, beaming.

"Flora Devere, Ferdy Devere. Amber Overwood."

Amber bounded to the front, red-gold plaits whipping madly around her head. The twins sauntered out, like glamorous angel supermodels.

I could feel my palms getting sweaty. Don't say she called my name when I wasn't listening, I prayed.

Hold on, Melanie, I thought suddenly. You're carrying on as if you CHOSE to come here!

I blinked with surprise. So I was. Why was that? It's not like I ever saw the point of normal school. Why in the world would I want to go to some goody-goody Angel Academy? Not to mention that I'm not an angel, I reminded myself.

Then something eerie happened.

The woman with the list looked up and smiled at me as if she'd known I was there all along. "And finally, Melanie Beeby. Welcome to the Academy, Melanie. We all hope you have a happy and productive time here," she said.

My knees went to jelly. They'd got my name on their heavenly list!

They actually *believed* I was an angel! You'd think real angels would recognise an undercover human when they saw one. But she seemed totally taken in. When I didn't move from my seat, she gave me another encouraging smile, presumably thinking I had stage fright.

OK, Mel, I thought. Here's your big chance to own up.

"Oops, sorry, Miss. I was miles away," I muttered. And coward that I am, I floated to the front on my jelly legs.

"I knew it," Lola burbled. "The minute I saw you, I KNEW we were going to be in the same class. That's Mr Allbright over there. The guy in the hat. Isn't he a duck?"

With his tufty hair and beaky nose, our teacher did look amazingly like a duck. A sweet, absent-minded little duck. "Did you have to put that duck idea in my head?" I hissed. "I'm going to die laughing every time I look at him."

I knew it was dumb, to try and make Lola like me when I was only passing through. But I couldn't help it somehow.

"I only meant he's cute," Lola was saying. Then she slid her eyes in Mr Allbright's direction and collapsed in hysterics. "Omigosh," she squeaked. "He really *does* look like a duck!"

By this time, cute Mr Allbright was heading briskly out of the hall. Our class started to follow him. Not knowing what else to do, I followed him too.

"Are you OK?" Lola asked, as we walked across the school campus. "Because back in the hall, I thought you didn't look OK."

She looked so concerned, I was tempted to tell her everything. But until I'd worked out what I was going to do about this bizarre angel situation, I couldn't take the risk.

"The thing is," I said, choosing my words carefully, "the actual thing is, I can't quite get my head round this angel stuff." I wasn't exactly lying.

But I still felt like a total fraud.

Lola groaned. "I forgot. You only just got here, poor thing. Did you whizz down a tunnel? I didn't get a sniff of a tunnel. I felt totally cheated."

"Uh-uh," I said. "No tunnel. But I heard some really cosmic sounds."

"Me too!" cried Amber, her eyes sparkling. "Isn't it amazing how you don't even feel scared?"

"It is actually," I agreed. I was quite impressed at myself for being able to talk about my death in such a mature way. Plus, I couldn't help noticing Amber had a tiny blue jewel in the middle of her forehead. I wondered if it was her own personal jewel, or some kind of funky angel accessory, and if so, where you got them.

Don't be silly, Mel, I told myself. You're not staying, remember.

We were passing a stunningly beautiful glass building. Cloud reflections skittered over its walls like playful lambs.

I stared up at the sky. There wasn't a cloud to be seen anywhere.

I gawped back at the building, completely confused. "How do they DO that?" I breathed.

"I have no idea," admitted Lola.

"Hey," said Amber brightly. "I hope we're all staying in the same dorm!"

I stared at her. "No-one told me this was *boarding* school?"

Lola gave me a funny little smile. "Well, you can't exactly go back home at nights, Melanie."

Amber giggled. "Ooh, Lola, you're so mean! Poor Mel. She just needs time to adjust."

I forced a smile. Amber was probably a genuinely sweet person, but I got the feeling that hanging out with her could do some serious damage to a person's tooth enamel.

The class came to a standstill in a beautiful little courtyard, full of tropical plants. Sand and seaweed were scattered around as if left behind by the tide. A salty breeze blew my hair into tangles.

I noticed hammocks strung between the palm trees, their canvas bleached by the sun. Then I gave a squeak of surprise.

"Is that the sea over there?" I whispered to Lola. "Is that the *beach*?"

This school is something else, I thought. It almost made me wish I was attending the Academy for real, instead of just faking it while I figured out my next move.

"That's the great thing about this city," Lola was saying.

It had never occurred to me that Heaven might be by the sea. And I'd definitely NEVER imagined cities.

Lola hoisted herself into a hammock. "It's great to be back," she said.

Some of the other kids grabbed hammocks too. Flora and Ferdy casually took up advanced yoga poses under a palm tree.

I couldn't believe the way Mr Allbright let everyone mess around like this. Poor lamb, I thought. He's got "pushover" written all over him.

Our teacher gave me an absent-minded smile. For a nasty moment I thought he'd actually read my mind. Then I decided Mr Allbright was just enjoying some private teacher-type joke.

"Right," he said, tugging at his ear. "You'll all be wanting to go and settle into your dormitories, so this is just an introductory session—"

I put up my hand, totally confused. "Erm," I said. "I thought we were going to our form room."

"You thought right," said Mr Allbright. "And as you see, here we are." He waved his hand at the little courtyard.

Suddenly I knew exactly how Alice felt when she fell down that rabbit hole.

"But this is outdoors!" I said.

"Absolutely," Mr Allbright agreed warmly. "I can't stand being cooped up, can you? As I was saying, lessons don't start until the day after tomorrow, so we'll keep this session short and sweet."

I wasn't going to risk a hammock in case I fell out in front of everyone. So I plonked myself on the sand and sat moodily arranging shells into patterns, while Mr Allbright talked us through our timetable. Yawn yawn yawn, I thought.

Amber nudged me. "Cheer up," she whispered. "After your first term you can choose a special subject."

Ooh, goody, I thought sarcastically.

Mr Allbright started dishing out book lists. I glanced at mine and nearly fainted. EEK! You're out of your depth here, babe, I thought.

"Oh, before you go," said Mr Allbright. "I've been asked to remind everyone about this term's HALO awards."

He tugged his ear again. "I'm not a fan of awards in general," he confessed. "But the HALO is different. It isn't about individual glory. It's about being a link in a divine chain, a valuable member of a team. I hope that this term I'll see at least one HALO go to someone in this class."

He started going on about how HALO work had to be done outside school hours (yeah, right!). But I had totally tuned out. One of my least favourite words in the dictionary had to be "TEAM". Unlike some people, I was proud to be a unique individual, and I wasn't about to become some boring link in anyone's divine chain, thanks very much! I mean, HALO awards, perleaze!

Twenty-four-hour brainache might be some people's idea of heaven, but it wasn't mine. Get out, Mel, I told myself. Get out now. You are not angel material and angel school is not for you. Just because you've died, doesn't mean people can push you around.

This decision was such a relief, I can't tell you.

Now all I had to do was tell Mr Allbright.

CHAPTER FOUR

Even as a little kid, I had this ability to wriggle out of tricky situations. Miss Rowntree said I was a natural escape artist. She said every time I'm faced with a situation which I find personally threatening, I slither out of it faster than Houdini in a buttered bikini.

So it took me twenty seconds to figure out how to get out of being an angel. This was my plan. On our first proper day of lessons, I'd make sure Mr Allbright saw me slaving away at my angel science or whatever. By lunchtime I'd be visibly stressing out (pale, sniffing back tears, etcetera).

Then I'd ask if I could speak to him in private. Through choking sobs, I'd tell Mr Allbright I was out of my depth. The Academy was WAY too advanced for a girl like me, and I'd never keep up with the others in a million years. Finally, I'd do that Bambi thing with my eyes and I'd be home and dry. By the time they figured out I was never an angel in the first place, I'd be gone!!

In my mind, I was already off the hook. I don't know about you, but relief makes me really chatty.

"So, what do you guys do after school?" I said.

"Oh, stuff," said Lola vaguely. "Shopping."

Yeah right, I thought. Shopping in Heaven!

Amber's eyes misted over "Oh, Melanie," she said. "I don't even know where to start. You are going to have the best time."

I took a nice calming breath. OK, so Amber was just a little too sweet. But I could put up with her for forty-eight hours.

"That's all for now, kids," beamed Mr Allbright. "I look forward to meeting you again, the day after tomorrow."

Lola stuck up her hand. "Sir," she said. "Shouldn't you tell us where we're staying this term?"

Our teacher looked astounded. "Did I forget to do that?"

"Yes, sir!" everyone yelled.

Mr Allbright hastily produced yet another list and reeled off names. I couldn't help feeling a happy little buzz when I found out I was staying in Lola's dorm.

Amber looked wistful. "I'll say goodbye then."

Everyone started moving off. "Hope we run into you soon, Melanie!" called one of the girls.

"Very, very soon," agreed her friend.

They looked as innocent as newborn babes, yet I had the definite feeling they were up to something.

"Ignore them," said Lola. "So do you want to go straight to our dorm, or what?"

I'd been dying for the moment when Lola and me could start swapping life stories. And it turned out she felt exactly the same! We drifted towards the dorms, talking our heads off. I got totally over-excited when I discovered Lola was from the twenty-second century!

"That is SO amazing!" I said. "You were born more than a hundred years after me, but here it's like we're the same age!"

"This place takes getting used to," Lola agreed. "People from different times mixed up together. That's why they have a dress code."

I was stunned. All this groovy gear I'd been seeing everywhere was Angel Academy *uniform*!

"I'll take you into town tomorrow to get yours," Lola suggested. "We'll go right after your – er..." Her voice trailed off.

"After my what?"

For some reason, Lola had gone really red. "Who knows!" she giggled. "Sometimes even I don't know what I'm talking about."

"Oh, me too," I said sympathetically. And to show Lola I totally understood, I started chattering on about the time I practically got expelled for lopping six inches off my school skirt.

All at once Amber came dashing back, bubbling with excitement. "Guess what! I went to sign up for the history club. And it's filling up really fast. So if either of you is interested, you should get down to the library right away."

"Oh, thanks, Amber," I said, trying to keep a straight face.

She blushed. "It's no trouble. I missed some brilliant opportunities when I first got here, just because I didn't know they were available. Anyway, got to go. Bye!" She sped away, plaits bouncing.

Lola grabbed my hand. To my astonishment, she

was shaking. "Mel, is it OK if we check out the dormitory later?"

"Sure," I said, surprised.

"Come on, the library's back there!" Lola launched herself into an impressive sprint.

I tore after her, totally baffled. Lola couldn't be getting this psyched about some geeky school club, could she?

Apparently she could. "I'm so glad Amber told us," she gasped out. "I am desperate to join this club. I couldn't even get on the waiting list last term."

"You're really that crazy about history?"

Lola looked amazed. "Aren't you?"

"I think I'd rather eat my own head," I said truthfully.

The library turned out to be the magical glass building I'd seen earlier. Instead of rushing in to sign up, Lola dithered outside. "I won't pressure you if history's not your thing," she said. "Wait here if you like."

I shrugged. "OK."

To my surprise Lola looked incredibly fed up. She disappeared through the revolving doors. Next minute she was back, eyes blazing. "I can't believe it!" she fumed. "When I saw you, I thought, that girl is my soul buddy."

"I thought that too," I said nervously.

Lola stamped her foot. "Then why aren't you jumping up and down at the idea of travelling through time?"

I gasped. "They do *time-travel* in this club?"

"Of course," said Lola. "Did you think we'd just learn a bunch of dates?"

"Well – yes," I admitted.

We both burst out laughing. At that moment I made up my mind. "Erm, Lola," I stammered. "I've got to tell you something—"

"Yikes!" shrieked Lola, ruining my big confession. "Look at that queue! Let's get inside!" She dragged me in through the revolving doors.

There are certain words which make me lose all will to live. "Sensible" is one. And "library" is definitely another. But guess what? The Angel Academy library is completely not like that.

For one thing, it has the coolest ceiling. You can actually watch stars and planets performing their *amazing* celestial manoeuvres.

Lola joined the queue for the history club. I tagged along, telling myself I was just keeping her company. It wasn't that I'd changed my mind about staying.

I got a shock when I saw who was signing us up. If I hadn't known they were angels, I'd have taken them for FBI. Suits, blank expressions – the works. I was positive our guy was getting security-type messages down his ear-piece. But I had a peek and what do you know? There was no ear-piece.

"Who ARE these people?" I hissed.

"Oh, they're from the Agency," said Lola airily, as if this was obvious.

Before I could follow this up, a boy's voice said, "Hi, er – Melanie isn't it?"

Do I know any boys in heaven? I wondered, amazed.

Then I turned and saw his face. *Omigosh*, I thought.

You could so totally tell he was an angel. One of those beautiful Italian-type angels you see in old paintings.

"I was meant to meet you at the gate," he explained. "But I got held up. You know how it is."

I managed a dazed nod.

"Still, it looks like you survived," he said calmly.

Some girls had turned to look at him. They were

like sunflowers, turning their heads to follow the sun. I don't know why, but that really annoyed me. Huh, I thought. I bet girls get tongue-tied around him all the time. And with a mighty effort I found my voice.

"Oh, yeah!" I said, in my most unimpressed tone. "I'm having a great time, thanks."

"Well, yell if you need anything," he said, and went back to his friends.

"'Yell if you need anything'," Lola mimicked. "Except Orlando didn't actually remember to tell you his name! That boy lives on a different planet."

"Nice eye candy, though," I said casually.

"Gorgeous, I'd say. He's also the best student the Academy has had since for ever. The Agency sends him on tons of assignments already. Ooh Melanie, just think!" teased Lola. "If they accept us into the history club, we'll actually be working with him!"

I'll admit this idea did make me go very slightly weak at the knees. Then I mentally replayed what Lola'd just said.

"*Accept* us? You're not saying we have to take a test?"

"No need," she pointed out. "They know everything about us already."

"That sounds really sinister. You mean the Agency like, runs the school as well?"

Lola sighed. "It's just common sense. The Agency is in the angel business. Hey, it IS the angel business!" she grinned. "Though we're supposed to call them agents these days."

I nodded to show I was keeping up.

"Ultimately, if we get through our training, some of us just MIGHT work for the Agency when we leave," Lola explained. "And naturally, the Agency likes to keep an eye on its future employees."

I'd always imagined angels as just hanging around, being effortlessly holy. I'd never thought of them having to WORK at it. Suddenly I had a worrying thought. "And these Agency guys can tell if we're, you know, for real?"

Lola laughed. "Talk about nowhere to run! When they look at you, it's like a total soul-scan!"

"Lola Sanchez?" called a bored voice.

"Totally luminous! They opened another queue," shrieked Lola. "See you outside, Mel!"

This was my cue to make a speedy getaway. But before I could run for it, an Agency official conferred with his invisible ear-piece and beckoned me to the front.

I couldn't believe my bad luck. He must have peeked at my soul when I wasn't looking. Oh-oh, I panicked. I'm going to be exposed as a bogus angel in front of everyone!

"I can explain," I stuttered. "There was like, a complete mix-up. And—"

"Ah yes, Melanie," he said smoothly. "Perhaps you'd like to tell me why you want to join the school history club?"

And with a terrifying WHOOSH, I was watching myself in flashback – sound, vision, everything.

I was seven years old and a total elf. Mousy hair scraped into bunches, eyes way too big for my face and a pointy little chin. At this point, Mum still dressed me in sweatshirts with cartoon characters on them. But that was OK, because secretly I was a time-traveller.

Whenever I got bored or lonely, I'd whizz off fearlessly to all the times and places which had the coolest costumes, and have imaginary adventures. Unfortunately, once or twice I made the mistake of shifting into time-travel mode when I was at school. "Control to Melanie," my teacher would sneer. "Feel free to return to Earth at any time."

Pretty soon I learned that I wasn't time-travelling at all, just daydreaming, which everyone knew was a total waste of time...

I came back to the angel library with a jolt.

"Yep," the Agency guy said into his collar. "No, you were right, Mike. She's a natural. I'll tell her." He glanced up. "Michael says congratulations," he said. "We'll be in touch."

I stumbled out through the revolving doors. Lola was waiting on the steps. Her face lit up. "You're in! That is SO cool!"

"Lola," I croaked. "Did you ever hear of a person who was an angel and didn't even know it?"

She patted my shoulder. "Come on. We'll go back to our dorm. It'll be a dump. It always is. But I'll make you some of my special drinking chocolate. What do you say?"

I took a long look at Lola Sanchez, the soul-mate I'd somehow known for ever. And I got the definite feeling my Houdini days were over.

"Sure," I said, as if she'd asked a different question entirely. "Why not?"

Chapter Five

Lola was right. Our dormitory was a total let-down. My room was more like a cupboard. As for the bed, I've seen cosier ironing boards.

Lola's hot chocolate was sinfully delicious, however. It was so frothy it was like drinking through a chocolatey cloud.

"I can't believe you can get this stuff in heaven," I burbled. "It has to be about a zillion times more wonderful than the Earth kind."

Lola pulled a face. "Actually, Mel, it *is* Earth chocolate. It's my grandmother's secret recipe."

I grinned. "That's OK! Where I come from, twenty-second-century hot chocolate would be considered unbelievably cool! How come you can get it here?"

"Didn't you know?" said Lola. "We're allowed anything from our own time period which is totally essential to our well-being."

I felt a little rush of relief. "You mean like, we can still listen to all our favourite music?"

She giggled. "Well, I couldn't survive without music, could you?"

"No way," I agreed happily.

After Lola had gone off to her own cupboard for the night, I stayed up, gazing out of my window at the city lights.

The air in Heaven has this fabulous champagne fizz, giving the impression there's always some wonderful nonstop party going on. But that night, it felt like a party I hadn't been invited to.

I'd never been totally on my own before. Not without the TV nattering in the background. I wasn't sure I'd cope. How would I sleep without Jade's snuffly breathing for company?

Of course, as an angel, I didn't *need* to sleep at all. We do get tired, incidentally. But it's not like on Earth. It's more like your spiritual batteries run out of juice, if you get me. What Lola calls angel electricity.

But like eating and shopping, sleep is a habit I'm in no major hurry to give up. So eventually I washed my face, put on the baggy T-shirt I'd borrowed from Lola and plonked down on my economy-size mattress.

I lay in the dark, telling myself that I had this amazing new life and was not in the least homesick. Then it gradually dawned on me that I could hear something.

It was my cosmic music. Those wonderful sounds which pulled me clear out into space, all the way to the gates of the Angel Academy.

And the longer I lay listening, the less I felt like a tiny ball-bearing in a divine game of pinball, and the more I felt I had truly come home.

I must have gone to sleep, because next thing I knew, someone was having a coughing fit outside my door.

I unpeeled my eyelids. It was still pitch dark. "I don't believe this," I groaned.

"What do you think you're up to, Lola Sanchez!" hissed a voice.

That's Amber, I thought.

"You minx, Lolly!" whispered a third voice. "You'll ruin everything!"

BAM! My door flew open. Eight or nine girls charged in. As well as Lola and Amber, I recognised Flora and the giggly girls from my class.

"Hey!" I said.

"I'm SO sorry, Mel!" wailed Lola.

"Up you get!" said Flora sweetly.

"Yeah? Going to make me?" I clung grimly to my sheet.

But peachy little Flora was stronger than she looked. She yanked my arm so hard, she totally pulled me out of bed.

"It's an old school tradition!" Lola was saying in a pleading voice. "It's really not personal."

"It feels personal to me!" I snarled.

The girls bundled me, kicking and struggling, down several flights of stairs, out into the grey light of dawn. We seemed to be heading for the beach.

"Now what?" I panted, as we scrunched over pebbles and bits of shell. "Are you going to drown me?"

"Will you relax!" Flora snapped. "Or we just might have to drop you!"

"Mel, I'm so jealous!" Amber was burbling. "Didn't you ADORE your initiation ceremony, Lollie? I would SO love to have mine all over again."

"Be my guest!" I growled.

I noticed that Lola was carefully avoiding my eyes. I got the impression she was totally feeling for me.

About half-way down the seashore, the other trainees dumped me down on the wet sand. We eyed each other uneasily.

"Is that it?" I demanded. "Can I go back to bed now?"

"No way," said Flora in a spooky voice. "It's just begun!"

And they joined hands and began to circle self-consciously around me on the sand, like kids playing "Jenny is a-weeping". They were giggling at first. Then they sobered up and started chanting some eerie little rhyme.

At the end of each chorus, they edged closer, moving me with them further and further down the beach, until everyone was ankle-deep in sea foam. Flora and Amber exchanged meaningful glances. And next minute, those sadistic trainee angels lifted me up and dunked me right down in the sea.

I scrambled up, and tried to wring some of the salt water out of my T-shirt. "Oh ha ha, how totally hilarious!" I yelled. "How old are you guys, exactly?"

But my tormentors melted away without a sound. And then I saw why.

There was a golden gleam on the horizon. And walking across the water towards me, out of the sunrise, were crowds of angels.

For a minute I forgot to breathe. The angels paid no more attention to me than a tree would, or a star.

I couldn't help myself. I stepped on to the silky surface of the waves and walked out to meet them. It wasn't weird or anything, like walking on jelly or glass. The sea behaved just the same as always. It was me that had changed. My bare feet splashed and scuffled across the sparkling waters of the ocean, as if I was, well – *paddling*.

I can't sink, I thought. I'm as light as air!

The thought was so incredible I didn't know whether to laugh or cry.

As I drew closer, an angel dipped his finger in the sea.

Omigosh, I thought. I could see clear to the bottom of the ocean, fathoms below. I saw shoals of fish shimmer to and fro beneath us. I saw monster crabs scuttling across the ocean floor, like jagged giant scissors. My angel senses were so acute, I actually saw a baby pearl secretly forming inside its oyster.

A jolt of pure happiness went through me. And for a fleeting moment I understood *everything*.

Then without me moving an inch, I was back on solid ground in my sopping wet T-shirt. And the angels were nowhere to be seen.

Lola was waiting, hugging her knees, still carefully not looking at me. "I brought you some clothes."

I took them without a word. I felt totally spaced and peculiar.

Later Lola told me that I was so silent on the way back, she was convinced I hated her! When we reached my door, she stared down at her boots. "So do you still want to go shopping or what?" she mumbled.

I was back to normal in a flash. "Are you *serious*? We can really go shopping in heaven?"

Lola burst out laughing. "But first I'm going to buy you the best breakfast you have ever had!"

I was amazed to discover that our school campus was only one tiny part of an incredibly vibey city. "What's that yummy smell?" I said as we walked into town.

"This is the Ambrosia district," Lola explained.

"Where all the best cafés are."

She took me to her favourite hang-out, a café called Guru. A bald waiter called Mo brought us the biggest breakfast on the menu.

We stuffed our faces with the most delicious pancakes I have had in my *entire* existence. And while we ate, Lola and I had an excellent heart-to-heart. She told me about her gran, who brought up Lola and her four brothers after their mum died. I told Lola about my mum and little sister, and how our lives totally cheered up after mum got together with Des.

"I'm scared I'll forget about them," I said.

"That's not how it works. What changes is, it stops hurting so much."

There was a short silence. "So how did you – er...?" I asked cautiously.

Lola had a wicked glint in her eye. "How did I croak?"

"Don't say, if you'd rather not," I said.

"Hey, it's not a problem, honestly. But it's funny how it's only new kids who ask that," Lola mused. She cleared her throat. "If you really want to know, I erm – got in the way of a bullet."

I gasped. "Someone *shot* you?"

"Only by mistake," she sighed. "It's no biggie, Mel. Trust me, after you've been here a bit longer, none of that stuff will seem nearly so important." She grinned. "You don't fret about losing all those cute little baby teeth now, do you?"

I frowned. "You're not trying to tell me that being *shot* is in the same league as losing your milk teeth?"

Lola shrugged. "There are worse ways to die in my city, I promise you."

I stared at her. "But you were just a kid!"

So was I, I thought. And I suddenly felt this lonely little ache inside.

Lola slurped up some of her smoothy. "It's like this, Mel," she said. "Some lives are really long and complicated, OK? They just go on and on, like, like – I don't know, *symphonies* or something."

I gave her a watery grin. "We listened to a couple in Music. There was this one that had about a gazillion endings, like durn, durn DURN! And then, blam, blam BLAM! And it *still* wasn't over!"

"Exactly," she beamed. "But *our* lives, Mel, yours and mine – they just went flashing by, like songs from a car radio. You know those vibey little tunes that put you in a great mood for the rest of the day?"

She hummed a catchy little riff, then broke off.

"Do those songs need to be any longer?" she demanded. "I don't *think* so, Melanie! They are perfect, just the way they are."

I couldn't help laughing. Lola certainly had a way of putting things. Though personally I'd have preferred a combo-option. A vibey, feel-good, Melanie Beeby symphony with a gazillion endings.

"You know this morning," I said, "when you all rushed into my room? You knew what was going to happen, didn't you?"

"Oh, Mel! I feel so terrible about that!"

"Not the stupid initiation," I said. "The angels. Are they...?" It was hard to explain what I felt. "I mean, one day will *we*, like, grow into *them*?"

Lola shook her head. "The ones you saw perform really specialised cosmic tasks. They deal with the natural world mostly. They don't have much to do with humans or feelings."

"Or shopping?" I suggested.

Lola giggled. "OK, OK. I can take a hint, you know!"

On our way out, I was interested to see that Lola didn't actually hand over any money. She just flashed her ID at Mo.

"See you later, Ms Sanchez," he grinned.

"Hey, do I get one of those?" I asked hopefully.

"Sure, once you get through your probationary term."

I was horrified. "You mean the Academy sometimes kicks people out?" Isn't the brain weird? Yesterday I was prepared to tunnel my way out with a teaspoon. Now suddenly I wanted to be voted Heaven's Most Popular Angel!

Lola shrugged. "You'd have to really screw up to get expelled. Don't look so worried," she said sympathetically. "It's never going to happen. And you'll know the instant your probation's up, because that's when you get your like, real angel name. Honestly, that is the coolest moment!" She went all dreamy, remembering.

I felt a pang of jealousy. I wanted to know my angel name too. "Do you know mine?" I pleaded. "Can't you tell me? Just a little sneak preview?"

Lola shook her head, still dreamy. "You're the only one who knows it. It's like something that's already locked inside you. And one day the key turns, and you hear it. And it's like you always knew."

A vague memory stirred at the back of my mind. "That's so weird," I whispered. "When I was little—"

But Lola had jumped up. "Come on, Mel! It's

time to spend spend spend!"

My mood changed in a flash. "But I don't have ID!" I wailed. "How am I going to pay for it?"

Lola's eyes gleamed. "Melanie Beeby," she said. "You are so going to love this place!"

She was right. But several hours later, as Lola and I walked back into Guru with at least a dozen carrier bags, I *still* couldn't believe it.

The instant Lola told the salespeople who I was, they let me have everything I needed. Just like that! OK, I didn't strictly *need* that sweet little grey dress with all the beading. But after Lola said how great it looked on me, I couldn't bear to leave it behind.

While we waited for our smoothies to arrive, I gazed around Guru, happily admiring the decor. Also, I have to admit, the boys!

Something occurred to me. "It's lucky everyone speaks such great English here," I said. "I am SO useless at languages."

Lola looked so tickled, that I felt myself turning red. "What did I say?"

"That's so cute! You really think we're talking in English!" Lola patted my arm. "Mel, you're an angel! You understand every human language ever invented. But in this city, you speak, well – Angel.

Like the rest of us."

I let my head fall on to the table. "AAARGH!" I growled. "This place is too angel for words! Angel this, angel that. Now you're telling me there's some weird angel LANGUAGE?"

"Languages," Lola corrected. "If you want to get technical." She knocked back her smoothy. "Let's head home and you can give me an exclusive fashion show."

"Now *that's* my language," I said promptly.

We walked home, taking a different route this time. It was getting late and a soft blue twilight was falling on the streets. On the way, we passed this kind of Greek temple building, set in really dreamy gardens. They were like the most beautiful wild flower meadows you could ever imagine, only with that extra heavenly something...

Suddenly I stood still. Between the stone pillars, I could see shining beings, quietly moving to and fro. Each of them was surrounded by a haze of coloured light. I was too far away to see what they were doing, but it was so peaceful, it made me want to cry.

"What's this place?" I whispered. "I mean, is it

like some special angel hang-out?"

Lola stared at me. "Oh, you're good!" she said slowly.

I felt my cheeks getting hot. "Did I say something stupid again?"

"I'm serious," she said. "You really pick up on vibes, don't you? I mean, apart from the Agency building, the Sanctuary has to have the *most* angel vibes in this entire city."

"But what are they all doing in there?" I asked.

"It's a kind of hospital," Lola said. "The guys who work in there specialise in angel healing arts."

I was just going to ask why in the world angels would need to go to hospital, when quite without warning, a sensation of utter horror flashed through me. It was so strong, I totally doubled up.

Lola shivered. "They must be bringing some agents back."

As we stood there, hypnotised, beams of white light came strobing down from the sky. The instant the light-beams touched down, hosts of heavenly paramedic types stepped out. The Sanctuary angels came hurrying to meet them, and both sets of angels started ferrying fleets of gauzy stretchers into the sanctuary.

From the smooth way they conducted this

operation, I got the feeling this was not an unusual event. Everyone really knew the drill. No-one ran. No-one yelled. Everyone was totally calm. Yet there was an electric urgency that you could almost taste.

"If I didn't know this was Heaven, I'd think they'd been airlifted out of a war zone or something," I whispered.

Lola looked as sick as I felt. "You'd be right. They just came back from Earth."

I forced myself to look at the wounded agents being carried past us. It's not easy to describe, but they all had this identical look. Some of them had terrible injuries, but from my new angel perspective, I somehow knew those visible injuries weren't the point. The true damage was deep down. It showed in their eyes and skin, but most of all it showed in their deadly stillness. It was like all their wonderful angel radiance had been drained out of them.

Suddenly Michael was coming towards us through the crowd.

"Lola, Melanie," he said quietly. "You should get back to school."

One of the sanctuary staff came out to meet him. They disappeared inside, looking deadly serious.

I realised Orlando was standing next to me. I must have looked like I was in total shock, because he said, "Are you OK?"

"I don't get it," I whispered. "Aren't we immortal now? I mean, how come people can still hurt us like this?"

Looking back, I can see that Orlando really didn't want to be the one to break this to me. His expression was so grim that I started shivering, even before he said the words.

"Those agents weren't hurt by humans, Mel."

I was bewildered. "Then who?"

He sighed. "Their name tends to vary, according to time and place. We generally just call them the Opposition."

Such a harmless word, but it shook me to the core.

Until that moment, I'd been living inside some rosy bubble, where angels automatically lived happily and stylishly ever after.

Now the dream was over.

Chapter Six

If there was a dance called the Melanie Beeby, it would go like this. One step forward, two steps back. One step forward, two steps back...

It's not that I *forgot* the scene outside the Sanctuary when I got back. It's more that it really scared me. So I told myself I totally didn't need to know about any gruesome old Opposition. It was one of those grown-up things, like the ozone layer, which needn't concern me.

Next day we started school, and I had more important stuff to think about. Mr Allbright might look sweet and fuzzy, but that guy didn't let us get away with a thing.

I know what you're thinking. Melanie Beeby, hitting the books – this is a joke, right? But for your information, I had TOTALLY turned over a new leaf. To be honest, it was mostly down to Mr Allbright. He's a *brilliant* teacher.

In our science class he showed us these cool little atoms grooving away, as if life was one big cosmic party. He said the point of showing us these little guys was so we'd know that absolutely everything in the universe is alive.

"What, even stones?" I said wittily.

"I'm glad you said that, Melanie," Mr Allbright beamed, and before you could say "Big-mouth Beeby," he'd dragged the whole class down to the beach.

"I want each of you to choose a pebble," he said excitedly. "And tune into its wavelength."

Oh, perleaze, I thought. But I had to eat my words. My pebble was SO deep, you have no idea. Luckily stones aren't all that interested in chatting, so Mr Allbright said I totally didn't need to feel bad about ignoring them up until now.

Incidentally, the history club was a complete non-event. Flora and Ferdy were members for one thing. More annoyingly, Orlando didn't turn up. I'd made up my mind to be v. unimpressed the next time I saw him. I'd been practising for DAYS.

Also Lola had completely got it wrong, because time-travel simply didn't come up. All that happened was some guy from the Agency gave us a long lecture about team work (yawn yawn yawn). Then he handed round a humungous book list and said they'd be in touch.

I checked a couple of the books out of the library (Lola made me) but I was too fed up to read them. Well, I never said I was a *total* goody-goody!

I couldn't face the Angel Handbook either, even though Mr Allbright insisted it was essential reading. I got as far as *Chapter 1: FINDING YOUR FEET IN HEAVEN*. Then I came over all dizzy and put it back on the shelf.

That was the day I found out we weren't allowed to take even an occasional sicky. Angels never get sick, apparently. This is very good news obviously. But it made me feel totally trapped. How was a girl supposed to get some rest?

Luckily, according to the timetable, Wednesday afternoon was our Private Study period. I couldn't wait. Finally, some chill-out time with my best friend, Lola.

But when I knocked on her door, Lola was on her way out.

"Sorry, Boo. I do singing on Wednesdays," she said. (I have NO idea why she calls me Boo. Lola invents these weird nicknames for everyone.)

"Oh, poor old you," I said, assuming Lola had been roped in for some kind of holy hymn singing. Then I did a truly noble deed. "I'll come with you, if you like," I suggested. "You know, just this once."

But Lola explained that Private Study meant you had to go off and do something by yourself. It sounded pointless to me. Why do something by yourself if you can do it with your mates?

I'd hate to give you the wrong idea, though. My new life might be confusing, but it had some excellent moments.

For instance, I'd been dreading the martial arts class. I've always been hopeless at PE. The first session was just a joke. Every time I staggered back on to my feet, another kid knocked me flat.

Just as I was in danger of becoming one big bruise, Mr Allbright told us we were going to work in pairs. I'd been praying I'd get Lola for my partner. So I was not amused when Mr Allbright paired me with Reuben, the kid who was dripping sea-water in assembly, if you remember.

"Why are we putting ourselves through this?" I grumbled. "I thought angels were supposed to be gentle and holy and stuff."

Reuben gave an amazed snort of laughter. "You're kidding! If we let ourselves get too soft, the Opposition would have us totally overrun."

That chilling word again. I quickly told myself I hadn't heard it.

"They used to teach us to fight with swords, way back," Reuben explained cheerfully. "I'm talking thousands and thousands of years ago. But these days the Agency prefers us to learn angel martial arts."

"And that's another thing," I growled. "I don't understand how Time works any more."

"That's because it doesn't," said Reuben. "Cosmic Time isn't something that WORKS. It's something you PLAY with. We play with Time in martial arts constantly."

I pulled a face. "Uh-uh, that's way too deep. Translate into bimbo-speak, please!"

Reuben shook his head, grinning. "I see your little game, Beeby. Ten out of ten for the distraction technique. Now, no more questions, OK? Not until after the class, anyway."

To my surprise, Reuben turned out to be a wicked martial arts teacher. He didn't mind how often he demonstrated a move. And he never once made me feel stupid. In fact he praised every tiny little improvement, until I almost started to believe I could do this stuff.

Suddenly, to my astonishment, I was flying through the air like a Ninja angel. Wow, I thought, this is so cool. Then I landed on my bum.

Reuben helped me up. "Isn't this great!" he beamed. "You're learning to trust those angel vibes."

"I am?" I said doubtfully. It seemed like a complete accident to me.

"Sure you are," he said confidently. "You stopped being scared, and you just flew, right?"

I mentally replayed what had just happened. "Hey!" I said. "You're right!"

And for five whole seconds, I was really thrilled with myself.

Then Reuben launched himself into a sequence of gravity-defying moves. Other kids joined in, including Flora and Ferdy. Soon there was this amazing martial arts dance going on. They did some moves in such dreamy slow motion, it really did look as if they'd actually stopped Time.

That's what Reuben meant, I thought.

It was pure magic.

Amber and Lola clapped and whooped with excitement. But all at once I felt unbelievably depressed.

"I'll never be that good," I sighed.

Reuben flipped himself the right way up. "Give yourself a chance! Besides, think of all that stuff you do without even thinking. Stuff which is like – impossible for me."

"Yeah, right," I said bitterly. "Just think."

But Reuben was serious. He was genuinely desperate for help, only he was too embarrassed to ask.

We found out quite by accident a few days later.

Reuben, Lola and me were relaxing near our favourite fountain, when a bunch of nursery-school kids skipped past looking totally angelic.

Then it hit me. They *were* angels. Tiny little angels.

"That's awful!" I gasped. "They must have died when they were little dots!"

"Uh-uh," said Reuben. "Some angels never

incarnate. Like me for instance." He flushed and looked away.

"Erm, is that a bad thing?" I asked cautiously.

"Incarnating is when you put on a human body," Lola explained. "It's what you have to do to live on Earth. But little Sweetpea here never got to make the trip."

I was amazed. "You never left Heaven?"

Reuben sighed. "Don't rub it in. It's been like, my big dream ever since I can remember."

"I can't believe it," I said. "You never even had a *peek* at Earth?"

Reuben looked wistful. "Not close-up. I've done Angel Watch in practicals."

"So how come you never went?" I persisted.

"The Agency won't let me," said Reuben. "Not until I pass my Earth Skills paper. Unfortunately I just failed retakes. *Again.*"

Quite suddenly I got it. Reuben had to be a totally different kind of angel to me and Lola!

"Lollie, you never told me there were two kinds of angels!" I grumbled.

"There are about a gazillion kinds actually," said Reuben. "But yeah, basically they divide into human-angels and angel-angels."

And in that moment I absolutely KNEW Orlando was an angel-angel. Plus I had deep suspicions about Flora and Ferdy.

"That explains your eyes!" I said.

Reuben looked offended. "Are you saying I've got weird eyes?"

"Not weird. They're kind of…"

"Pure," suggested Lola wickedly.

Reuben scowled. "Isn't that another way of saying weird?"

"My sunrise angels weren't weird," I said. "Stars aren't weird. Nor is a snowflake, or – a tiny newborn baby."

"Exactly," said Lola. "They're pure!" She grinned at Reuben. "Like you, my little Sweetpea!"

"So how does it work, being an angel-angel?" I asked him. "I mean, did you start out as a tiny cherub and grow up? Or is it that you just look like a typical thirteen year old, but you're actually totally ancient inside?"

"Poor Melanie, that old T-word has you all confused," Reuben teased.

"Don't tell me, I know," I sighed. "Time doesn't really exist in Heaven, wah wah wah."

"Oh, it exists! It just behaves totally differently."

He gave a sheepish grin. "I've never quite got my head around the Earth kind, to be honest. But isn't it something like – there's never ever enough of it to do the things you want to do? And once you make a mistake, that's it. You're stuck with it for ever?"

Lola nodded vigorously.

"I suppose," I agreed.

"Well, Cosmic Time is different. It isn't this irresistible force you're constantly wrestling with. It's more like this – this never-ending playground, where you can have all the Time you need. You can grow up fast or slow, backtrack a bit, make a few corrections. Whatever!"

"Actually, Cosmic Time IS quite cool," Lola admitted.

I clutched my head. "Sorry, this is way too weird for me."

"Now you know how I feel about Earth Skills," said Reuben gloomily.

Out of the blue I had this brilliant idea. "I've got it!" I squeaked. "You helped me with martial arts, Reubs. Why don't I help you with your Earth Skills? You'll help too, won't you, Lollie?"

I truly thought Reuben was going to burst into tears. "I can't believe you mean it!" he kept saying.

"I've been feeling like such a loser!"

But by the end of Reuben's first lesson, Lola and I were practically tearing our hair out. It wasn't that Reuben was dim. Actually I think he was some kind of angel genius. He just could not get the hang of the most elementary Earth concepts. Things like bank accounts or bombing foreign countries totally mystified him. "But what is war *for*?" he kept wailing.

"It's not FOR anything, Sweetpea," Lola sighed. "It just IS."

"Let's leave war out of it for now," I suggested. "I just got some music from home. Let's have a little bop instead."

Reuben had never heard Earth music before. But he was totally into it.

"They really play this stuff on Earth?" he said amazed.

"In my time, yeah," I said. "In Mum's time—"

"Don't get back on to Time," Reuben shuddered. "I'm still recovering from war."

What with one thing and another, the days were whizzing by. Mostly I was really happy. Other days I'd find myself missing things from my old life. Silly things, like hitting the late-night garage for emergency M&Ms!

But no matter how good or bad things were, I could NOT figure out what I was meant to be doing on Private Study afternoons.

To begin with, I used it to catch up on those girly chores. Hair, nails, that kind of thing. But I noticed that the others came back, kind of glowing.

The whole thing started to drive me nuts. I felt like the only person in the school who wasn't in on this big secret. Clearly Private Study was not for doing regular school work. It was also not the same as free time. So what WAS it?

Without actually mentioning the mysterious glow-factor, I cunningly quizzed the others about what *they* did.

Reuben practised martial arts. No surprises there. Amber said she played her musical instrument (the harp, presumably). Flora and Ferdy said they did angel mathematics. Yeah, right!

This sounds really sad, but I totally started dreading Wednesdays.

"Everything OK, Melanie?" Mr Allbright asked, finding me brushing tiny grains of sand off the hammocks, as I put off going back to my room for as long as possible.

"Oh, I'm fine, Mr Allbright," I said brightly. "Really settling in."

Somehow I couldn't bring myself to tell a high being like Mr Allbright that I was so shallow I couldn't stand my own company for one measly afternoon a week.

When I got back to the dorm, I decided to wash my hair. It didn't need it. I just wanted to kill some time. But as I flipped the little doodad on the shampoo bottle, Miss Rowntree's voice started up inside my head. "There's more to life than makeovers, Melanie," she sneered.

I'm not sure there is, I thought miserably. Not for me.

I was in trouble and I didn't know what to do. "Help," I whispered. "I need help."

I didn't really think anyone was listening. But they must have been.

Because a few minutes later, help came.

Suddenly, and for no apparent reason, I got this violent urge to go to the beach. It was totally weird. One minute I'm fretting about Private Study, the next my head is full of waves and sea-sounds. It was like this irresistible call.

Yet again I found myself splitting into several Melanies. One is saying, "What are you ON, Mel?" Another is whispering, "Come to the seashore, NOW!"

All at once I grabbed my jacket and rushed out.

I stormed along, telling myself I wasn't in jail. I was perfectly free to walk down to the beach if I wanted to.

Sure, if it was actually your *idea*, bird-brain, the regular Mel pointed out.

But once I was sniffing that warm salty breeze, all the Mels magically calmed down.

This was so not like me, you can't imagine! The old Mel *never* did stuff by herself. Yet here I was, walking by the edge of the water, squidging damp sand between my toes.

I've always loved the sea, ever since Mum took me on a day-trip when I was three years old. The instant we got out of the bus, something inside me went, "YES!"

I loved *everything*. The glitter of light on the waves, the salty breeze, the screams of huge seabirds. And all that SPACE!

Suddenly, the memory that had almost surfaced that morning in Guru came floating into my head.

Mum was holding a shell to my ear, so I could hear the sound of the waves. But I was convinced it whispered my name. "The shell called you Melanie?" said Mum. "Not *that* name," I kept saying. "My real name." But I couldn't explain what I meant.

I smiled to myself, remembering.

Just then some little nursery-school angels came racing across the sand. "We found you!" they shrieked. They danced me round, giggling. None of them looked any older than four (in Earth years, that is), and they were totally full of beans.

I was bewildered. "You *found* me? You don't even know me."

"Yes we do. You're Melanie," they giggled.

A little boy tugged at my hand. "Come and play," he insisted. He had the calmest face I ever saw and absolutely no hair. He looked exactly like a tiny buddha.

"I can't," I said wistfully. "I'm supposed to be doing Private Study."

"Oh, pooh," said a little girl with a sparkly hairband. "They just want you to use the Angel Link."

My heart sank. Kindergarten angels know more than you, Mel, I thought.

"The what?" I said miserably.

"It isn't the Link that matters," my little buddha explained in a gentle voice. "It's what happens after that."

"Yeah, like what?" I said, still depressed at being the slowest learner in Heaven.

His eyes shone. "You plug into the angel power supply and find your very best self!" he said.

"And you feel all safe and smiley," said the hairband girl.

"Smiley," echoed the littlest angel hoarsely.

"It actually makes you glow!" said another little boy.

I couldn't BELIEVE what I was hearing. In two seconds flat, these tots had solved my problem!

"And that's all?" I gasped.

"Not exactly ALL," he admitted. "Miss says we'll understand the rest when we're ready."

"But how do you, you know, plug in?" I asked.

"Oh, that's lemon squeezy," boasted the sparkly hairband girl. "Here's what you do, OK? First you get really quiet inside."

The littlest angel waved her hand. "Let me, let me!"

"Go on then, Maudie," everyone sighed.

Maudie took a big breath. "You let yourself feel all

safe and smiley," she recited in a hoarse little voice. "Then you picture being the best self you know! And then guess what!" she beamed. "You ARE it."

"Miss says when we use the Link, we're connected to every angel that ever was or ever will be," my little buddha explained.

"Come on," said the hairband girl impatiently. "Miss Dove says to bring Melanie back with us."

The children started tugging me along the beach.

"Miss *said* we'd find you here," the little buddha beamed.

I stopped in my tracks. "But how did she know?"

"You asked for help, silly!" whispered the littlest angel.

She clearly saw nothing weird about pre-schoolers picking up someone's personal distress signals. But I was in a total spin.

Melanie Beeby, I scolded myself. Four-year-olds know more than you. You should be ashamed. Go home and read your Handbook from cover to cover.

I didn't, though. Want to know what I did instead? I spent the afternoon in nursery school!

First we did cutting and sticking, involving more glitter than you could possibly imagine. Small angels *adore* anything sparkly, apparently.

Then Miss Dove said we were going to grow tiny orange trees in pots. I thought this sounded almost as boring as normal school. But all the little angels immediately went "Yay!" like this was some big treat!

"You too, Melanie," Miss Dove beamed.

"Oh, that's OK, I'll just watch," I said hastily.

But it turns out no-one EVER just watches in Miss Dove's class. She wouldn't take no for an answer, just briskly handed me my personal tree-growing kit: a little pip and a pot of dirt. And we all solemnly planted and watered them.

At this point, things got a little different to my usual school seed-planting experiments. Miss Dove made us hold our pots in both hands. "Now I want everyone to go quiet inside and plug into the angel power supply," she said in her special nursery-teacher voice.

And guess what! With no effort at all, I pictured myself being the best self I could be, like Miss Dove said, and all at once I felt all that cosmic electricity whooshing through me, as if I really was connecting with all the angels in existence.

Next Miss Dove showed us how to beam this energy into our little pots of dirt. "Gently, gently," she kept saying. "We don't want to fry them, children, do we?"

Then we all popped our pots on the window-sill in the sun, and Miss Dove told the children to sing me a new song they'd been learning. I don't know why, but something about their little voices reminded me of those wonderful cosmic sounds which lulled me to sleep every night.

But during the singing, something extraordinary happened. Our orange pips began to put out shiny green shoots! By the time the children had reached the last verse, each pot contained a perfect miniature orange tree!

And I know this sounds silly, but mine seemed to recognise me, because when I picked it up, it instantly burst into sweet-smelling blossom.

I was enchanted. "I grew a tree!" I burbled. "That is so sublime!"

At last it was time to go home. All the children in Miss Dove's class shrugged on their cool little rucksacks (designed to look exactly like wings), and went racing out of school.

Miss Dove said I'd been *invaluable*, and invited me to pop in any time I was free. I repeated her words to my tiny orange tree, all the way home.

"You were invaluable, Melanie," I whispered. "Invaluable."

The minute I walked into my room, I saw myself in the mirror. And guess what? I finally had that authentic angel glow!

Lola popped her head round my door. She gave me a swift once-over, then grinned. "I see you finally cracked Private Study then!" she beamed.

"Really?" I breathed.

"Erm, have you checked your post, Boo?" she asked innocently.

I shook my head. "Uh-uh."

"Tarraa!" Lola waved an envelope with my name on it. "We've got tomorrow off! The Agency is having a Dark Study Day. It HAS to be something to do with the history club."

"Omigosh!" I screamed. *"We're going time-travelling!"*

Chapter Seven

The minute Lolly went back to her room, I took my little beaded dress out of the wardrobe and tried it on. I told myelf this had nothing to do with impressing Orlando. I just wanted to wear it.

Supposing grey isn't dark enough for Dark Study Day? I panicked. Maybe I should wear black?

Then I had a good look at my reflection. I was looking unusually delicious, if I say so myself. Nah, that's dark enough for anyone, I thought. The dress was a bit on the short side, but so what?

Next morning Lola and I walked downtown to the Agency headquarters.

I was dying of curiosity. I'd been hearing about

this mysterious Agency ever since I got here. I couldn't wait to see it for myself.

I'd forgotten that in this city, it wasn't just what something looked like, it was what it *felt* like.

We were still a couple of streets away when a violent tingling started up in the soles of my feet. Then we cut down a side street, and right in front of us was this amazing futuristic skyscraper.

It looked like it was made out of the same magical glass as the Academy library. But instead of a built-in cloud feature, the Agency's tower was continually washed by lovely waves of colour.

In the time it took us to reach the entrance, the building shimmered right through glowing sunrise to twilight lavenders and blues.

The tower was so tall that the upper windows were actually up among the clouds. But through the curly white wisps I glimpsed violent bursts of light. They seemed to occur about a heartbeat apart.

"What's happening up there?" I breathed.

"Oh, the usual comings and goings," said Lola casually.

My mouth dropped open. "You mean those are agents like, zooming out of Heaven?"

"Or zooming back again," said Lola.

I threw my arms around her. "Totally luminous, Lollie!" I shrieked. "That's going to be US!"

Amber was waiting for us outside on the steps.

"You look great, Mel," she beamed. "Erm, but are you sure you'll be able to run in that sweet little dress?"

I glared at Lola. "You never said we'd have to *run*!"

"It's a training day, Boo!" Lola grinned. "I thought you'd work that out for yourself."

We stared up at the Agency building, working up courage to go in. By this time, its high tingle-factor was making me feel incredibly light-headed. But Lola is not a girl who is easily intimidated.

"OK, we'll do it on three," she announced. "One, two, THREE!"

We dived into the revolving doors and came out, giggling. Unfortunately, the Agency lobby is the size of a cathedral. The tiniest whisper echoes on for *ever*. The three of us tiptoed across acres of highly polished marble, trying not to laugh, and Lola gave our names to the guy at the desk. Then we stepped into a lift and went whizzing up into the sky for miles.

Now that I was actually inside it, the Agency's whizzy energy levels felt quite normal. But I noticed Lola and Amber had suddenly acquired this extra-special angel glow, so probably I had too.

We hurried along a warren of gleaming corridors, following the signs to the Training Day.

The Dark Study area was crowded with alarmingly advanced angels, all standing around and using angel jargon until I thought I'd scream.

You could just tell none of them would *ever* stoop to taking advice from toddlers.

I was almost relieved to spot Flora and Ferdy coming through the crowd. A few metres behind them was Orlando.

Just in time I remembered that I had not dressed to impress him, plus I was not one of his sad little groupies. So I gave him my briefest smile and said, "Oh, hi."

At that moment Michael came in. I was more clued-up about archangels these days. But I'd noticed that despite Michael's awesome cosmic responsibilities, he never acted as if he was in any way above the rest of us. Sometimes he reminded me of a big brown bear, right down to his podgy tummy. Then I'd see those eyes, blazing with terrifying intelligence, and have to look away.

"Thank you for coming at such short notice," he said. "The fact is, we're facing a celestial emergency, and we need all the help we can get."

I was stunned. This amazing being was actually asking *me* for help!

"As you know, certain eras in human history present the Agency with greater challenges than others," he went on. "The Dark Ages is an obvious example."

I couldn't quite believe this was happening! I'd only been an angel for about five minutes, but here I was at the cosmic hub!

"The greatest drain on our resources, however, comes from the twentieth and twenty-first centuries," Michael said gravely. "As some of you will know, we recently received a severe set-back, and a large number of agents were wounded in the field."

Then he launched into the usual team-work speech, and how connecting with each other through the Link was normally effortless.

"Unfortunately, on a turbulent planet like Earth, it does take more concentration," Michael went on. "Just remember that the principle is the same. Through the Link, you are instantly connected with your heavenly power supply. And the Opposition will have no power over you."

My eyes accidentally drifted to Orlando, who was sitting down at the front. Pay attention, Mel, I scolded myself. This isn't school assembly. It's real.

"The Opposition naturally prefers humans to believe they are alone in a hostile universe." Michael took a sip of water. "It will do its utmost to prevent you carrying out your mission, either by separating you from your team, or by cutting you off from the Link. These Dark Study courses simulate the kind of trouble you can expect."

We were all divided into teams. All six Academy kids were in one team. Orlando was our team leader.

"Just take a moment to establish the Link," said Michael.

I sent up a silent thankyou to Miss Dove. Thanks to her, I now knew that the Link was some kind of heavenly internet. Luckily, since my afternoon in nursery school, I totally had it down.

I took a big breath, went quiet inside, and WHOOSH! I was connected.

It was effortless, just like Michael said. I felt so peaceful, I knew nothing could ever hurt me again. I could see everyone else felt the same.

Then two agents sprang up from their seats and went to stand on either side of a door. Michael gave them a nod, and one of them pressed a button. The door slid back. When I saw what was on the other side, my mouth went as dry as cotton wool. I'd secretly been hoping for castles and knights in armour. But there was just darkness. Icy cold darkness.

"GO, GO, GO!" chanted the agents, and they began pushing people through the door, one at a time.

Oh-oh, I thought. This is scarier than I thought!

"You'll be OK, Mel," said Orlando quietly.

I gave him a withering look. I didn't care if Orlando had just read my most private thoughts, I refused to seem impressed.

But at that moment, the agents grabbed my arms and booted me into space.

FLASH! It was a frosty night and I was in a crowded fairground, a disappointingly modern one. Not a bustle or crinoline in sight.

I should explain that Agency simulations faithfully recreate what happens when a celestial agent first hits Planet Earth. Which is basically that it's completely mad.

Suddenly my angelic senses were bombarded with about a gazillion signals.

Can you imagine being forced to listen to all the radios, TVs and stereos in existence? Only Earth isn't just blasting you with a cacophony of *sounds* – it's also broadcasting this nonstop uproar of thoughts and feelings, all rushing through you like light waves. Not only is it scary and overwhelming, it actually *hurts*.

I clutched my head. "Ow," I whimpered.

FLASH! Lola appeared beside me. Amber appeared next, then the twins, followed by Orlando.

Ferdy instantly clutched his head. "Oh-oh! Total brain overload!" he gasped. We were all in genuine agony at that point, but everyone cracked up. It was the most human thing I'd ever seen Ferdy do.

Orlando quickly showed us how to tune most of this hubbub out. You just focus on the Link, and the other stuff fades into the background.

But as it turned out, brain overload wasn't the weirdest thing we had to deal with. Amber gave a muffled shriek. "Eek!" she shuddered. "That woman walked right through me! I know she's only a hologram, but it felt SO indecent."

"Get used to it," grinned Orlando. "On Earth, people walk through you constantly." He cleared his throat. "Now, we're looking for a kid who's run away from home. Just one problem – the Opposition is after him too. So you're also keeping your eyes skinned for the bad guys. Only, they won't necessarily LOOK like bad guys. They may not look like guys, full stop."

"So how will we recognise it, erm, them?" asked Amber.

"Practice," said Orlando tersely.

I gave a mock salute. But secretly I thought Orlando made an excellent team leader.

Actually, the training exercise was really interesting. We had to run all over the fairground looking for our runaway. We jumped on the dodgems and searched the cars. We hitched a ride on the Ferris wheel. We even went whistling through spooky tunnels on the ghost train.

Unfortunately my dress was totally embarrassing me. I was definitely going to have to rethink my outfit before I went on an actual mission.

Then, like someone throwing a switch, everything changed. You know when the sun goes behind a cloud, how all the light drains out of everything? It was like that. I felt a prickle of horror.

"They're here," said Orlando softly.

"I can feel it!" I whispered.

"Ugh," said Amber. "Slime."

Lola was deathly white. "Not slime, treacle," she

muttered in a sleepwalking voice. "Evil cosmic treacle, oozing everywhere."

That's when I found out that the Opposition can only be recognised through experience. It's pure evil intelligence which can disguise itself any way it likes. If Orlando had actually explained this, I think I'd have panicked. As it was, all my angel senses were suddenly functioning on red alert. But they were totally focused by this time, so it didn't hurt.

And all at once I heard the boy. Or rather, the boy's thoughts. We all did.

Flora's brow crinkled. "Melanie," she said in her clear little voice. "Does Earth have a thing called a Hot Dog Stall? Because if so, he's there. His name is Curtis and he's nicked his mum's purse." She frowned. "I *think* that's what he's saying."

We all went dashing off to the hot dog stall, and there was Curtis, shivering in a flimsy jacket and hungrily polishing off his frankfurter.

We weren't a minute too soon. Some menacing older kids were heading right for him. In a flash, I saw what was going to happen. Those kids were going to get Curtis into heavy-duty trouble. All because he'd made a stupid mistake.

"Curtis," I said. "It's OK. Go home and tell your mum you're sorry and everything will be all right."

"Yeah, but you'd better clean up your act, boy," scolded Lola.

"No more *nicking*, young man!" said Flora, shaking her finger.

"Erm, nice try, but use the Link, OK?" suggested Orlando. "It's more effective."

We gathered around Curtis so closely that I could smell his hot-dog breath. Then we linked him up with our angelic power supply and *bombed* him with heavenly vibes. Curtis's thoughts calmed down at once. Not only that, the evil treacle phenomenon totally evaporated. It was as if the Opposition simply lost interest. As for those menacing kids, they sailed past Curtis as if he didn't exist.

"They didn't even SEE him," breathed Amber.

"Well done, team," said Orlando quietly. He snapped his fingers. "End program," he said.

FLASH! We were back in the Training Area.

People were patting Flora on the back.

"What a star," I told her.

I actually felt quite fond of her. You know, temporarily.

"That hot-dog thing really threw me off," Ferdy was saying.

But I'd stopped listening. I'd realised something incredibly important.

"Lollie," I hissed. "I want to specialise in Time! And when I graduate, I'm going to try out for the Agency."

"Do you mean it?" Lola gasped.

Was she kidding? From now on, I was going to be the hardest-working, most responsible team member ever. Together we'd blaze through time and space on a cosmic crusade. Goodbye, shallow human, I thought deliriously. And hello, wise angel.

But you can't say that kind of stuff aloud, even to your best friend. So I just said, "Yeah, Lollie, I mean it."

Several hours later, we were sprawling on Lola's rug, sipping hot chocolate. "I'm so happy, it's ridiculous!" I told her.

"Ridiculous is right," she yawned "You've got yourself a serious chocolate moustache, Boo."

It was after midnight. We'd taken part in so many simulations, I'd lost count. We were shattered, but we couldn't quite get up the energy to go to bed. It might sound weird, but outwitting the Opposition in a simulation burns up nearly as much angel electricity as the real thing.

"I wish I'd known this stuff when I was alive," I said suddenly.

"Stuff?" Lola mumbled.

"Those times I thought I was alone, when all the time the Agency had everything under control. I wish someone had told me."

"Oh, totally," said Lola.

"Lollie, there's something I still don't get," I said.

"Hmmn?" said Lola.

I swallowed. It was like I could hardly bring myself to say the name.

"I haven't got a clue what the Opposition really is," I confessed.

Lola sat up, frowning. "Do they have computer viruses in your time, Mel?"

I nodded. "They're like sinister virtual life-forms."

"So why do you think humans fool around with them?"

I ran my finger round my chocolatey mug and licked it thoughtfully.

"I think some people just enjoy committing major sabotage, period."

"Exactly!" said Lola. "No-one really knows how the Opposition got into the cosmic system. And frankly, who cares? It's out there now, doing major sabotage. And the Agency can't ease up, or the Opposition would totally get the upper hand."

"So it's just like – a cosmic glitch. It isn't real, right?" I asked uneasily. I think I just wanted Lola to comfort me. Because deep down, I already knew the answer.

Lola took a long time to reply. Then she said quietly, "No, it's real, Boo."

"But the guys in white suits always win in the end, though, don't they?" I pleaded. "Don't they?"

But Lola silently started getting her stuff ready for school next day.

Suddenly I had to go to bed, before my brain went into total melt-down. I stumbled to my room, and I was asleep before I even hit the pillow.

As a trainee angel, you lead this totally double life. Next day I went to school feeling like the angel equivalent of Buffy the Vampire Slayer, and received a serious shock.

While some of us had been playing thrilling cosmic war games, the rest of the class had started revising for exams.

Remember the words I mentioned? The ones which freak me out? Well for me, EXAMS is right up there with NIGHTMARE.

That night I had my recurring one, where I'm climbing a ladder to the stars and one by one the rungs start breaking off in my hand.

The famous Beeby curse had struck again.

It works like this. The more desperately I want to do well, the more incapable I am of picking up a book. The less work I do, the more desperate I become. As the days went by, I slid into a major depression.

Then one night Lola really told me off.

"You're talking yourself into a corner, Mel. You're not weird, you're not doomed and you're not alone. You've got me and Reuben to help you now."

Lola's pep-talk broke the spell. She seemed so confident I could do well, I actually believed her. Night after night, Lola, Reuben and I tested each other on all the subjects Mr Allbright had taught us.

When I finally tottered into the examination hall and turned over my first exam paper, I practically fainted. I understood *all* the questions!

After the exams, a gang of us went out to Guru to celebrate. I was still fizzing with relief. "I don't want to max it or anything," I told Reuben. "I just don't want the Academy to chuck me out."

"I just hope I scrape a pass in Earth Skills, finally," he sighed.

"Sure you will, Sweetpea!" grinned Lola. "And we'll all zoom off to Earth together like the three cosmic musketeers!"

Hours later, I let myself back into my room, and was surprised to hear the chirp of an Agency telephone. Last time I looked, there hadn't been a phone. Yet here it was, beside my bed.

I pressed TALK. "Erm, Melanie speaking," I said, feeling extremely silly.

"Congratulations," said Michael. "Your Dark Study team did extremely well."

"Oh, th-thank you," I stuttered.

"Now let's see how you deal with the real thing. We don't normally send trainees out into the field so soon, but as you know, we've got a crisis on. An Agency limousine will collect you in a few minutes."

"Oh, where are we going?" I squeaked. "I mean *when*?" I added hastily.

Michael's voice sounded as calm as always. "You'll be doing angel duty in the London Blitz," he said. "1944 to be precise."

CHAPTER EIGHT

Minutes later I was staring into my wardrobe in deepest despair.

Lola hammered on my door. "Melanie!" she thundered. "Get yourself out here!"

"I'm still in my party dress!" I wailed.

"The Londoners won't care if you're wearing a tiara! Most humans can't see angels, remember?"

"You'd better be right," I muttered.

The limousine picked up Amber and the twins on the way, then sped downtown to Agency Headquarters, where Michael and Orlando were waiting.

You could tell the night staff didn't think a girl in a sparkly mini-dress had ANY chance in the unending war against cosmic evil. But Orlando didn't seem to notice. That boy is SO on a higher level, it's unbelievable!

I wasn't sure how I felt about spending forty-eight hours with Orlando. Luckily I didn't have time to think about it, because Michael whisked us through Departures at top speed.

Then he handed out angel tags – little platinum discs on lightweight chains. When mine caught the light, I made out a tiny heavenly symbol in 3D.

"These insignia show you're on Agency business," Michael explained. "They also strengthen your link with your heavenly home."

My heavenly home, I thought. This is really happening!

We crowded into the time portal.

"Incidentally," said Michael casually. "I thought you'd enjoy going by the scenic route."

The door slid shut.

"Next stop Earth," whispered Lola.

Seconds later, the portal lit up like a Christmas tree, and we were catapulted into the slipstream of history.

These are some of the amazing sights we saw. Dinosaurs lumbering around in a steamy dinosaur world. Horsemen in hats with bizarre earflaps, galloping furiously towards a fabulous Eastern city. Egyptian slaves sweating over what would eventually turn out to be the Pyramids.

But my favourite moment has to be when we crowded into an attic in long-ago Italy, where a young man was painting by candlelight.

To my surprise, the room was already bursting with angels, all dressed in gorgeous Renaissance-type clothes – except for the cherubs, who just wore tiny wisps of gauze. The angels all had soulful eyes and dark curly hair, like Orlando. They murmured politely as we came in, then went back to zapping the artist with inspirational-type vibes.

"That's Leonardo!" said Orlando.

Lola gasped. "The da Vinci guy?"

Orlando nodded. "He's a major Agency project."

I edged up to Lola. "How come there's all these like, old-fashioned angels here?"

"Sometimes Earth angels get posted back to their own time period," she whispered. "To help out with some special mission."

"It feels just like home," breathed Flora.

It was true. Leonardo's attic room had the *most* angel electricity flying around. I suppose that's how he managed to stay awake all night, creating masterpieces, while everyone else in Italy just snored their heads off.

Then we were away again, whirling through history like divine dandelion seeds.

This time I got the definite sense that some historical periods were, well – DARKER than the rest. Suddenly it dawned on me that these parts just might have something to do with the Opposition. Then I wished I hadn't had this particular thought. Because minutes later we arrived in wartime London, and there was no light anywhere.

I know it doesn't sound very angelic, but I felt a moment of pure panic. The place looked totally empty. Then I saw dozens of feeble little torches bobbing along in the dark.

Lola froze beside me. "Why is everyone creeping about like spies?" she whispered.

"It's the blackout," I hissed. "People aren't allowed to show lights."

"So what's all that luminous spaghetti up there?" she said. Shafts of white light were criss-crossing the rooftops.

"Searchlights," I told her.

Amber looked impressed. "Boy, you've really been reading up on this."

"Not really. We did it in History," I whispered. "Plus I must have seen about a gazillion war films on TV."

It's not often I get the chance to show off my superior knowledge, right? Maybe I should have milked it a little longer. But I was in shock.

I totally didn't recognise this depressing city, with all these jagged spaces where houses ought to be. At night-time, *my* London blazed with every kind of light. Car headlamps, street lights, neon signs. This London was too dark and dismal for words.

There was a bomb crater right in the middle of the street. But the local Londoners just calmly walked around it, like it was no big deal.

There was a sickly smell of leaking gas, plus a smell of burning like you wouldn't believe.

We'd landed outside a pub called the Angel. I think that was probably Michael's little joke. Inside, people were having a singsong, belting out that really cheesy one about bluebirds and the cliffs of Dover.

Flora winced. "They're in tremendously good spirits," she said bravely.

Suddenly an eerie wailing filled the air, wavering up and down the scale. My tummy looped the loop.

Oh-oh, I thought, that's the air-raid warning.

"We'd better get going," said Orlando.

We joined the crowds streaming into the Underground. It was really uncomfortable. People barged right through me as if I was thin air. I told myself it wasn't personal. I'd probably walked through a few angels myself in my time.

But when we reached the platform, I almost bolted straight back up to the street. Practically the entire neighbourhood had come to spend the night in the tube. The air stank of underground trains and stale smoke, plus that sour pong of people who could use a really good shower. Friends, relations and total strangers all squashed together like factory chickens, cracking jokes and eating sandwiches, even knitting, as calmly as if they were in their own living rooms.

The younger children were mostly tucked up, fast asleep, unaware of the planes droning overhead. Except one tiny kid who couldn't stop coughing. His cheeks were hot and red and he was getting really upset.

"Hey, small fry!" Lola said softly. "Would you like me to fix that mean old cough?"

The little boy's eyes opened wide. He stretched out his arms, smiling.

"He can see her!" I breathed.

"Of course he can!" said Orlando. "Toddlers are much smarter than grown-ups."

There was a huge explosion overhead. I squeaked with fright.

"Don't tell me the Agency's sending babies now!" said a clipped British voice. "Enjoying the pretty fireworks, darlings?"

Orlando grinned. "Hiya Celia! How's it going?"

And suddenly I saw that the tube station was full of Earth angels, all wearing elegant 1940s clothes. They waved briskly, then went back to work.

"Splendidly, thanks," Celia was saying. "Luckily you've come on a quiet night. Absolutely no sign of You Know Who."

And she and Orlando launched into one of those advanced angel conversations which I totally couldn't follow.

"So what are we supposed to do, exactly?" I asked Amber.

She looked surprised. "Just be yourself, of course."

But Celia's glamorous army made me feel totally inadequate. I felt like some sad girl who was just *pretending* to be an angel. I looked around for Lola but she was still cooing to her toddler.

I can't do this, I panicked. I shouldn't have come.

Then I saw Molly.

She couldn't have been more than six years old, but she had the wisest eyes I've ever seen on a human being. The other kids were all in big family groups. Molly was just with her mother. Her mum was really young and full of beans, more like a big sister really – kidding around and pulling her daughter's pixie hood over her eyes.

"I want you to tell me a story," Molly kept saying.

"Slave driver," sighed her mum. She put on a posh voice. "All right, which story does Modom require?"

Molly's mum was a wicked storyteller. Her version of *The Princess and the Pea* was a hoot.

And with a brilliant flash of inspiration, I saw how I could make myself useful. I crept up really close to Molly and her mum, linked myself up with my power supply and began radiating lovely vibes.

Other kids began to edge closer. Soon Molly's mum had this crowd of spellbound children lapping up every word. I decided I could get seriously hooked on being an angel. Between us, we'd created this charmed circle, and now everyone was desperate to be inside it.

All at once, there was another massive explosion. You could see people shudder, wondering if it was their street, their house, which had caught the blast. But without missing a beat, Molly's mum carried right on describing how the old queen made up the bed with twenty quilts and twenty feather beds. And she kept going until she reached the part where everyone got to live happily ever after.

"Go on, missus," said one of the older kids wistfully. "Tell us another."

Ahhh, this is SO sweet, I thought. Then I almost jumped out of my skin. Scary Celia was standing next to me!

"Well done, dear," she said. "When humans and divine personnel work together, that's when miracles happen!"

I looked round to see who she was talking to. But she meant *me*!

"Keep up the good work!" said Celia. And she whisked away down the platform to terrify someone else.

CHAPTER NINE

That night our shelter absolutely rocked! But at last the enemy planes went droning away towards the English Channel and everyone could get some sleep.

Before daybreak, I glanced up and saw Orlando watching over a sleeping soldier.

"Poor guy just came back to find his house a pile of rubble," he said. "No-one can tell him where his family's gone."

The man's eyelids began to flicker, and his exhausted face took on a strangely peaceful expression.

"He's dreaming," I said softly.

"He used to be a gardener," Orlando sighed. "Before he went off to fight. I thought he could use a restful garden dream."

"You can send dreams?" I breathed.

He gave me one of his heartmelting smiles. "It's no big deal. I'll teach you some time – if you're interested," he added shyly.

Neither of us spoke after that, but it wasn't an awkward silence. Actually, it was lovely.

Shortly after dawn, people began to stir, gathering up babies and belongings.

"Button your coat, Moll," her mum grumbled. "I've got to be at work in half an hour."

"My fingers won't wake up," Molly complained.

I felt really sad as they hurried away. I'd watched over them all night. Now I knew their hopes and fears as well as my own. I know that tuning into human thoughts must sound like some major celestial ability. But the fact is, once you're an angel it's impossible *not* to. They just jump out at you like radio waves.

That's how I knew that Molly's dad had been killed in action, less than six months ago. Now they were all alone.

By a strange coincidence, I'd lost *my* dad when I was Molly's age. He didn't die though, he left. And I know this is corny, but for ages after that, I was terrified Mum would leave too. One time she was late picking me up from school, and it was like my whole world totally crumbled. So I had a pretty good idea what Molly was going through.

Lola nudged me. "Control to Melanie," she teased.

I blinked. Celia wafted up. "I probably won't need you chaps until tonight," she said. "Why not make yourselves useful upstairs?"

"Excellent," crowed Lola. "We can be time-tourists!"

We emerged into a November dawn. It was wonderful to breathe the damp London air after our long night underground.

"Omigosh," said Amber suddenly.

A family were eating breakfast in their living room. Dad in his collar and tie, Mum in her apron, plus three little kids, all politely sipping tea and passing the toast and marge. It was like a scene from a picture book. Except for one thing. The front had been blown clean off their house.

And I remembered Reuben saying, "But what's war for?"

Lola had both hands pressed tightly to her mouth. "Whatever kind of bomb does that?" she whispered.

"The Germans have started sending over these weird buzz bombs," Ferdy explained earnestly. "They're like aircraft, except they don't have pilots. They just point them in the right direction, then when they arrive – BOOM!"

"My Great Nan called them doodlebugs," I said. "She said the first time one came over their house, she almost wet herself." I had a sudden thought. "Ferdy," I said, "how come *you* know so much stuff about 1944?"

When Ferdy tosses his hair about, it means he's going to say something wildly superior. "Don't you *ever* use the Link?"

"Me?" I bluffed. "Never! I prefer to like, improvise."

"Boo, you are so-o bad!" giggled Lola.

Everywhere, we saw constant reminders of the war. Queues outside food shops, sticky tape over the windows, sandbags in doorways. But instead of letting themselves be crushed, people just sprang up again like daisies, totally surprising you.

I don't want you to think we were *just* being time-tourists. Lola and I spent hours with a really good-looking fireman, while his mates dug him out from under a pile of rubble.

He was more of a fire*boy* really. His name was

Stan and he'd been searching a bombed house for survivors when the roof fell in. He was in a lot of pain, but he kept up a stream of daft jokes.

Finally the firemen lifted him free. As the ambulance doors closed, we heard Stan yell, "Tell those two pretty girls to wait for me, do you hear?"

"Poor Stan," muttered one of his mates. "He's really concussed."

I jumped up, tugging down my dress as far as it would go.

"This is your fault, Lollie," I blazed. "I can't believe I've been sitting here in this little dress and Stan the fireman could SEE me!"

Then we heard a low growl in the distance.

"Erm, I think that's a buzz bomb," I said.

"One flying bomb's not so bad," said Amber brightly.

Ferdy was looking unusually nervous. "Actually, they send them in relays."

People were already hurrying for the nearest shelter.

The siren began its stomach-churning wail.

As the bomb came nearer, the air was literally juddering with vibration, as if it was compressing itself into some terrifying new element. I think

Orlando saw how scared I was, because he suddenly grabbed my hand.

"We'll do this the easy way," he yelled. "Touch your angel tags and focus on the shelter. On a count of three. One, two – three!"

I obediently shut my eyes and FLASH! We were underground, as everyone came fleeing down from the street.

BOOM! The first buzz bomb exploded overhead.

Celia appeared, looking wonderfully chic. "Chaos, isn't it?" she said. "Let's see what we can do for the poor dears, shall we?"

We started beaming angel vibes at the traumatised Londoners.

I realised Orlando was standing really close to me. I tried not to dwell on the fact that he'd recently held my hand.

"How did you do that cool fast-forward trick?" I murmured.

Orlando sighed. "Mel, you really ought to read your Handbook!"

We went back to work. It probably sounds terribly hippie-dippie, but transmitting angelic vibes in a crisis is actually just common sense. Negative emotions make it that much easier for the Opposition to home in.

But for some reason I kept looking up every time someone came down into the shelter. The stream of arrivals slowed to a trickle. As the third buzz bomb exploded overhead, I realised what was bothering me.

Molly and her mum weren't there.

In an instant of total clarity, I knew Molly was in danger. I've got to go to her, I thought.

But Orlando completely put his foot down. "You know the score, Mel," he said firmly. "No heroes, no stars. Just links in a divine chain. Those are the rules."

I took a deep breath, trying to stay calm. "I'm not trying to big myself up, I swear. But Molly's only six and she's all alone in an air raid. I *saw* her. Orlando, it's like I'm meant to save her or something. It's — it's –" I searched desperately for the right words. "A genuine cosmic emergency!"

But Orlando was not remotely impressed. "Remember that time outside the Sanctuary? Those agents had a cosmic emergency too. And the Opposition picked them all off like apples."

I really lost my temper then. "Well, EXCUSE me," I yelled. "But I think a little girl is more important than some old rule!"

"Boo," Lola whispered. "Everyone's looking."

Celia's angels were staring in horror. It was like being back at school, only about a billion times worse. Plus now even my best friend was against me.

"I know it must seem harsh," said Orlando quietly.

"Not harsh," I said through gritted teeth. "Inhuman."

Orlando's calm expression didn't flicker. "Just get on with your work, Mel, OK?"

I stared at him. Couldn't he see that Molly and her mother *were* my work? Obviously I'd have to take care of this all by myself.

I sneaked a last yearning look at Orlando. Get real, Mel, I told myself. A gorgeous genius and an airhead with attitude? It was never going to happen!

I didn't try to hide what I was doing. In front of everybody, I touched my angel insignia, and focused on Molly with all my heart.

FLASH! I was outside a terrace of tall thin houses in the fading light.

A weird-looking aircraft hovered at rooftop level. Angry flames jetted out of its ugly backside. A distinctive buzz-bomb growl filled the air. Then it stopped and there was a deathly hush.

The buzz bomb dropped behind the terrace like a stone. Then BOOM! The whole world came crashing down. Jagged shards of glass, clouds of brick dust, actual bricks, half a chimney pot.

Out of instinct I dived into a doorway.

"You're an immortal being," I reminded myself. "Get a grip."

At that moment I heard a scared whimper. "Mum? Where are you, Mum?"

I scanned the street, until I saw a basement door swinging on its hinges. "Hold on Molly!" I called ridiculously, though I knew she couldn't hear me. "I'm coming."

I found her crouching under the kitchen table, whispering the same words over and over. "Come home, Mum," she was whispering. "Please don't be dead, Mum. I'll make you a cup of tea just how you like it. Please don't be dead, Mum."

I couldn't bear it. I completely forgot I was an angel.

"You don't have to be scared. I'm here now," I said softly.

But as I reached for her, I caught a stealthy flicker of movement in the hall. Just the tiniest flicker. And suddenly it was impossible to breathe.

Then I heard a voice so intimate, I seemed to have known it for ever.

"Hi Molly," it said. "I've come to take you down to the shelter."

The tiny hairs rose on my neck.

A boy was lounging in the doorway. He wasn't looking at Molly. He wasn't looking at anything. He was just *there*, smiling at some private joke.

He had bleached blond hair and the bluest eyes I've ever seen. I remember thinking how out of place he looked in that 1940s kitchen, in his black T-shirt and jeans, the image of this boy I'd secretly fancied at my school. Right down to those beautiful dangerous eyes.

This is so unfair, I thought dreamily. They never told me the Opposition could be beautiful.

"We can take any form we like," said the boy softly.

He snapped his fingers like a magician. Suddenly, shadowy little creatures were swarming everywhere, blindly bumping into each other, falling into the sink. The sound they made was out of my worst nightmares – a skittery insect sound which got right inside my head.

"I'm scared, Mum," Molly moaned.

Her voice shook me out of my panic. Call yourself an angel, Melanie Beeby? I scolded myself. This is your basic good-versus-evil type situation. So just pull yourself together!

I stepped in front of the boy, holding out my divine insignia. I was shaking all over.

"Maybe I don't look much like an angel," I quavered, "but I'm here on official Agency business and Molly's under angelic protection. So don't even try to touch her."

The boy laughed. "Oh, but I haven't come for Molly. I've come for you!"

I froze. Total brain melt, I thought. I am so stupid.

I'd made it so easy for them. Leaving my mates in the lurch. Deluding myself I was on a cosmic mission. I had this wonderful new life, I thought. And I threw it away. All for nothing.

"That's right," said the boy. "And by the time we've finished with you, that's exactly what you'll be. Nothing."

He looked straight at me, and his beautiful eyes were totally empty.

"NOTHING," he repeated.

Now I'm a girl who, if someone says I look pale, faints right on cue.

115

And I'm not proud of this, OK, but I immediately felt myself dissolving like a sugar cube. *It's happening*, I thought despairingly. I'm not a person. I'm not an angel. I'm no-one, I'm nothing. Soon I'll just be an empty space. It's all over...

Except, it wasn't.

"Erm, hang about!" I said suddenly. "What am I meant to be scared of exactly? I've already lost everything I care about. I've got nothing left TO lose. Apart from wowing me with your naff special FX, there's not a thing you can do." I drew myself up to my full height. "So stop wasting my time, moron!"

He blew me a scornful kiss. "Diddums. Like I actually care."

But the Opposition's gruesome FX were already fading like a bad dream.

"There's the door," I said in my snottiest voice. "Mind it doesn't hit you in the backside on the way out."

I turned my back as if he'd ceased to exist. And suddenly I could breathe again. He'd gone.

Given my record, I probably wasn't the best angel to save Molly, but I *was* the only angel available. So I touched my angel tags, and with a

WHOOSH of cosmic energy, I willed myself to become visible.

There was a gasp from under the table.

I'd done it! I'd actually materialised! I was so thrilled with myself that my mind went a total blank. What shall I say? I panicked. Then vaguely familiar words floated into my head. I was only six when I played the angel in our school nativity, but it came back like yesterday. Well, kind of.

"Erm – fear not!" I said huskily. "For lo! I am the angel Melanie and I have come to let you know you are not alone."

Molly crawled out, her eyes filled with awe. Then I caught sight of my reflection in the hall and my eyes filled with awe too.

The mirror glowed with a rosy light. Inside the rosy halo was a wonderful being with wings, the kind a terrified child would instantly recognise as an angel.

My moment of weird glory lasted all of five seconds.

Then Molly's mum rushed in, her face absolutely white. "Thank heaven!" she sobbed. She scooped Molly up in her arms and hurried out of the door.

"It's all right Mum," I heard Molly gabble. "I saw

a beautiful angel and she said don't be frightened, so I wasn't."

My knees went to jelly with pure relief. I closed my eyes and a silly smile spread slowly over my face. I don't think I've ever felt as happy as I did in that moment. I saved Molly all by myself, I thought. I really really did it.

Then an unearthly light burst upon my closed eyelids. When I opened them, Michael was standing there. He held out his hand for my angel tags.

"I'll have those, thanks," he said coldly.

CHAPTER TEN

I'd tried every trick I knew to get myself to sleep. I'd had a long bath by candlelight. I'd helped myself to Lola's stash of twenty-second-century drinking chocolate. I'd even listened to my favourite late-night music turned way down low.

I'd tried everything and I was still as jumpy as a Mexican bean. In normal circumstances I'd have died of fright. But angels can't die. Not even angel failures like me.

Typically I never did get around to reading that Handbook, so I had no idea what we did instead. I just hoped it wasn't like that depressing fairytale, where the little mermaid turns into sea foam.

I switched off the light and got into bed. But the dark didn't make me sleepy, just lonely. I padded over to the window and gazed out over the beautiful, beautiful city. Its lights sparkled like millions of fallen stars.

My eyes prickled and blurred. Don't think, Melanie. Don't think about that wraparound sky so blue that you can't tell where it leaves off and the sea begins. Don't think about Lola and Reuben, or that sweet-faced boy Orlando. You had a once-in-eternity opportunity and you blew it.

When I first got here, I used to imagine how gobsmacked Miss Rowntree would be if she ever learned that her most troublesome pupil had been picked for angel school. I was constantly dreaming up dramatic situations where I zoomed back to Earth and wowed my old teacher with my amazing skills. "Melanie," she'd gasp. "I'm truly sorry I misunderstood you. You had hidden depths, which I completely failed to see."

But now it seemed I hadn't changed after all – just gone round in one big dreary circle.

After I was brought back in disgrace, Michael quietly listed every one of my misdemeanours. Abandoning the other members of my team, thus putting them at risk; materialising to a human child without permission; claiming to be on Agency business when actually it was all my own stupid idea...

I'd broken so many celestial rules, it was probably some kind of record. I couldn't blame the Academy for wanting to throw me out.

"It's out of my hands," Michael had said quietly. "The Academy Council will deal with you in due course. Until then you will not be permitted to leave the school grounds."

And he'd looked so disappointed, I'd have given anything to be human again so I could just crawl off and die.

Yet I didn't regret what I'd done. Once I had that moment of clarity in the tube station, I had to do what I believed was right. Even though it turned out to be totally, totally wrong.

It's like, up until that moment I'd just been playing a beautiful magical game called Angel. But the instant I walked away, that was when it became the real thing.

I hadn't set eyes on my mates since I got back. Our entire class had gone off on an end-of-term jaunt to some exotic wildlife park. The dorm was totally dead, and I preferred it that way.

I just couldn't face them after what happened. By the time they came back, it would all be over. I'd be sea foam, or whatever.

I caught sight of my stricken face in the mirror. "We were meant to be the three cosmic musketeers," I whispered.

Now I'd never go time-travelling with my friends, or learn to send dreams like Orlando.

"Stop torturing yourself, Mel," I said aloud. "Try to get through the night with a bit of dignity, OK?"

I'd been summoned to appear before the Council early next morning. But I was so nervous I got there way ahead of time.

"I don't think they're quite ready for you, Melanie," said the school secretary, avoiding my eyes. "Perhaps you'd care to take a seat."

I could tell she despised me. But I was too numb to care. Get used to it, Mel, I thought drearily. In ten minutes you'll be a fallen angel. The lowest of the low.

The chamber door had gorgeous stained-glass panels. I sat staring at it for so long, I could have drawn it from memory. From time to time I heard raised voices. There was a major debate going on. I caught glimpses of swirling robes as various archangels swept past.

I'd never met any archangels, apart from Michael. But Lola once told me they made space aliens seem almost cuddly.

I felt utterly alone. Desperate for comfort, I reached for my angel insignia to reassure myself, but my hand closed around air.

Then I seemed to hear Lola's voice. "What are you doing, Boo?" she demanded. "Sitting here like a total turkey while these terrifying beings decide what to do with you. DO something, girl!"

"Yeah, Mel," Reuben teased. "Put your Houdini powers into reverse and stay put for a change!"

It was like my best friends were actually with me in the waiting room!

"OK," I whispered. "I will."

And I stood up, tugged down my skirt and knocked on the door.

There was no answer, so I took a deep breath and went in.

With so many archangels in one room, the light levels were truly awesome. Michael was there, to my relief. And from what I remembered of our angelic history lessons, I guessed I was also looking at Gabriel, Raphael, Uriel, Jophiel and Chamuel. Just don't ask me which terrifying face belonged to which archangel.

The archangels stared back, appalled. I willed my jelly knees to hold me up.

"I don't mean to be disrespectful," I croaked. "But you've got to let me stay. You've just got to."

The secretary rushed in. "I am so sorry," she panted. "I distinctly told Miss Beeby to wait outside."

"That's quite all right," said a remote voice. "We're most interested to hear what she has to say for herself."

I closed my eyes. "Um," I said. "First, I want to let you know, that I do realise I really messed up badly."

"Hardly a controversial insight," said an identically distant voice.

"I know that," I said humbly. "But you truly can't imagine how sorry I am. I've learned a lot since I've been here."

One of the archangels gave a weary sigh.

"It's the truth," I said quickly. "Mr Allbright is a great teacher and my friends helped heaps, and I think that one day I could shape up to be a really wicked trouble-shooter. Brilliant trouble-shooter, I mean," I corrected hastily.

"Melanie," Michael began. "I don't think this is—"

I rushed on desperately. "I let my team mates down and that was wrong. But that doesn't mean you guys were wrong when you picked me to be an angel." My voice cracked with misery. "If you'll just give me a second chance," I pleaded huskily, "I'll never let you down again. I'll work night and day. I'll even read my—"

An irritable voice interrupted me. "Enough! This is extremely touching, my dear, but I'm afraid you left it too late. We came to our verdict a few minutes before you burst in. And as you know, the Council's decision is final."

I felt a total fool. "Oh," I said. "I'm – I didn't…"

I was suddenly blinded with tears. I was done for. My angelic career had finally crashed and burned. I blundered towards the door.

"Melanie?" said Michael softly. "Don't you want to know what that verdict was?"

I turned in despair. "I suppose, that sinister sea foam thing," I whispered.

"Sea foam?" said Uriel, or possibly Jophiel, looking utterly baffled.

Michael took charge. "Melanie, the Council unanimously agreed that you may stay," he said.

I could feel a leftover tear tracking down my chin. "Stay?" I echoed blankly

It's a dream, I thought. I'll wake up in a minute

and I'll have to go to the *real* Academy Council.

"You did remarkably well in your exams, Melanie," said Michael. "In fact you got a distinction."

I think it was Michael's smile that made me know I wasn't dreaming. I felt it right inside my heart. Suddenly I heard what he'd said.

"A distinction!" I shrieked. "Totally luminous!"

"You also lost your team a much-deserved HALO award," Gabriel or Chamuel pointed out.

"Oh," I said, ashamed. "I didn't know."

"And your angelic presentation skills still need a little work," he added sternly. "I quote: 'For lo! I am the angel Melanie', etcetera etcetera."

My face burned. There are SO not any secrets in Heaven!

Then Uriel – it was definitely Uriel – said something so beautiful, I just know I'll remember it for ever.

"However," he said gently, "a trouble-shooting angel, far from Heaven, must sometimes improvise. And your heart, as humans say, was very much in the right place."

CHAPTER ELEVEN

The morning of the end-of-term party, Lola and I went on a major shopping spree.

"So what was he like?" Lola said, holding up a sugary pink baby-doll dress patterned with little love hearts.

"Yuk!" I said. "Nightmare."

"He was yuk?"

"The dress, dumbo. The Opposition guy was in a totally different category of nightmare. Did you still have horror films in your time?"

Lola shuddered. "My brothers loved those things. Me, I couldn't see the point. All those gruesome special FX."

"*That's* the category," I said. "The spooky thing was, he looked exactly like this boy I fancied at school."

Lola giggled. "A really *bad* boy, I bet."

We went back to hunting along the rails.

"Boo, do you even know what you're looking for?" Lola sighed.

I showed her a scarlet leather catsuit. "What do you think?"

"Miaow!" grinned Lola. "Maybe you should go for something more discreet!"

And she picked out a Clark Kent-type suit. We went into fits of giggles.

"Ooh, yes! All I need is those sexy black-rimmed spectacles," I told her.

"OK," said Lola. "We've got exactly one hour to get this perfect look together. Then we've got to do some serious cooking for the party."

I remembered something. "Lollie, did you and Reuben like, transmit good vibes to me or something, when I was in with the big guys?"

Lola suddenly looked vague. "Maybe. I don't remember."

"Sure you don't." I gave her a hug. "Thanks. I got them."

Exactly one hour later I had the perfect trouble-shooting outfit – cropped top, combats and some cool boots. To me that look says committed, it says *now*, it says ready for action. I mean, I'm an angel, so I should look totally divine, right?

We held our class party down on the beach. Everything was so lovely, I kept thinking it couldn't possibly get any lovelier – but each time the party morphed effortlessly into a whole new phase.

At one point I found myself standing beside Flora. "Sorry about losing you guys that award," I mumbled. I thought she'd be furious, but she just gave a cool little shrug.

"There's always next term."

People can SO surprise you. Take Amber for instance. It turns out she doesn't play the harp at all. Would you believe, bongo drums?!

Incidentally, Reuben aced his Earth Skills paper. Trust me, until you've seen a happy angel-angel, you do *not* know what happiness is!

Lola and I had the most fun teaching Reuben terrestrial-type DJing. In no time he'd developed his own style, mixing earthly and heavenly sounds and rhythms like you would NOT believe.

"Ya-ay! DJ Sweetpea is in the house!" yelled Lola.

Then suddenly my bare arms were covered with goosebumps. Someone was calling me and I had to go.

I slipped down to the seashore, and there was Michael, waiting. He didn't speak, just picked up a beautiful shell from the water's edge and, with the sweetest smile, put it into my hand.

I held it for a moment, just to feel its smooth curved shape. Impulsively I put it to my ear. And then it happened, just like Lola said.

"Helix," whispered the waves.

"It's my name," I breathed. "My true angel name."

losing
the plot

With special thanks to Maria and to local angels,
Chrissie and Hazel

CHAPTER ONE

Try to forget I'm an angel for a minute, and put yourself in my shoes.

Once upon a time, not so long ago, I lived on Earth like you. I attended your standard hell-hole comprehensive, where I spent most of my time hanging out with my mates, nattering about boys and clothes, and waiting for my real life to begin.

Don't get me wrong. I wasn't your actual, tattooed-in-rude-places bad girl. But I don't think even my best mates would have voted me Girl Most Likely to Become an Angel! My teacher, Miss Rowntree, thought I was a waste of space. "An airhead with attitude," she called me.

You know how it is. If enough people tell you

you're dim, you start to believe it, don't you? So when I found myself at the Angel Academy, I automatically assumed there'd been some big celestial screw-up. Clearly they'd confused me with some genuinely deserving kid.

Only they hadn't.

Believe it or not, I turned out to have a natural gift for angel work.

I'm not saying I'm this like, angel genius or anything. I made some really stupid mistakes when I first got here. But the great thing about the Angel Academy is they expect you to get down to the nitty gritty stuff right away. Unlike on Earth, where you have to wait till you're practically grown up before you're allowed to do anything interesting.

To my amazement I passed my exams with flying colours. And at the end of last term, I finally got my true angel name (it's Helix if you're interested). As for my new home, well. Picture your dream holiday destination and times it by a zillion, and even that doesn't begin to do this place justice.

Sounds like I've got it made, I know. Here I am, literally living in Paradise, doing something I'm actually good at. For the first time, I'm part of something. And to top it all, this very morning, my first ever angel ID had arrived in the post.

I should have been the happiest person alive. But I wasn't. Alive that is, or happy. Because I knew that somewhere in a tiny council flat, in a distant galaxy far away, my mum was crying herself to sleep, totally convinced her eldest daughter had been tragically snuffed out, like some little candle flame. When all the time I was safe and sound on what my Great Nan likes to call The Other Side.

I know what you're thinking. What kind of loser feels unhappy in Heaven? My mates were thinking exactly the same thing. In fact, they had a real go at me.

"You never come out with us any more, Mel," Lola complained. "You're practically a hermit these days."

"I'll come next time, I swear," I mumbled guiltily. "It's just that I volunteered to do Angel Watch tonight."

"Yeah, right," said Reuben. "That's what you said last time, and the time before, and the time before that."

"You've got to come, Boo. Today's your big day!" Lola wailed. "You finally got your ID!"

"Yeah, you're a bona fide trainee angel," Reuben coaxed. "So let's go downtown and party like we planned."

I shook my head. "I told you, I can't."

Lola glowered at me. "I thought we were your mates, Mel Beeby. But it's like you're deliberately avoiding us. How can we help you if you won't tell us what's wrong?"

It probably doesn't seem that way, but Lola Sanchez is my soul mate. The moment I set eyes on her I felt as if we'd known each other for ever, and she felt just the same way. Before she died, Lola lived in the twenty-second century, in some tough third-world city. And sometimes you can totally tell!

Reuben's the complete opposite. (Lola's nickname for him is Sweetpea.) Quarrels actually make him feel ill. But don't get the wrong idea. Reuben's no light-weight. He does martial arts, so he's got serious muscles. But unlike me and Lola, Reuben actually *started* life as an angel. He's only ever lived in the Heavenly City and finds humans totally baffling.

Usually, the three of us are inseparable. The Three Cosmic Musketeers, Lola calls us. We're all doing Earth History for our special subject. That probably sounds like we're always memorising dates and reading history books, right? Wrong!

OK, we have to do a bit of studying, but we also make actual field trips to like, different eras in Earth's history. And like Lola says, the sheer buzz of time-travelling totally makes up for the other stuff.

But lately, I couldn't seem to muster any enthusiasm for anything. I was much too homesick. For days now, I'd been completely churned up about my family. It wouldn't have been so bad if I could let them know I was OK. But this was out of the question. Which is why I tried to take my mind off things by doing something practical, like Angel Watch.

It was getting on for midnight as I hurried across the city, and stars glittered over the skyscrapers like huge diamante brooches. I could hear the soft swoosh of traffic, and another sound – a sweet steady throbbing like a cosmic humming top. Once I'd asked Reuben where this mysterious music was coming from.

"Everything!" he said calmly.

I still don't understand how it works. I only know it's the loveliest sound I've ever heard. It's the first thing I heard after a joyrider accidentally booted me out of the twenty-first century and into the Angel Academy. These days I mostly notice it as I'm drifting off to sleep, or when I'm alone with my thoughts.

I was heading for the Agency building, way the other side of town. The Agency is the administrative hub of the entire cosmos. In other words, Angel HQ. We're generally referred to as "cosmic agents" these days, rather than angels. This has the advantage of sounding dead crisp and professional, not to mention totally up to the minute.

The Agency is based in this futuristic glass tower. Its upper storeys literally disappear into the clouds. Gorgeous colours wash over it in waves. Every few seconds there's a burst of light overhead as celestial agents arrive or depart. Because of all the high-level cosmic activity going on inside, the tower gives off amazing vibes. I get tingles while I'm still like, *streets* away.

On this particular night, I went in through the revolving doors, tiptoed across the marble foyer, and flashed my new ID casually at the guy on the desk. Then I stepped into a lift and went humming up into the sky.

The Angel Watch centre takes up an entire floor of the Agency building. It's a massive open-plan area with hundreds of work stations. The minute you walk in, you hear a vast murmuring sound, like an invisible tide washing in and out. I was totally blown away when I realised what I was hearing. Human thoughts. Wave after wave of them. Sad, happy, funny, lonely, please-please-help-me thoughts. And thanks to the Agency, every single one is heard. They're extremely proud of this heavenly aftercare service. Though when I was living on Planet Earth, I personally had NO idea this scheme was available.

One of the night staff handed me a list. "Here again, Mel!" she joked.

"I like coming here," I said defensively.

It was true. It made me feel slightly less guilty about my cushy new life. Plus I got a genuine buzz out of helping people. Assuming I *was* helping them, of course.

I spotted a free booth next to Kwan Yin, this v. serene girl from the Academy. As I passed, I caught a glimpse of her screen.

It was horrifying. Kids, so coated in dust they looked grey, were picking through rags and Coke cans on some vast rubbish tip. One of them was about the same age as my little sister, Jade.

"Omigosh," I said in dismay. "What can anyone ever do to help them?"

"This," said Kwan Yin calmly and went on beaming angelic vibes.

Once I was in my booth, I adjusted my swivel chair, and kicked off my shoes. Then I consulted my list and tapped in the access code for someone called Jordan Scarlatti.

A tiny bald baby flashed up on my screen.

New-borns often find Earth a shock to their systems, so the Agency surrounds them with homey angel vibes while they adjust. It's like goldfish. You don't dump them in chilly tap water right off, do you? You acclimatise them gradually.

Baby Jordan was in an incubator, wired up to this beeping hi-tech machine. His mum sat holding his teeny doll-sized hand through the hole in the incubator. I think she was the one who'd called us for help.

"OK, let's see what we can do," I whispered.

Using Angel Link is totally second nature to me now. It's a kind of heavenly internet, only you don't need a machine to access help or info, just pure concentration.

First I mentally linked up to every angel in existence. And once I felt those familiar vibes whoosh through me, I transmitted them to Jordan for all I was worth.

When I'd finished, I couldn't resist plonking an angel kiss right on Jordan's button nose. Sometimes we breathe on the back of their necks or their bare tummies, a kind of angel tickle. Babies adore angelic vibes, and Jordan's baby thoughts instantly went haywire. "Mum, Mum, an angel kissed me!"

"Ssh, it's our secret," I said softly.

A ripple of laughter went round the centre. The other night workers were pointing at something above my head, so naturally I looked up too.

A crowd of party balloons was floating towards me. Suddenly one gave a loud POP! Sparkly streamers fell out and draped themselves around my head, making me feel a real wally.

"Surprise, surprise!" sang a familiar voice. And Lola and Reuben burst in, clutching cartons from our favourite Chinese takeaway.

As I'm sure you guessed, trainee angels are not encouraged to smuggle Shanghai noodles and crispy seaweed into the Agency building. Not to mention balloons, and heavenly party poppers.

"Are you off your heads?" I wailed, when I could get the words out.

"It's your fault, Boo," said Lola cheerfully. "Since you wouldn't come to the party, we had to bring the party to you!"

She dumped her stylish takeaway cartons on my desk and started peeling off tinfoil lids. Delicious smells filled the air. "I don't know about you guys, but I'm starving," she announced.

But at that moment, I noticed Reuben staring past her with an appalled expression. I followed his gaze. Omigosh, I thought. We are SO in trouble.

Lola saw my face and spun round in alarm.

Standing behind her was our headmaster.

CHAPTER TWO

Let me explain that Michael is not, repeat NOT, your typical headmaster.

As well as running our school, he's a v. big cheese at the Agency. He's also an archangel. Plus he *totally* doesn't take care of himself. On this particular night, he wore a beautiful suit which already looked as if he'd slept in it.

Rather surprisingly, he didn't mention the balloons or the takeaway, just said, "Here again, Melanie? That's three times this week."

Michael has this terrifying ability to see into your soul, which I completely didn't need.

"I LIKE doing Angel Watch," I said. "Is that so hard to believe?"

"Not at all." Michael dragged a chair into my overcrowded little booth, which smelled suspiciously like a tiny Chinese restaurant.

"Oh, Jordan's looking much better," he beamed. "I'll just check his light levels." He touched a key with a fancy L on it (which I'd totally never noticed) and the incubator filled with golden sparkles.

"Wow!" I breathed. "How did you do that?"

Michael laughed. "I didn't! *You* did."

But I couldn't really take it in. I could feel Lola and Reuben silently panicking behind me. Should they whisk our Chinese goodies out from under Michael's nose? Or act like it was nothing to do with them and hope he didn't ask awkward questions?

To my amazement, Michael solved the problem by helping himself to a spring roll. "Did you get these from The Silver Lychee?" he asked.

Lola gave a cautious nod.

"Thought so," he mumbled happily. "The chef's a genius."

Sitting next to an archangel is an experience. Seeing one sploshing on the soy sauce is something else. Suddenly Lola cracked and reached for a spring roll. Soon we were all tucking in.

Michael took off his gorgeous jacket and hung it over his chair. "Who's next on your list, Melanie?"

Light levels really soar when there's an archangel in the vicinity, so we whizzed through my list with no effort whatsoever.

"That about wraps it up," I said at last. "Thanks for your help."

I was expecting Michael to put on his jacket and go back to his office. But he said, "Erm, how's the time-travel going, Melanie?"

"It's OK," I sighed.

But it's impossible to lie to an archangel, so after a few seconds I came clean. "I can't really see the point," I admitted. "All that hanging around being immortal and invisible. I thought we'd at least get to materialise. But Mr Allbright said very few angels develop the ability."

I'd felt unbelievably depressed when Mr A told us this. I was like, "Then why bother?"

"Your teacher's right." Michael's eyes twinkled. "Though agents have been known to make a fluke appearance in an emergency!"

"Oh ha ha," I said. You see, on my first ever time-trip, I got a teeny bit carried away. I materialised without Agency permission, and almost got myself expelled.

By this time I was starting to wonder what was going on. We'd finished the takeaway ages ago, but Michael showed no sign of wanting to break up the party. Plus he kept doing that church steeple thing with his fingers, as if he was working up to asking us something.

"I'm sorry you're having doubts, Mel," he said at last. "You see, we've got this, er – situation on Earth. I'd been hoping you three could help out."

Something inside me instantly sprang to attention. When archangels ask for help, it's got to be major.

"What kind of situation?" Reuben asked.

"It's actually more of a glitch. But if it isn't caught—" Michael corrected himself hastily. "I mean, *monitored*, it could be dangerous. Perhaps even catastrophic."

Words like these are music to Lola's twenty-second-century ears.

"You said the three of us," she said eagerly. "You mean we'd be going by ourselves?"

"You do work exceptionally well as a team. But if Melanie's lost interest—"

"She hasn't. Have you, Boo?" Lola interrupted.

"I haven't?" I said.

"No way," said Reuben firmly.

Michael cleared his throat. "I should warn you this is one of the more volatile eras in Earth's history. A time of love, hate, treachery."

"Sounds like fun," grinned Lola.

"So when is this glitch exactly?" asked Reuben.

"It's not an actual glitch yet," said Michael confusingly. "More of a *potential* glitch. If it does appear, it will probably show up in Elizabethan London, around 1579, say."

"So this is like, a research trip, not an actual mission, right?" I was pretty sure the Agency didn't send new trainees on solo missions.

"That's right," Michael agreed, just a shade too quickly. "Technically speaking, it's not a mission as such. As I said, it's a delicate situation."

I was puzzled. Usually Michael is the most straightforward being in the universe. But tonight, it was like everything he said had this weird double meaning.

"I don't get it," I said. "Are you saying we can do stuff, so long as we do it like, unofficially?"

Our headmaster began to construct a new steeple with his fingers. "Just remember that you didn't hear it from me," he said very quietly.

I stared at him in bewilderment. What kind of an answer was that?

"Erm," said Lola, "What if we don't find your glitch?"

Michael suddenly looked weary. "I can't really go into details at this stage."

"Can't or won't?" I said cheekily.

Michael's expression was cagey. "All you need to know is that if it isn't checked, it will leave the way wide open to the Opposition."

I still feel queasy when I hear that word. I was totally shocked when I found out there were evil forces which wage war on angels for like, fun. The Agency refers to these forces as the Opposition. My mates and I call them PODS, as in Powers of Darkness.

Unlike us, they have no actual shape of their own. But over the centuries they've developed a scary ability to take on any shape they like.

On my first time-trip to Earth, I tangled with a PODS agent who was the image of a boy I fancied at my old school. This boy (the human one) was gorgeous, but really bad news, so for obvious reasons, I'd kept this humiliating crush to myself. Yet somehow the PODS Agency had all this deeply personal info about me. It made me hot and bothered just thinking about it.

I realised Lola was talking to me. "Mel, are you OK?"

"Er, yeah," I said. "When do we go?"

"As I was saying, now would be best," said Michael.

"Oh, wha-at? Can't we at least go home to change?"

I have these perfect trouble-shooting outfits in my wardrobe, but nine times out of ten, I have to charge off in what I happen to be wearing at the time, which is usually something v. short and sparkly. Just what you need, when you're off to do battle with the Powers of Darkness.

"All right," Michael sighed. He ruffled my hair affectionately and I felt about a zillion angel volts sizzle through me. "But be quick."

And with archangel fingerprints tingling all over my scalp, I said hoarsely, "I will."

"Do you guys get the feeling this mission could be really big?" Reuben said, as we hurried back to school.

"Really vague, more like," I grumbled. "I mean, first it's a situation. Then it's a glitch. Ooh, then it's only a *potential* glitch. And we're not on a mission, we're just taking a look. Erm, no, scrub that! I should have said *unofficially* taking a look!"

"It has to be vague, Mel, you know that," said Reuben. "Humans have free will. You can't say what's *going* to happen. Just what *might* happen."

"Oh, honestly! Will you just listen to yourself?" I complained.

"Hey, what's your problem?" said Lola.

I took a deep breath. "We're supposed to be

divine messengers, or whatever. Only we never actually materialise, so most humans never get the message! Duh! So can someone please tell me what we're FOR!"

My friends stared at me in surprise. I was quite surprised myself. Michael was right. I did have doubts, loads of them. Now they'd all come splurting out at once.

"I just want to know what we're for," I repeated in a quieter voice. "Like, if humans have this free will everyone goes on about, how come we're allowed to influence them, anyway?"

"You said it," said Reuben. "We *influence* them. Beam vibes, help them remember who they are. We don't make them do stuff."

"Totally," agreed Lola. "The PODS put on enough pressure as it is."

Reuben grinned. "If it helps, just think of angels as alarm clocks."

I couldn't help laughing. "As *what*?"

His eyes glinted. "We wake humans up!"

Lola put her arm round me. "Come on, Boo. You should be wildly excited. Can you believe they're letting us do a solo trip?"

"Yeah, this sounds more up Orlando's street," Reuben agreed.

Orlando is one of our seniors. Not only is he an angel genius, he's heart-meltingly gorgeous. But he's so into his studies, he genuinely doesn't notice the effect he has on girls.

Lola gave me a sly nudge. "Melanie wishes Orlando was coming too."

"I do not," I said huffily.

"He's probably off on some hush-hush Agency project," said Reuben.

"They didn't pick us because Orlando's unavailable, you know," I objected. "They picked us because we're good."

"Oooh!" teased Lola. "Someone's feeling better!"

I was, actually. "Hey," I said suddenly. "Do you think angels are wired so they like, *need* to do angel work?"

My friends exchanged weary glances, zipped their lips and threw away invisible keys.

"OK, OK, I'll read the boring cosmic manual!" I sighed. "Now can we just drop it?"

Back at the school dorm, I put on my new T-shirt, a pair of low-slung Triple 5 Soul jeans and big funky boots. I swapped a couple of hoop earrings for business-like little studs. Then I threw a few girly necessities into my rucksack, grabbed my jacket and I was ready to go.

I checked out of the window and saw an Agency limo already waiting, its lights blinking in the dark. Lola tapped on my door. We're such close friends, we're practically twins. And our taste in clothes is so similar, it's spooky. Except that being from the future, my soul-mate always looks that bit more outrageous!

Tonight, she had on the coolest sunglasses, with misty blue lenses. One lens had a tiny diamante star in the corner. "You look great!" I told her.

The limo dropped us back at HQ, then we hurtled down to Departures. Michael looked pointedly at his watch.

"We aren't *that* late," I panted.

Lola grinned. "Plus, like you always say, Time doesn't actually exist."

Michael hustled us along corridors, giving us a last-minute briefing as we went. "You'll be splitting up, I'm afraid. Each of you has been allocated—" he coughed. "I mean, will be monitoring a different human."

"So much for the research trip," I mouthed at Lola.

"I *think* I'm right in saying it's not a plague year," Michael was saying.

Workers in white fluorescent suits were giving our portal a last-minute service. The chief maintenance guy gave us a bashful grin. On Earth, Al would be an ideal heavy, a doorman at a nightclub or something. But he's actually incredibly shy. He makes these agonizing little jokes but he totally can't look you in the eye.

Michael dished out our angel tags while we waited. We always wear them when we're on official business. They help us stay in contact with other angels through the Link. Plus they're v. useful if we want to get somewhere in a hurry. Since we were going to Earth without a supervising adult, we also got issued with these really hi-tech Agency watches.

"Ready when you are, kids," said Al, and we stepped into the portal.

Reuben was singing under his breath. I recognised the lyrics of a tune he'd been working on. "*You're not alone,*" it went, "*You're not alone,*" over and over.

"That's a cool tune, Sweetpea," Lola said. "Let's put a little harmony in there." Lola has a beautiful voice. She literally sings like an angel.

I sing like a frog, basically, but I joined in just the same.

When Michael heard us singing in the time portal, he got this weird look on his face. At first I thought it was because his regular agents don't tend to sing on take-off. But he didn't look like, annoyed. He looked sort of touched and upset. He actually made a move towards us, as if he was going to say something. Then at the last minute, he checked himself and gave Al the thumbs-up.

"Remember," he called to us, "stay alert."

The door slid shut.

"Yeah, the Agency needs lerts," Lola quipped under her breath.

I waved at Michael through the glass, trying not to laugh.

"What's plague, Mel?" Reuben hissed into my ear.

I explained that the plague was one of the most terrifyingly contagious human diseases ever. I'd just reached the part about those disgusting purple boils, when our portal lit up like a fairground and we were blasted out of Heaven and into the slipstream of history.

Time-travel, Agency-style, is unbelievably speedy. Entire centuries flash past your eyes in a multi-coloured blur.

Shortly after take-off, we passed a major Opposition outpost. They're quite easy to spot, generally showing up as whirlpools of dark icky energy. The Agency only sends really top-flight trouble-shooters there. Personally, just whizzing past one gave me the chills.

Then I remembered something that Mr Allbright said. He said *nothing in the cosmos ever stays the same*. Like, a golden era can collapse in ruins and a dark one can have a major change of heart.

I remembered something else too. He said it only takes *one* wide-awake human to make a difference!

But as we hurtled towards our destination, we started getting a weird strobing effect. Dark light dark light dark light. Like a cosmic zebra crossing.

It looked as if we were heading for a time and place where the forces of light and darkness were *totally equal*. It was deeply disturbing to look at. I hastily put on my shades.

"Erm?" I said. "Aren't fifty-fifty set-ups incredibly dangerous? Aren't they the ones which easily tip like, either way?"

But I never got my answer. With a final blinding burst of light, we were catapulted into Time. When I opened my eyes, the time-portal had vanished. So had my friends.

I was alone in Elizabethan London.

It was raining heavily. And there was no light anywhere.

CHAPTER THREE

Eventually I twigged. This was not Cosmic Darkness with a capital D, it's just that street-lights hadn't been invented yet.

"Aargh! What is *that*?" I clapped my hands over my nose.

Think of your local rubbish dump on a sweltering summer's day, add a spot of raw sewage and a dash of wood-smoke, and you'll get an idea of the extreme niffiness of Elizabethan London.

My Agency watch flashed, informing me I'd been on this mission for exactly thirty, oops, thirty-one seconds.

We're meant to run through this three-step procedure, as soon as we touch down. Luckily, I'd memorised this section of the manual.

"STEP ONE," I recited. "Adjust angel senses, if necessary. Conditions may be primitive, causing distress to divine personnel."

Tell me about it! I hastily made the necessary adjustments, doing my best to avoid taking in any actual oxygen. To my relief, the pong became more bearable.

I was becoming aware of low grumbling sounds. Suddenly my surroundings lit up with a lurid blue light. The lightning lasted long enough for me to see scruffy thatched roofs and timber house-fronts, all leaning every which way, and several rats scavenging in the garbage. Then I was back in darkness.

Since I became an angel, I kind of tolerate rats, but I'm not what you'd call a fan. I carried on bravely with my check-list.

"STEP TWO. Acclimatise to local thought levels..."

Elizabethan thought-levels turned out to be soothingly low-density. Plus, they had a bubbly feel-good vibe, which I totally wasn't expecting.

My watch let out a beep. Time for Step Three. Should be homing in on my subject any minute now.

The rain was hammering down by this time, and the flashes of lightning were v. close together.

Two men in cloaks hurried past. One held up a

burning torch to light their way. It gave off a strong, vaguely familiar smell, like creosote or tar.

Roars of laughter were coming from a house with a green bush over the door. Stale beer fumes and savoury cooking smells wafted out. The door opened and someone lurched into the street, singing at the top of his voice.

This is the place, I thought. I can't explain how I knew. It's an angel thing. Like a tiny zing of angel electricity inside your heart.

I took a deep breath and went in.

Inside, yellowish candles gave out a spluttering light and a strong smell of fat.

I dutifully scanned my immediate environment, like Mr Allbright says we should, in case any other cosmic agents were passing through. They weren't, which I found quite surprising. We usually spot loads of Earth angels knocking around.

The tavern was crowded with customers, all quaffing ale and tucking into platters of stew. It was a real mix. Well-off types wearing starched ruffs and gorgeous silks and velvets, mingling cheerfully with poorer people. Though I think there must have been some law which said the poor had to wear depressing clothes, because the majority of the customers were dressed in these like, dingy dung colours.

All this candlelight was highly atmospheric, but unfortunately it didn't quite reach into the corners. I had to wander around, peering foolishly into shadows. Where oh where was my human?

One corner was filled by a huge snoring drunk. As I watched, he scratched furiously at his head. Still totally zonked, the drunk then began foraging in his armpit. Hey, fleas *and* body lice, I thought. Groovy!

In another corner, a young man was scribbling on a piece of parchment, between mouthfuls of stew. Hmmn, homesick foreigner, I decided. Possibly French. Could this be my human? He was WAY the most stylish dresser in the tavern.

I listened hopefully to my heart. Uh-uh, I decided regretfully. No zing.

A plump woman was ferrying flagons of ale between the tables, looking hot and flustered. "Where's that girl got to?" she complained to a man in an apron. "It's all me and Nettie can do to keep up."

Being an angel, I understood her perfectly, but her words had an almost American twang; nothing like English speech in my day.

"Don't be hard on her, wife," said the man calmly. "'Tis my brother's last night in port. He and Cat will be saying their farewells."

ZING!

That's her, I thought. That's my human!

I made my way around the tavern, as if I was being pulled along by an invisible string, until I reached a dark winding staircase. By the time I reached the top, it wasn't a pulling sensation. It was a shout. *She's here!*

A girl's voice floated through an open door. "Why won't you take me?"

I slipped through the door into a little room. By modern standards it was empty. Bare floorboards, a bed, a wooden chest, a jug, and a small basin. Two stubs of candle gave a flickering light.

Cat had her back to me. She seemed to be in the middle of a big argument with a wild-haired man in seaboots. He was big and burly with an impressive collection of scars. A pearl the size of a pear-drop dangled from his ear.

"I told you before! It's no life for a little maid at sea."

"I'm not a little maid, I'm thirteen," Cat snapped. "And I can do anything a man can do and more."

She turned and I saw her properly for the first time.

She was beautiful. Even in this light, I could tell her eyes were green. But it was the colour of her skin which really took me by surprise. It was like Demerara sugar, at the exact moment it melts into caramel.

I am so dense. I had no *idea* there were any black Elizabethans.

Cat twiddled a wiry black curl which had escaped from her cap. "Don't leave me," she pleaded. "Living here, I feel like a freak at a fair."

She put on a bumpkin voice. "What shall we do tonight, Ebenezer? Oh, let's go to the Feathers and gawp at the blackamoor. 'Tis said her father is the most fearsome pirate on the Spanish Main."

Her voice shook with unhappiness. But I'm ashamed to say I was totally thrilled. A pirate's daughter! This had to be my coolest assignment yet!

Her dad sounded upset. "Was I wrong to bring you to England?"

"No," she admitted. "I was happy when I was little." She clutched his arm. "Take me with you. Please."

Her father sighed. "Not this time, my honey." He gave her an awkward pat. "Come, let us part as friends. It may be many months before we meet again."

Cat fingered a string of cowrie shells around her neck. Her face had gone totally blank and her emotions were so guarded that even *I* couldn't tell what she was feeling.

"You look just like her," her father said huskily.

She dropped her shells. "I know who I look like!" she spat. "I see myself in the glass each morning. So if you mean to leave me behind again, go! And don't bother coming back!"

The pirate's face grew dark with anger. Moving surprisingly quietly for such a bulky man, he left without a word, closing the door behind him.

Cat instantly threw herself face-down on her bed. She cried so hard, I felt the bed shaking, yet she didn't make a sound.

I sat beside her in agonized sympathy. "Please don't," I begged her. "He hates leaving you. Angels know these things."

After bawling for five minutes max, Cat sat up and gave herself a fierce shake. "The world is full of orphans," she said aloud. "They manage well enough."

She splashed water on her face from the basin, tied an apron around her waist, blew out one candle and used the other to light her way downstairs.

"Catherine Darcy, you'll be the death of me!" her aunt scolded through the uproar. "Me and Nettie's rushed off our feet. You can start by serving these fine gentlemen by the window."

I learned a lot about Cat as I watched her serving customers, demurely dodging the hands trying to pinch her bum or sneak down her bodice, and ignoring stupid remarks about her skin colour rubbing off. She totally didn't let it touch her. Even though her life was deeply depressing, she had this queen-like dignity which I really envied.

Suddenly the door opened and two youths burst in. "Didn't I tell you I'd make Rosalind love me?" the tallest boy was saying. He kissed his hand to the air. "Oh, fair Rosalind, soon you will be mine!"

"You just love the chase, Nick Ducket," grinned his friend. "The moment she's yours, you'll moon over sweet Beatrice or lovely Helena!"

It was hard to believe they'd been out in the same rainstorm. Nick's companion looked half-drowned, while Nick himself was just fetchingly rain-sprinkled.

As well as being good-looking (he had the most gorgeous blond hair!), Nick had bags of confidence. And his clothes were sublime.

I know it's not a nice thing to say, but his mate wasn't in the same league. His boots were so old and worn that water was actually leaking *out* of them. And his wet hair was plastered to his scalp, emphasising his large, rather vague eyes.

Suddenly I felt my skin prickle, which is generally a sign that other angels are in the vicinity. Maybe Michael's checking up on us, I thought.

So I was completely astonished when my mates

appeared. They rushed over and we had a quick hug.

"What are you doing here?" I demanded.

Reuben nodded at the boys. "Following them."

Nick was waving frantically to Cat. She hastily shooed them into an empty corner.

"Have pity, sweet Cat," he wheedled. "Chance and I haven't eaten since yesterday noon."

She glanced around nervously. "All right. But pay for your drinks, or my aunt will get suspicious."

Nick threw down some coins. "Some spiced ale, Cat, if you please!"

She rubbed her thumb across her fingers. "*And the rest, Master Ducket.*"

"You do not love me," he complained.

She gave a scornful laugh. "Rosalind may drop at your feet like a dead pigeon the instant you fire a poem at her! I have more sense." Flouncing her skirts, she bustled off to fetch their ale.

Nick grinned. "I'll have to tame that little wildcat in a year or so."

His friend didn't answer. He had an oddly misty expression. Actually, I started to wonder if maybe he wasn't quite all there.

"It's so weird that they're friends,' I said to the others. "Why didn't the Agency say so in the first place?"

A grubby white puppy appeared from somewhere. It made an immediate beeline for Reuben, collapsing beside him in a sprawl of gangly paws, looking up adoringly. Animals *love* pure angels. It's like hanging out with Doctor Dolittle.

Cat sneaked two huge helpings of stew to her mates while her aunt wasn't looking. "Here's some bread to mop up the gravy," she whispered.

"Stay, Cat," Nick coaxed her. "You're looking so pretty today."

Chance started eating ravenously. "Yes, stay, Cat," he mumbled. "Nick's got a proposition for you."

Cat's eyes narrowed. "Another one?"

Nick acted hurt. "This will make us rich."

"Don't tell me," she scoffed. "With his dying breath, an old alchemist gave you the recipe for turning lead into gold. But you're prepared to share it with me, in return for some more stew."

Nick clutched his chest, as if she'd just stabbed him through the heart. "So young, yet so cruel!"

Cat grinned. "I'm young, but I didn't just fall out of the nest," she called, as she flew off to serve new customers.

I quickly gave my mates the lowdown on Cat's unusual family history.

"Nick's amazing too," said Lola loyally. "He

knows Greek and Latin, plus he plays the lute. And he writes poetry."

"And what a dish," I sighed.

Reuben was tickling the puppy's tummy. To the customers, of course, it looked as if it was just rolling around on the ground in sheer puppy high spirits!

"What's your boy called again?" I asked politely.

He gave a deep sigh. "Chance."

"That's a funny name."

"No comment," Reuben said darkly.

Chance had really perked up now he'd eaten. Only unfortunately, he'd gone to the other extreme. When Cat joined them, he started on some involved story about how his landlord just slung him out for no reason. I've got to admit, Chance had quite a knack for storytelling. He seemed to know how to make dead ordinary things sound incredibly dramatic. But it was like no-one could get a word in!

Cat was sweet, though. "Don't worry. We won't let you sleep on the street."

His eyes lit up. "It wouldn't be the first time I've been homeless!" he said eagerly. "Did I tell you about when I came to London? It was the middle of winter. Snow was falling—"

"I thought you arrived in May," she objected.

"So I did," he said promptly. "There was an unusually late fall of snow that year. One night, I woke up in a doorway, half-dead with cold, and found myself covered in a thin layer of white, like a poor man's shroud—"

Reuben rolled his eyes. I felt sorry for him. Me and Lola both had v. cool humans to take care of. Chance was just really sad!

Unfortunately, Lola picked that moment to put the boot in. "I've got this feeling Nick might be really famous when he grows up,' she bragged.

Reuben shuddered. "Famous? Him? After what he was saying about cock fights, on the way here?"

She scowled. "Animal rights haven't been invented yet, you idiot. They don't know any better."

Suddenly I noticed several men moving stealthily towards the Frenchman's table.

"Erm," I said uneasily, "I'm getting bad vibes."

Then someone shrieked, "The traitor has a knife!"

And next minute total chaos broke out.

Chapter Four

The Frenchman's chair was pulled from under him, sending him sprawling. Then the table went over. Ink and leftover stew flew everywhere.

Someone bellowed, "Stand up, you Spanish dog! Fight like a man!" And someone else yanked the Frenchman to his feet.

"The knife was only to sharpen my quill, monsieurs," he stammered.

But the men started shoving him around, trying to make him fight.

Naturally, we were doing our best to transmit helpful vibes, but it took some concentration, believe me. Luckily Cat's uncle came charging up from his cellar and calmed things down. And after a lot of extremely unpleasant name-calling, the Frenchman was allowed to leave unharmed.

Lola was horrified. "Will someone tell me what's so wrong with Spain?" she demanded.

As it happened, the Tudors were about the only thing I'd liked about history lessons at my old school. I think it was that irresistible combination of blood, gore and fashion! So I was able to give my mates a speedy history lesson.

"The Spanish wanted a Protestant to rule England. Sorry, I mean a Catholic," I added hastily. "That's right, they definitely wanted Queen Elizabeth to turn Catholic, so she could marry their king. But she said, 'No way, José,' so they plotted to get rid of her."

Reuben was shocked. "You mean like, *kill* her?"

"They tried everything!" I said knowledgeably. "Poisoned dresses, hired assassins."

"Poisoned dresses!" Lola was impressed.

"One time they sent warships to invade England," I told them. "But the English beat them off."

Then I did a hasty calculation. "Oh, hang on. Maybe the Spanish Armada hasn't happened yet…Oh, I don't know! Anyway, I'm telling you, this Spanish thing dragged on for like, decades."

Reuben looked confused. "Mel, the guy wasn't even *Spanish*!"

Lola shrugged. "He was foreign, wasn't he?"

I could tell the incident had put her totally on edge.

Michael warned us it would be like this, I thought. Elizabethans are SO intense. One minute everyone's having a mellow time, then suddenly, total mayhem!

I think the bad vibes had got to Chance too. Because with absolutely no warning, he jumped up and started doing acrobatics. Back-flips, cartwheels, walking on his hands.

"What on earth?" said Reuben.

Everyone was staring open-mouthed. No-one knew what to make of this lunatic.

Once he'd got everyone's attention, Chance somersaulted across the tavern at electrifying speed. Then, like a character in a musical, he jumped on a chair and started to sing. An extremely rude song to judge from the actions.

By the time he reached the last verse, the customers were laughing so much, they could hardly stand!

"Where did you learn tumbling?" Cat hissed as he took his bow.

"Oh, the gypsies taught me," he mumbled.

Nick came bounding over to join him. After some conferring, the boys launched into a drinking song. Nick had a wonderful voice, heaps better than Chance's. When they'd finished, Chance left Nick to charm the punters with a truly beautiful ballad.

Afterwards, everyone bought them drinks, and before long everyone was getting happily smashed.

Lola was full of admiration. "Chance totally changed the atmosphere," she said. "That was pure genius!"

"Pure adrenaline, you mean," Reuben scoffed. "It's like he *had* to do something, even if it meant making a total spectacle of himself. Have you noticed how tense he is? That kid is hiding something."

I kind of agreed with him, actually. Something about Chance just didn't add up.

During the singsong, I'd noticed three girls chatting to Cat. What with their lurid make-up and worldly-wise expressions, it didn't exactly take a rocket scientist to figure out how they earned their living. After a bit of arguing, they called Chance over.

"Cat says you need a place to stay," said a girl with a mole on her cheek. "We've got a cubbyhole you could use, haven't we, Nell?"

"Tell us about yourself," suggested Nell.

"Oh, please don't," Reuben groaned.

But Chance was off like a wind-up rabbit, telling them how his family had fallen on hard times. Desperate to help out, he'd gone out one night to poach the squire's deer, and got caught. Luckily a mate helped him to escape from the local lock-up.

"There was nothing to do but come to London and seek my fortune. It was the month of May, but instead of blossom, snow was falling. One night I woke up in a doorway, half-dead with cold –"

"All together now," Lola giggled.

"– and found myself covered in a thin layer of white, like a poor man's shroud," we chorused.

But by the time Chance had finished this ridiculous yarn, the girls had agreed he could stay.

"We'll take care of your sweetheart, Cat!" they teased her, as they got up to leave.

"We're going to the playhouse tomorrow," Nick reminded Chance. He pinched Cat's cheek. "You come too."

She glowered. "You just want me to help you with your plan."

"I'll call for you," Nick insisted.

Reuben followed Chance and his new landladies

into the night.

"Don't do anything I wouldn't do," I called, as my soul-mate skipped off with dishy Nick.

After the last customers had stumbled home, Cat took a candle-stump and climbed up to her little attic.

I'd have fallen straight into bed, personally. But she patiently peeled off layer after layer, including a rib-crushing corset (a *corset*!), until she was only wearing her petticoat.

She washed herself thoroughly with squishy-looking home-made soap, then said her prayers. And at the end she gabbled quickly, "Please bring my father safely home," which I presumed meant she'd forgiven him.

Then Cat climbed into bed, snuffed out her candle, tucked her hand under her cheek, and instantly fell asleep.

Watching humans sleep is really touching. Their daytime disguises just fall away, and you see right into their souls.

Cat's dreams bore absolutely no resemblance to her daytime life. They were filled with crying gulls and the snap and billow of sails. And when she strained her eyes, she could see the shore, a blue shadow on the horizon.

But then the sun came up over the rooftops and birds began twittering outside her window. And it was time for Cat to start another day.

Nick turned up shortly after ten.

"*Omigosh*," I sighed. "He's even better looking by daylight!"

I noticed Lola behind him, pulling faces. "Hands off! This human's mine," she teased. Strangely, she didn't sound quite as pleased about it as she had the day before.

Cat grudgingly consented to take Nick to Chance's lodgings.

"I have not agreed to anything. I want to see how he is, that's all," she said and immediately went marching off. She had brought bread and cold meat for Chance, wrapped in a cloth.

The street was dazzlingly bright after the tavern. Lola and I put our shades on, and I hooked my arm through hers. "So what's Golden Boy's place like?"

She rolled her eyes. "Messy! You know boys!"

But I thought Lola sounded just a bit too perky. I don't know why, but I got the feeling she was keeping something from me.

I couldn't believe how noisy London was in these times. Wooden carts thundering over cobbles, bells pealing, plus all the street-sellers shouted practically non-stop.

Nick bought a red rose from a flower girl and stuck it in his cap.

Oh, what a poser! I thought. And I decided it was high time gorgeous Nick was dislodged from his pedestal. I gave Lola a nudge. "Bet the flower's for that Rosalind bimbo."

She gave me a hurt look. "I think it looks really good on him."

"Ooh," I teased. "Looks like you're carrying a bit of a torch."

Lola glared at me. But luckily at that moment Cat and Nick got a spurt on and we had to go galloping after them.

Cat went beetling off down a maze of alleyways, until she reached a rickety tenement built of wood and thatch. Nick caught her up at the door, and started nosing in Cat's bundle while they waited for someone to let them in. She slapped his hand away.

"I see you have favourites, Cat," he said huffily. "Chance gets breakfast, yet I must buy my own."

"If you're hungry, it's because you squander your father's money at cards," she snapped. "Chance has nobody to care for him."

"Push the door, Cat, and walk in," called a girl's

voice.

We piled in after her into a little front room where Reuben was calmly practising martial arts knee-bends.

"You survived then," I teased.

He grinned. "Naturally. The girls are cool. Can you believe they've got him writing love letters to earn his keep!"

We quickly moved in to do a spot of angelic eavesdropping.

Chance was at the table in his shirt-sleeves, scribbling away. The girls clustered around him, with awed expressions.

One of the girls was mending Chance's doublet for him.

Nick pulled a sour face at Cat. "Poor Chance has *nobody*," he mimicked.

Chance turned to Nell. "This is what you said. 'Dearest Jem, I remember your sweet face as we walked by the river...'"

As she heard her words read back, Nell blushed to her ears. "Tell me how to end it," she begged.

"As quickly as possible," Nick suggested in a sarky voice.

Chance tried to ignore him. "Did Jem give you that half a sixpence around your neck?" She nodded. "How about something like, 'I wear your token night and day. It shines as brightly as when you first gave it to me.'"

"Hurry up, man," said Nick impatiently. "We've got better things to do than listen to your bad poetry."

Chance looked hurt. "It's not supposed to be poetry. It's a letter."

Sympathetic Nell came to his rescue. "It's three years since I saw my Jem," she said. "My letter can wait."

The other girl bit off her thread and gave Chance his doublet back. "Farewell, Tom," the girls called after him affectionately.

Lola and I almost banged heads in the doorway. "Farewell *who*?" we said simultaneously.

Cat had gone storming out. The boys had to run to catch up with her, and so did we. She kept up her cracking pace for a few minutes. Then she glared at Chance. "Why do you *do* that?"

He gave a baffled shrug. "What?"

"All these lies! You even lie about your name. 'My friends call me Chance', that's what you said."

"It's true!" he blustered.

"Really! What about that man who came for you, wasn't he looking for someone named Robert? And now you're Tom or Dick or is it Harry?"

Chance looked completely panic-stricken. He was actually cringing, like a dazed little mole being dragged into daylight.

Nick tried to interrupt but Cat was unstoppable. "You have more names than the tavern dog! Customers call him Snowball one day and Killer the next until he—"

She stopped abruptly. Desperate to shut her up, Nick had whipped the rose out of his hatband and presented it to her with a bow.

"No more of this," he laughed. "For what's in a name? Would not this rose smell as sweetly, if it were called turnip or herring, or – or *hairy nostril*!"

I felt the weirdest tingle. Like I'd already heard these words, or something very like them, before. They had a similar effect on Chance, because he stopped looking like a dazzled mole, and broke into a delighted smile.

But Cat just stared at the rose. She had forgotten to close her mouth and there was the faintest flush under her golden skin.

Oh-oh, I thought. Complications! I nudged Lola. "I think Cat fancies your Nick," I whispered.

Reuben looked smug. "You've only just noticed, haven't you."

"When did you notice then?" I said sullenly.

He gave me his most seraphic smile. "The first time I saw her."

Suddenly Lola took off her sunglasses. I was horrified to see she was crying.

"Lollie, what is it?"

But she could hardly get the words out. "It's Nick," she wailed at last. Then she glowered through her tears. "He's the bad guy, OK? Dumb old Lola got the doofus."

"Hey, where did that come from?" I said, startled. "This isn't a contest, you know."

"I wouldn't say he's an out-and-out bad guy," said Reuben comfortingly. "He's just a bit full of himself. It's probably hormones."

Lola was in such a state, that she actually stamped. "It's not his hormones. It's his *heart*, you idiot! All he thinks about is getting people to do what he wants. He's on the make, twenty-four hours a day. It's like he can't stop."

And she told us that after Nick left the Feathers the previous evening, he'd stopped off at various shady gambling dens, ending up at some total dive where people were forcing this poor ape to ride around on a horse.

"You're kidding," I said.

"These half-starved bulldogs were just waiting for it to fall off! And Nick watched," she choked.

I put my arm around her. "But that doesn't make him a bad person, Lollie. You said yourself, animal rights haven't been invented yet."

"Boo, he was actually laughing. He thought it was funny!" Lola hid her face in her hands. "Then we finally got back to his place, and he fell asleep and all that cruelty just melted away. And I watched him sleeping. He has such beautiful dreams," she said earnestly. "And it's like I saw the real him."

I had a flash of inspiration. "You think he's our glitch, don't you?"

"Yes. No. Oh, I don't know," she said wretchedly.

As we watched, Nick pushed back his hair and smiled into Cat's eyes.

Lola's right, I thought. It has to be him. He's clever and gorgeous, but he's just too smooth for his own good.

Reuben beamed at Lola. "This is great! We finally know what we're doing here."

"Yeah! Dingaling!" I did a bad impersonation of an alarm clock. "We have to wake up Golden Boy and save him from himself."

I told myself this was the right, the only, decision. Chance was a real character but basically a loser.

Cat was fabulous, but as an Elizabethan girl, her career prospects were painfully limited.

We're professionals, I told myself bravely. We aren't *allowed* to have favourites. And on that basis, we have to nominate talented go-getting Nick as Elizabethan Human Most Likely to Succeed.

"So that's settled," I said. "We'll get dishy Nick Ducket back on track and everything will be cool."

"Phew! What a relief," said Reuben.

And like people in a toothpaste ad, we gave each other big cheesy smiles.

CHAPTER FIVE

We were down by the docks, dangling our feet off a jetty, three angels and three humans in a row, listening to Nick pitch his latest money-making scheme. Well, Chance and Reuben were listening.

Me and Lola tuned out, the minute we realised Nick was proposing some dodgy gambling scam. I'm thick when it comes to cards and Lola was just depressed. Here we were, mad keen to help Nick become his new improved self, and he totally wouldn't co-operate.

I'm fairly sure Cat was thinking about her dad. She kept glancing wistfully at the sailing ships riding at anchor in the harbour.

I love the smell of docks: salt and tar and fresh

wood shavings. Mmmn! I shut my eyes to have a good sniff, and was impressed to see gold sparkles dancing past my eyelids. "I'm getting cosmic sparkles!" I announced excitedly.

Lola instantly shut her eyes. "Me too! Wonder what that's about?"

"Could it be something to do with that little feel-good vibe they've got going here?" I said tentatively.

"I suppose!" Lola lifted her face to the sun, enjoying the rays.

"Maybe it's because the Elizabethan world has like totally opened up," I suggested. "Exciting new lands to explore. New discoveries and stuff. You can practically taste the excitement in the air."

Especially down here, I thought dreamily, with all these beautiful ships getting ready to sail who knows where.

Lola frowned. "I'll tell you what's weird, Boo. I mean, this has to be the vibiest time we've visited so far."

"Totally," I agreed.

"So, why isn't the place *stiff* with angels? I haven't seen a single cosmic agent of any description, have you?"

"Actually, no—" I began.

"Will you shut up!" Reuben grumbled. "I'm trying to make sense of all this underworld lingo Nick's spouting. What is a 'fingerer', anyway?"

Lola sighed. "He's trying to involve Cat in a sting."

"A what?" said Reuben.

"A hustle," I suggested. "A scam?"

Reuben still looked blank.

"OK," said Lola. "Did they tell you about gambling on your Earth Skills course?"

Reuben looked cautious. "Kind of. Not sure I got it, though."

"Nick wants Cat to dupe someone into thinking he's playing cards with a pair of total bozos, then he and Chance will take him for everything he's got."

"No way. Cat will never go along with it," Reuben said firmly. "Will she, Mel?"

Lola sighed. "In case you haven't noticed, Nick has this amazing way of making people do what he wants."

"I'm talking about some law student freshly up from the country," Nick was saying smoothly. "If we don't empty his pockets, someone else will."

Cat frowned. "And if we get caught?"

"We won't," he said impatiently. "Besides, Chance and I are taking all the risks. You will simply be our innocent go-between."

She chewed her lip, trying to give the impression that she was calmly weighing up various pros and cons.

Poor Cat, I thought. I completely understood what she was going through. I mean, she didn't want Nick to think she was a pushover. On the other hand, no-one wants to look like a wuss in front of their mates, do they?

Plus I think Nick giving her that rose had made Cat feel all mixed up inside. And the bottom line was that she fancied him too much to say no.

"All right. Just this once," she agreed reluctantly.

Nick was delighted. "That's my Cat!"

Huh! This boy is way too cocky, I fumed to myself.

"I'll buy you a new necklace out of our winnings," he said impulsively. "Instead of those childish shells you wear."

Cat glowered at him. "Just give me my share, and I'll buy my own jewellery, Nick Ducket."

The trio set off in the general direction of London Bridge, with us angels following close behind. On the way, Reuben was fretting. "You can't blame Chance. He's permanently broke. Also he hero-worships Nick. But Nick seems like he's quite rich. And what if his scam goes wrong? What if the others come unstuck, because of him?"

"Maybe they won't," I suggested. "Maybe it'll be a doddle, like Nick says, and they'll just grab the money and run."

My mates looked shocked.

"Oh come *on*," I said. "Humans get away with dodgy stuff all the time."

The gaming house was attached to a riverside tavern called The Fleece. It was hardly a glitzy casino, just a room with too many tables, not enough light and almost no fresh air.

Serving wenches bustled about with refreshments, but you could tell food and drink were not the point of this place. Money – winning it, losing it – that was the point. The air was jittery with anxiety.

Just inside the door, an Irishman with a silky hypnotist's voice was making three cards fly around a table like a magician.

"Keep your eyes on the Lady, my fine sirs," he crooned. "Don't look away, no, not for a second."

But when the Irishman turned the cards over, the gamblers groaned with disappointment. He shook his head sorrowfully. "Didn't I warn you to be careful?"

Reuben was beside himself. "I just spotted a whatsisname! A sting!"

Lola burst out laughing. "I should hope you did! No-one ever wins Find The Lady."

Nick and Chance had been scanning the gaming house for potential victims. Now they'd clocked one, a shiny-faced law student, bragging to anyone who would listen.

At a signal from Nick, Cat moved in and went into this sexy simpleton routine.

"Two young gentlemen over there have been watching you play cards, sir," she said in a country voice. "And they noted your prow – prow – Oh, I dunno, 'tis a word which means 'great skill'."

Loudmouth scratched his neck inside its ruff. "Prowess," he corrected her conceitedly.

"Prowess! The very word." Cat gave him a wide-eyed smile. "Anyway, they sent me to inquire if you would care to play cards. They are willing to risk all the money they have with them, for the great honour of playing with such as you." She bobbed a little curtsey.

"Then I mustn't disappoint them," he smirked.

Nick really had a knack for knowing what made people tick. This student was greedy as well as boastful. Also not too bright.

The boys played so badly, it was embarrassing. Chance was even more bumbling and pathetic than usual. Naturally, Loudmouth cleaned them out. But just as their victim got up from the table, Nick gave this hammy gasp of surprise.

"I quite forgot! I have my rent money hidden inside my shirt, for safekeeping. Would you do us the honour of playing again?" he pleaded.

I couldn't believe Loudmouth would fall for it. But like I said, he wasn't too bright. His eyes lit up with pure greed. "Let's play for everything in our purses! And perhaps your luck will change?" he added, obviously thinking they were gluttons for punishment.

Their luck did change – dramatically. Nick and Chance revealed totally unsuspected gambling skills, and Loudmouth lost the lot, including the money he'd won from Nick and Chance.

Nick and his mates fled with their winnings, flushed with excitement.

"Smooth as cream," Nick gloated. "Here is your prize, Cat."

Cat hastily stowed her share inside her bodice. Eek! I do hope she isn't turning into a gangster's moll, I thought anxiously.

Reuben sagged with relief. "You were right, Mel. They pulled it off."

"Looks like it," I agreed.

Nick and Chance took Cat to the playhouse to celebrate.

We'd just joined this massive queue outside, when Nick frowned. "I forgot my pomander," he complained. "I'm going to buy some oranges." And he disappeared into the crowd.

Lola and Reuben exchanged baffled glances.

"Was that like, code?" said Lola.

I grinned. "Haven't you noticed those fancy fashion items some people have hanging from their belts?"

"Those pepperpot thingies?" said Lola.

I nodded. "Well, they're filled with incredibly strong perfume."

(OK, so I might have read up on the Tudors a *teensy* bit. I mean, once you get into it, it's quite juicy!)

"OK," Lola said cautiously. "And Elizabethans do this because…?"

"Because they have this theory that disease is caused by bad smells."

Reuben pulled a face. "And you can see why! Have you ever smelled so many unwashed humans in your life?"

Chance was wandering up and down the queue, chatting to various acquaintances. He had this incredible ability to get on with people from all walks of life. One minute he was talking about fetlocks to a groom, then minutes later I heard him swapping leather-making jargon with someone.

"Your boy's networking," I giggled to Reuben.

"My boy's a total chameleon, more like," he sighed.

When Chance rejoined her, Cat gave him one of her looks. "You are the strangest boy," she said. "You write like an Oxford scholar, yet you never know where your next meal is coming from. Don't you ever want to follow a trade like a normal person?"

Chance looked appalled. "Seven years working for the same master? The same work day after day, for no wages? Every day the *same*?" He shuddered. "I'd rather you sent for the constables and had me thrown in Newgate jail."

"But what will become of you?" Cat said in an anxious voice.

His eyes grew hazy with worry. "I don't know. I wake at night in a sweat, wondering why I was—"

But he was interrupted by a blare of noise. An actor from the playhouse was blowing loud blasts on a trumpet – our signal to go in.

Nick caught up with his friends, tossing an orange to each of them as they filed in through the great carved doors. They rubbed the peel on the insides of their wrists, solemnly sniffing the perfume.

"Oh, I get it," grinned Lola. "Smart move."

I'd only been to the theatre once before, on a school trip. It didn't leave much impression to be honest. I just remember miles of carpet and v. hard seats, which we had to sit on for like, hours.

Well, there was no carpet at the Lion. And the roof had a massive hole cut into it. You could actually see clouds floating overhead!

I'd assumed our kids' tickets would entitle them to seats, in this swanky grandstand affair at the side. But that cost an extra penny apparently (like, wow!). So we stood out in the open, with all the other hard-up folk. Groundlings, as you're meant to call them.

The posh patrons, lords and ladies and so on, had the spiffiest seats at the side of the stage. Actually, I think the groundlings enjoyed looking at them as much as the show.

At last several actors bounded on. The play had started.

To begin with, the audience didn't seem too fussed. They went on wandering about, chatting and cracking hazelnuts. But I was gripped. The play was nothing like my school experience. It was wild! Like circus and stand-up, pantomime and soap opera all jumbled together. Boys dressed as girls, actors nattering to the audience, and whenever things threatened to get heavy, the fool got everyone laughing again.

As it went on, the audience became totally involved, booing the villains, or screaming at the heroine to be careful. During a weepy bit near the end, a woman behind me was actually sobbing out loud.

"I always forget how much I love plays," Cat whispered to Chance.

"I could have a job here, if I wanted," he said at once.

"Here we go," sighed Reuben.

Cat looked impressed. "Really?"

"We could go backstage. I know some of the actors."

"Oh, yes?" said Cat sharply. "What name do *they* know you by?"

I couldn't help laughing. And then for some reason I glanced casually at the gorgeously dressed lords and ladies at the side of the stage, and my entire world went blurry.

There, sniffing his pomander and one hundred percent visible to the human race, was my number one cosmic enemy.

The last time I'd seen this particular PODS agent,

he'd been wearing a T-shirt and jeans. But apart from his bleached hair, the figure up on the stage could have stepped out of an Elizabethan painting. And I know this sounds stupid, but I was hypnotised by his jewellery – huge knuckleduster rings with great winking stones. I couldn't take my eyes off them.

Omigosh! I'd better warn the others, I thought.

But suddenly this seemed like a really dangerous thing to do.

What if it isn't him? I panicked. What if it's just some genuine Elizabethan aristocrat who only *looks* like him?

Check the eyes, Mel, I told myself. The agent had those scary dead eyes, remember?

So I had another frantic peek. And found myself looking at an empty seat.

I was totally confused. Had I just imagined the whole thing? Mr Allbright always said time-travel can play tricks with your mind.

The play finished in a storm of applause.

Nick gave a loud yawn. "At last!" he said irritably. "I thought it was going on for ever."

He began to hurry his mates towards the exit. "Come on! Those apprentices over there are spoiling for a fight and I don't want Cat mixed up in it."

"I was going to take her backstage," Chance

protested.

But as usual Nick got his own way.

Outside, the weather was changing for the worse. Clouds were blowing up from the river, swallowing the last of the sunset, making it seem much later than it really was.

Looking back, I know I should have told the others what I'd seen. But I mean, an actual PODS up on the stage in full view, blatantly interacting with humans? How likely was that? And how come my mates didn't see him? It's not like I was the only angel in the area.

Much better keep quiet, Mel, I decided. If you make a big deal out of this, you'll only embarrass yourself.

Since we'd left the playhouse, Chance had been trudging along, smiling to himself. Suddenly he looked dismayed. "We're almost at London Bridge!"

"Oh, so we are," said Nick, as if he'd only just noticed.

"Why did we come this way?" said Chance. "Cat said she had to go home."

"Yes," said Cat accusingly. "What's your game, Nick Ducket?"

Nick touched one of her springy fuse-wire curls,

and gave her his special smile. "I just thought, that since Lady Fortune has been smiling on us…"

"No, no, NO," said Cat. "I said I'd help you ONCE, Nick. I told you, my aunt is expecting me back."

"Come, Cat," Nick coaxed. "You know you have a natural gift for deception, like all your—"

He broke off in surprise. A raggedy procession was heading our way. Men, women, apprentices and children, all pointing and laughing.

I heard the wavery tooting of a flute, a clunky little drum, explosive cracks like gunshots.

As they got closer, I saw that the musicians were just dirty little kids with scared expressions. Close behind was their dad, grinning all over his face and cracking a long whip. That's why I'd thought I heard gunshots. He wore a sleeveless leather jerkin, exposing his muscly arms and most of his hairy chest.

"Ooer, it's Mister Muscles the Lion Tamer!" I joked.

Lola muttered, "That man's got more teeth than a shark!"

But Reuben didn't say a word. He'd gone totally white.

He'd seen the dancing bear.

CHAPTER SIX

I have never seen anything so sad as that bear trying to waltz. It was basically a bag of bones in a saggy fur coat, blind in one eye and covered with scars.

For some reason, it kept peering wistfully into faces in the crowd. It seemed to be looking for someone.

A shiver of wonder went through me. *Omigosh! It's looking for us!*

Unlike his bear, Mister Muscles was not a sensitive being, so it didn't occur to him there were angels in his vicinity. He had no idea why his beast was disobeying him, and he didn't care.

He cracked his whip violently, and the bear collapsed on to all fours. The crowd roared.

Chance had abruptly taken himself off down an alleyway. He seemed to be having a major argument with himself. For the first time since I'd known him, his thoughts jumped out at me.

I could seize his whip, break it into pieces. But I'm not as strong as he is. I'll just make a fool of myself and the beast will be no better off.

Like some dazed sleepwalker, Reuben started walking towards the bear.

"Don't do anything!" I yelled. "Don't do a *thing*!"

He did, though. Reuben did something I totally didn't expect.

He *spoke* to the bear in the most beautiful language I have ever heard. Actually, the soft mysterious sounds reminded me very slightly of that heavenly music, my cosmic lullaby.

When it heard these lullaby words, the bear grew very still. Very deliberately, it looked at Reuben with its one good eye, and Reuben looked back. And without worrying about its fleas, not to mention its smell (which was rank), Reuben put his arms around the bear. The bear looked totally blissful.

But Mister Muscles was desperate to get his show back on the road, so he started striking the bear with his whip again and again.

And to my horror, each time the whip cracked,

Reuben groaned and doubled up. I couldn't understand what was happening. I mean, humans can't injure angels. Everyone knows that.

Lola was quicker on the uptake. She was already running towards him. "The stupid boy's taking its pain, Mel!" she shrieked.

Five times the man struck at the bear, and each time Reuben almost fell. But on the sixth blow, someone caught the bear-keeper's arm in midair.

"I think it's had enough!" said a voice.

Everyone gasped, including me and Lola.

Nick calmly took the whip from Mister Muscles and my knees went to pure jelly with gratitude. Not only had he saved the bear, he'd saved my friend!

Nick might be a control freak, but he's a born leader, I thought admiringly. He can just walk into any situation and change it to suit himself.

I could actually feel the crowd switching loyalties. Beside Nick, Mister Muscles just looked like a cowardly bully. Suddenly nobody wanted anything to do with him. People began drifting away, muttering.

We rushed over to Reuben, but he insisted he was fine.

Nick smiled at Mister Muscles. "It's almost nightfall. Rest and let the beast rest too. And feed your little cubs while you're about it. They look as if they need it." He tossed some coins to Mister Muscles, who sullenly stowed them in his jerkin.

We watched the sad little circus trail down the alley to put up at The Fleece. Chance rejoined his mates, v. shame-faced.

Cat was glowing. "Nick, you were wonderful. That poor bear!"

We thought he was wonderful too. This was the *real* Nick. The boy Lola had watched sleeping. The boy with beautiful dreams.

"You see, Lollie," I whispered. "It's working. He's improving already!"

Nick's eyes slid away from Cat's. "We'd better walk you home," he sighed. "Unless you erm, changed your mind?" He gestured wistfully towards the gaming house.

I don't believe you, Nick Ducket, I thought.

Cat gave him a mischievous smile. "Oh well. Since I'm sure to get a beating, I may as well stay out and make a profit!"

She seemed genuinely cheerful, but I was confused. I just didn't get Nick. Moments ago, he'd done a genuinely good deed. But it was like he couldn't resist cashing in.

Lola's right, I thought miserably. He's always on the make.

Cat suddenly noticed Chance. "Where have you been hiding?" she laughed. "You should have seen Nick! He actually took that oaf's whip away!"

Chance forced a smile. "I saw the whole thing. I wanted to stop him myself," he added apologetically, "but I—"

"But you were puking your guts up," Nick grinned. "We know."

"Well, I'm fully recovered now and I'm VERY hungry!" Chance rubbed his belly, making fun of himself. "Didn't I see a pieman somewhere?"

"Just around the corner," said Cat promptly. "Maybe he's still there." She ran off, jingling coins.

The minute she'd disappeared, Chance said urgently, "Nick, let's walk Cat home, then perhaps she won't get a beating. We've won enough for today."

Nick's eyes grew cold. "Enough for you, perhaps. I am a gentleman with a gentlemen's expenses."

"Wouldn't your father help?" Chance asked tentatively. "You're not the first person to get into debt."

"How would you know?" Nick sneered. "Without me, you'd probably be starving in the gutter. Yet when I ask for help, it's different."

I couldn't believe he was being so horrible. I'd want to punch anyone who spoke to me like that.

But Chance just stood there, taking it. "Nick, you know I'd do anything," he began.

And at that moment Lola said urgently, "Mel! We've lost Reuben!"

We found our buddy in a squalid shelter in the tavern courtyard, giving the bear some angel TLC. He was singing under his breath as he tended its wounds. "You're not alone," he sang.

"You never told us you spoke bear," Lola said softly.

"It's not exactly bear," Reuben answered. "It's this language angels invented at the dawn of creation, to communicate with animals."

The bear gave Reuben a jealous nudge.

"He wants to come back with us," he explained. "I told him it's not his time."

The bear hung its head as if it understood.

On top of everything else, this was too much for Lola. Tears spilled down her face.

"Don't cry, Lollie. It'll be all right," I comforted her. Though I wasn't sure if I meant the bear, Nick's appallingly selfish behaviour, or the ultimate success of our cosmic fact-finding trip.

"But it looks so lonely," she wept.

"His name is Sackerson," Reuben corrected her. "And he's a very wise soul."

By the time we'd dragged Reuben back to the gambling house, Cat had already lined up victim number two. She brought him over to the boys table, desperately trying to keep a straight face, but at the last minute someone barred their way.

"I'm Big Ned," he slurred. "And this game is mine."

He sat down heavily, almost missing the chair. The boys grinned. A drunk was even better! And this one had obviously been drinking for hours. He kept dozing off and the boys had to wake him to take his turn. He still won, of course.

But just as Nick was psyching himself up for the final phase of their sting, Big Ned had an alarming personality change. His lids lost their drunken droop and this cold little gleam appeared in his eyes.

He picked up the cards, shuffling so fast, it sounded like pigeons taking off. And with a flick of his wrist, he sent all fifty-two cards streaming through the air in a perfect arc.

Cat's eyes went wide with alarm. "Run!" she hissed.

Two burly men appeared, grinning like crocodiles.

"Bad luck, young 'uns," Ned said cheerfully. "Tell you what, we'll play again. Maybe Lady Fortune will smile on you."

Nick was grey with shock. "We have no money!"

I recognised the "Find The Lady" con-man among Ned's heavies. "You haven't forgotten the rent money you put inside your shirt?" he said in his silky Irish voice. "Aah, well. Rufus here will help you find it."

"These have to be the resident crooks," Lola whispered.

"Yeah and I don't think they appreciate amateurs on their turf," I whispered back.

"We seen what you were up to this morning, young sirs," said Ned in the same cheerful tone. "Rufus wanted a little chat, didn't you, Rufus?"

Rufus glared, clenching his huge hands into fists.

Suddenly Ned grabbed Nick's doublet, jerking him to his feet. "So now you're back, I think we'll have that private chat after all. Down by the river, where it's nice and quiet."

The Fleece regulars seemed to know all about Ned's private chats. No-one even glanced up as the kids were bundled out into the yard.

It was pitch black, and the rain was hammering down again. All you could hear was rain and the river lapping invisibly nearby.

I was worried obviously, but not too worried. I was waiting for Nick to do his stuff, to turn the whole thing to his advantage, like he always did.

Only this time, he didn't.

It was like all his rich boy's confidence had suddenly deserted him. I've got this theory that he couldn't swim, because he started pleading with the men not to throw him in the river. He actually threw himself on his knees, whimpering like a little kid.

But the crooks calmly removed Nick's expensive shirt and doublet, saying he wouldn't need them where he was going.

Don't think we were hanging around like shiny Christmas decorations, while all this was going on. We were beaming vibes like crazy.

But absolutely nothing happened. Unless you count Rufus getting the torch to light finally. Now that they could see where they were going, the crooks began to hustle their captives across the courtyard towards the river.

They're going to die, I thought. Omigosh, they're really going to die!

And I completely freaked out.

"DO something, you idiot!" I screamed. "You're going to drown!" And I actually whacked poor Chance between the shoulder blades.

WHOOSH! A jolt of angel electricity sizzled down my fingers.

Chance jumped as if he'd been zapped with a cattle prod.

Lola was horrified. "Melanie! *Wake* them, we said, not shock the sassafras out of them!"

"I was upset," I wailed.

"Shush," hissed Reuben. "Something's happening!"

It's hard to describe how Chance changed. It was something in his eyes. Suddenly, they looked like angel eyes. This was Chance, but not as we knew him. It was Chance minus his fog. And he was not about to let anyone die.

"Murder us if you must," he said calmly. "But spare my lady, for she is not of woman born."

Big Ned stopped dead. "What say you, boy?"

"Human attendants are easily replaced," Chance explained. "But if you harm my lady, her people may deal harshly with you."

"Her people? You mean the Good Folk?" The Irishman almost whispered the words. He glared at Ned. "You swore she was a blackamoor."

Chance gave a chilling chuckle. "Are you blind? Have you not seen her eyes? They are as green as willows in spring."

The con-man thrust the torch towards Cat. What he saw made his hand shake. "Elf fire!" he hissed.

There was a pricklingly tense silence while Cat tried to look cold and heartless, like an elf king's daughter.

"See how she looks at you?" said Chance. "Would a mortal look at her captors so brazenly? But we should not talk of such things in the dark, only…"

"Only what?" barked Big Ned, sounding panic-stricken.

"Only, if my lady should let down her hair, run for your lives."

"What will happen?" whispered Rufus, completely under Chance's spell.

"Her father will appear in the guise of…" Chance let his voice tail off.

"Tell us, boy!" Ned pleaded. "In what shape will he appear?"

Cat had figured out what Chance was up to by this time. She began to hum dreamily. And as she hummed, she slowly removed her cap, letting her fuse-wire curls fall dramatically around her shoulders.

Rufus's eyes bulged. "*She's calling him!*" he hissed.

But it was really Reuben who saved the day. Just as I twigged that Cat was humming Sackerson's waltz, our brilliant buddy called out in that skin-pricklingly lovely angel language.

Only it didn't sound like a lullaby this time. It sounded like a war-cry.

Sackerson's sleep was already disturbed by the tune which tortured his daylight hours. Reuben's summons did the rest. With a great roar, the bear rose up out of the darkness.

Dropping the torch, the crooks fled, howling with terror.

A micro-second later, the bear ran out of chain and sat down heavily, scratching its bottom.

Cat was delirious. "Chance! It is *you* who have elfin blood, enchanting them with that wild tale!"

He hugged her. "What about you? You remembered its tune!"

"It just floated into my head," she said excitedly. "That poor beast did the rest."

Nick just stood watching, kind of flaring his nostrils and trying to look superior. Not easy to pull off, when you're shirtless and shivering in the rain.

Without a word, Chance whipped off his battered doublet and held it out to Nick.

Nick pulled a face. "Ugh, it smells of sweat and onions."

Cat totally exploded. "How dare you be so high and mighty, Nick Ducket?" she yelled. "If it wasn't for Chance, we might all have died!"

She was practically in tears.

"Well, I have learned my lesson," she went on

more quietly. "And I pray you have learned yours. For I fear this reckless life will be the death of you."

Nick studied his boots for a second. Then he gave her one of his winning smiles. Not his usual five-star variety, but a smile nonetheless.

"Everything you say is true," he said, to my surprise. "And I promise I will turn over a new leaf. I had been thinking of going up to Oxford, which would make my father very happy. And maybe one day I will write plays. Yes," Nick said dreamily. "I think I would enjoy that."

Chance beamed. "If I take that job at the playhouse, maybe I can act in them!"

But Nick didn't answer him and there was an uneasy silence.

He's ashamed, I thought. If it wasn't for Chance, Nick would be floating in the river, and he knows it.

Chance was staring wistfully at his best mate, desperate to get things back on their old easy footing.

And all at once he started doing this silly walk, imitating the fool at the Lion. He did it brilliantly and it worked like a charm. In no time, Nick was roaring with laughter.

But I had to turn away. Ten minutes ago, Chance's eyes had blazed with cosmic intelligence.

Now he was Nick's fool again. It was like watching Sackerson trying to waltz.

Still laughing, Nick draped his arms round his friends' shoulders. "Let us swear to be friends for ever! For you are the most faithful friends anyone ever had."

Cat laughed. "We swear!"

Nick snatched up the torch and they walked off, with Chance capering beside them, shouting, "We swear, we swear, oh great master!"

I started to follow them but Lola said softly, "It's over, Mel."

I felt a funny ache in my chest. "Are you sure?"

Nick's laughing voice floated back. "What about this for a stage direction, Chance? 'Exit: pursued by a bear'!"

And at that moment, as if someone had turned off a tap, the rain stopped and a big silvery moon came from behind the clouds. The scene had Happy Ending written all over it. Everyone was happy except me. But I totally didn't know why.

Reuben took my hand. "Ready?"

I stiffened. I'd heard the tiniest movement in the dark. "Did you hear that?"

"Rats," shuddered Lola. "Come on. Let's get back to civilization! 'Bye, Sackerson," she called.

"We won't forget you."

The bear closed his eyes as the beam of light came strobing down.

And with a whoosh of cosmic energy, we went zooming home.

CHAPTER SEVEN

On the way back, Reuben kept closing his eyes as if he felt dizzy. But when I asked if he was OK, he snapped, "Why shouldn't I be?"

I know now that I should have checked it out, but I was preoccupied with worries of my own. I had a bad feeling we hadn't found Michael's glitch after all. And lurking beneath that worry was a worse fear. I was scared our humans might be in danger.

I tried telling Lola, but she didn't want to know.

"Could you drop it, Mel?" she pleaded. "I want to get home, have a couple of hours' sleep, then grab my dancing shoes! Hey, I can't wait to go to that new place, The Babylon Café."

When Lollie starts babbling, like a girl who's had

too many mochaccinos, it's her way of saying, "I'm freaking out inside, but I can't talk about it yet, OK?"

So it was a big relief when the door slid open and rays of lovely celestial light flooded in.

"I can't wait to tell Michael," Lola bubbled.

Then her face crumpled. Our welcome party consisted of one person. Al, the maintenance guy.

"Mike's sorry, but something came up," he mumbled shyly.

Lola stared around the deserted Arrivals area in bewilderment. "But Michael *always* comes to meet us!"

I didn't feel too cheerful myself. I really look forward to that moment when I see Michael hurrying towards us, like he can't wait to hear every detail of our trip. Him *not* being there made everything feel unreal. As if part of me was still out there, adrift in time.

Al shrugged. "Mike was archangel on call, so what can you do?" He gave a bashful glance in my direction. "You'll never guess where he's gone." (Al and I have this little running joke.)

"Don't tell me," I sighed. "He had to bale out my century again."

Al faked amazement. "Incredible! How'd you know?"

I grinned. "A wild hunch!"

"Is it me, or was Al acting strange just now?" Reuben asked in his new tired voice, as we headed home in the limo.

Lola gave him her party-girl smile. "It's you, Sweetpea. He was trying to make up for Michael not being there, that's all."

I didn't have the energy to talk, so I just gazed out of the limo, watching familiar landmarks flow past.

Suddenly Reuben tapped on the glass between us and the driver.

"Can you drop me off at the dojo?"

Lola looked astonished. "Are you sure? You look like you need some rest."

"Pure angels don't need to rest," he said huffily. "A complete work-out, that's all I need."

I didn't think Reuben looked up to a martial arts work-out either. But you can't tell boys anything, so we promised to meet him at Guru next morning. Guru is our favourite hang-out and serves the best breakfasts in the universe.

"My treat," I reminded him. "I've got ID now, remember."

On the way back to our dorm, I caught sight of myself in the driver's mirror and hastily fluffed out my hair. Then I began to brush down my jacket. You are *such* a muck-magnet, Mel, I scolded myself. Where *did* all these hairs come from?

I examined one closely and felt a pang. A few of Sackerson's bear hairs had hitched a ride back to Heaven. And I had that weird floaty feeling again, as if I'd left an important part of me behind.

Several hours later I still couldn't sleep. Without knowing how I got there, I found myself over by the window, gazing out over the twinkling lights of the city.

Heavenly architects are something else. Even super-modern buildings are awesome here – glittering hi-tech domes and soaring skyscrapers.

"Aren't you thrilled to be back in this beautiful city, Mel?" I said aloud. "You can go back to doing all that fun stuff with your mates."

But I couldn't seem to remember what that stuff was. I could only think of all those long nights down at Angel Watch. Which set me off thinking about my mum and my little sister, Jade. If only I could let them know how much I loved them...

Then it hit me. "Oh, you little devil!" I scolded myself. "*That's* why you took all those night shifts! You were hoping the Beeby family would flash up on your screen one night!"

Under normal conditions, I'd have been shocked at myself. But part of me was floating in time, and all of me was exhausted, and absolutely nothing felt real.

Go to bed, Mel, I told myself. In the morning things will look better.

And I lay down on my economy-sized bed, and killed the lights.

You couldn't call it a dream exactly. It was more like a movie trailer. Three Elizabethan teenagers running through the rain, laughing and joking. There were gold sparkles dancing in the air, all mixed up with the rain and the night, and I heard myself saying, "Aren't fifty-fifty set-ups the dangerous kind?"

Then the trailer cut out and a new one started, almost identical to the first. Only for some reason there weren't so many sparkles, and the streets were darker and way more menacing.

I don't know how many times I had to watch that scene. Each time it got darker and more nightmarish. Even the rain was scary, thundering down overflows, flooding into rain barrels and puddles, crashing and slooshing. And suddenly I couldn't stand it. I sat up gasping for breath, my heart pounding.

I realised someone was tapping on my door. "It's me, Reuben."

I got up and let him in.

He was still in his baggy martial-arts gear and worryingly pale around the edges.

"Sorry, I know it's late." Reuben half-fell into my armchair, then winced and prised a leather boot out from under his behind.

"I hate to say this," he said, "but I've got the feeling we lost the plot back there."

"Me too." I told him all about my horror-movie trailer.

Reuben closed his eyes. "This isn't good," he said. "We must have tipped the cosmic balance the wrong way."

I was horrified. "But how? I mean—"

Lola stumped in, with a flamingo-pink robe thrown over her PJs, her curls sticking up like radio antennae. "Could you keep it down?" she grumbled.

"Are we bothering you?" I said apologetically.

"Yeah, with your stupid negative thoughts." Lola dumped herself down on my rug. "Plus I was already being bothered by my stupid negative thoughts," she admitted grumpily.

Reuben reached over and ruffled her hair. "Let's hear them. The stupid negative thoughts of Lola Sanchez."

Lola began ticking them off on her fingers. "One, Michael wasn't there to meet us. He's *always* there. Two, Al was tying himself in knots, using every word in his vocabulary, except 'You blew it, kids'. Three, I ran into Amber in the hall and she totally didn't know what to do with herself when she saw me."

"Four," Reuben interrupted. "It was just the same at the dojo. I started to feel like I didn't even exist."

"FIVE," Lola said loudly, "I feel as if we've just made a big mistake. I can feel it, in here." She thumped her chest.

I was horrified. "You honestly think Michael is giving us the cold shoulder because we screwed up our mission? He'd never do that."

"It's not like they're punishing us," said Reuben. "More giving us the space to figure things out for ourselves."

"Oh," I said.

But none of us had the slightest idea what we'd done wrong.

"Oh, well. We can't do anything until Michael gets back," Lola sighed. "We should get some sleep."

"I'm staying up, thanks," I shuddered. "I'm not risking that horror movie again."

And then, with a feeling like going down too fast in a lift, I had a chilling thought.

What if our depressing homecoming had something to do with my weird hallucination at the playhouse?

What if my imaginary PODS agent was real?

I was flooded with panic. Omigosh, Mel, I think you just screwed up BIG time.

I've got to tell them, I thought. I've got to tell them now!

But I couldn't make my voice work properly. "Lollie," I croaked. "Remember our first field-trip when I rescued the little kid in the air raid?"

"Do I! Reubs, you should have heard her yell at Orlando! She—"

I was desperately talking over her. "Remember that PODS guy?"

"Your gorgeous bad boy look-alike? What about him?"

I described how I'd seen him at the playhouse, passing himself off as human.

Lola almost went into orbit. "You're kidding! You saw him *again*?"

I buried my face in my hands. "I wasn't sure if I was imagining it. I am so STUPID."

Reuben's eyes had closed again. "Don't beat yourself up, Mel," he said in a tired voice.

"Why does it have to be me? Why didn't you guys see him?"

"Maybe it's you he's after, babe," Lola explained.

I felt myself turn cold. "Why? What have I done to him?"

"Who knows how their minds work," Reuben said, without opening his eyes.

But while Reuben was talking, I was mentally replaying those vital last seconds on Earth. The stealthy sounds in the darkness – that was the PODS too. He'd love to think of me remembering it when it was too late.

Then I thought, but maybe it's *not* too late.

And a weird thing happened. All my fear and self-pity fell away. As if I was looking down from some high mountain peak somewhere, and seeing everything with total clarity.

It's not that I stopped being scared. More that I saw our situation incredibly calmly. As if I'd thrown a dice, and was about to make my next move in some vast cosmic game, a game I totally didn't understand.

"We shouldn't have left those kids," I told the others. "Come on. We're going back."

Al is a highly-trained professional, so if he was surprised when three trainee angels showed up in the middle of the night, demanding to be returned to Tudor times, he didn't let it show.

Actually, I got the feeling he was incredibly relieved. Not only that, but he had a portal all ready to go. He ran the usual checks, then I noticed him shuffling his shoes a bit.

"Look, I don't know how much Michael told you, but the fact is, we have a situation. Which means I can't beam you back through the exact same time-window. I got to send you through the nearest *available* window, OK?"

"Sounds mysterious," said Lola.

Al lowered his voice. "Like I say, we got a situation. Didn't you ever wonder why the Agency sent you in the first place?"

"Well, actually—" I began.

"The fact is, Michael didn't want to do it," he said earnestly. "But it was send you or no-one, know what I'm saying? The only reason you guys were able to slip through was because of some cosmic loop-hole they somehow overlooked."

Reuben looked bewildered. "The Agency overlooked something?"

"He means the Opposition, Sweetpea."

Al looked queasy. "I don't discuss those people. Some words leave a bad taste, if you get my meaning?"

He doled out our angel tags. We put them on, slightly stunned.

"Hey, did I mention you got to swap humans?" he called as we climbed into the portal. "Sorry for any inconvenience, but it's Agency policy."

And the last thing I saw through the portal door was Al shyly giving us the thumbs-up, like he was saying, "Better luck this time."

CHAPTER EIGHT

We found ourselves in a crowd of happy, laughing Elizabethans. The soft chords of a lute drifted through the air. Everyone was carrying armfuls of white blossom. And from behind the houses and spires of London came the misty sound of a cuckoo.

Lola's face was a picture. "Did we just land in the middle of a wedding?"

"I think it's some kind of May Day celebration," I said.

Her eyes brightened. "Like a fiesta?"

Reuben was enchanted. "Do they do this in your century, Mel?"

"Erm, not where I come from," I grinned.

And to prove this wasn't a total Disney experience,

a woman opened a window and emptied a chamber pot into the street.

Our watches flashed and we made minor adjustments.

"Hey, they didn't split us up," pointed out Reuben. "That means our humans are in this crowd somewhere. I wonder who's got who this time?"

Lola's watch and mine both beeped. Seconds later, two familiar figures wandered past, holding hands.

And Lola went, "I don't *believe* it!"

I didn't believe it either. Was this honestly the first time-slot the Agency could manage? This Cat was two years older at least, and stunningly pretty, with her curls falling loose and a crown of blossoms in her hair. And Chance looked better in every way – happier, healthier, and just generally more *there*, somehow. The zing in my chest told me that he was my responsibility this time.

I won't deny that it was deeply disturbing missing out on such a major chunk of their lives. Time-travel is weird like that. But I was so happy to see them safe after my scary premonitions, that I could have kissed them. "Don't they look great?" I burbled. "And they're actually an item! How about that!"

We soon found out that Cat and Chance were on their way to meet Nick. This was more of a coincidence than it sounds. It seemed he'd been out of touch for months.

"He's longing to see you," Chance was saying. "He said he'd called into the Feathers several times but you're never there."

"With his fine new friend. I know, Nettie told me." Cat sounded wary.

"Nick is extremely fine himself, these days," he admitted. "I hardly recognised him when he came backstage. But he's exactly the same. A new sweetheart for every day of the week."

"What did you talk about?" she said curiously.

"Oh, he had erm, a business proposition." Chance sounded just a little too careless.

But Cat was blushing furiously. "Did you tell Nick – you know?"

He beamed at her. "He was happy for us. He said it was a pity the cause of true love did not always run so smooth."

She frowned. "That's a very strange thing to say."

"You're so suspicious, Catherine Darcy! Nick says you always think the worst of him. Let me go on with my tale. It's very tragic. Nick found one of the queen's ladies weeping in the garden. A beautiful lady apparently. Eventually Nick persuaded her to tell him her troubles."

"I can imagine," Cat said darkly.

"The lady made Nick swear to tell no-one—"

"Oh, no-one except you and me and Nettie and the town crier!"

Cat saw Chance's face. "Sorry," she said humbly. "Tell your story."

"It seems she is in love with a Spaniard, a very handsome one. But because of the climate at court, they cannot be seen speaking together."

Cat's eyes widened. "How sad! And how *silly*!"

"Isn't it?" said Chance eagerly. "But Nick has thought of a plan to help her. Not only that, he says it's an opportunity for me to earn a great deal of money. There's no risk. He says I'd just be the go-between."

Cat flung up her hands. "And you *believed* him?"

We had reached a green space between the houses, where a maypole was decorated with spring flowers and coloured ribbons. Some young people were doing a skippy-type country dance to the sound of flutes and fiddles.

"It's true!" I heard Chance say. "I'd be playing Cupid and making money at the same time. Money for us, Cat," he coaxed. "So we can be married!"

"People got married really young in these days,"

I explained to Lola, who was looking v. shocked. "Weird I know," I added. "I mean she's just a teenager, right? Why limit yourself?"

"You haven't seen Nick for months," Cat was saying earnestly. "Now suddenly he wants to help you. How do you know there's no risk? How do you know he doesn't wish you harm?"

Chance laughed. "Because he's my friend."

Cat opened her mouth, "But—"

"No buts, Catherine Darcy," he said firmly. "It's May day, the sun is shining and I intend to dance with the most beautiful girl in London."

And he swept her off to join the dancers.

Lola shrugged. "We must have been suffering from time-travel fatigue or something. They seem fine to me."

"I'm not sure about this scheme of Nick's," said Reuben doubtfully. "Wasn't he going to university? I think he's my human this time, so—"

"Oh, who cares?" said Lola. "He's doing well for himself. Now he's trying to help an old friend."

"Yeah, but—"

"No buts!" she teased him. "It's May day, the sun is shining and I intend to dance with the most beautiful Sweetpea in London!" And she danced away with him, giggling.

I watched the dancers dreamily, noticing that each time Cat and Chance met and linked arms, they smiled into each other's eyes, before whirling away in opposite directions. It kind of reminded me of how I feel with Orlando sometimes.

I came out of my thoughts with a jolt. Someone was standing beside me, a good-looking young man with a rose in his cap. Though I'd have probably recognised Nick without the rose, from his faintly superior smile.

He'd become incredibly stylish since the last time I'd seen him – slashed sleeves, gorgeous shoes. I was convinced the gold pomander hanging from his belt was studded with actual jewels.

Lola's right, I thought. All those dreams and dire premonitions, they were purely in my head!

There was a burst of clapping as Cat and Chance swung each other energetically between two rows of their fellow dancers.

I was watching Nick eagerly, waiting for him to recognise his old friends, so I saw the exact moment when his face changed.

And his eyes went totally cold.

Then he stepped forward, laughing, as they went hurtling past. And it was like nothing had ever happened.

But I knew it had. Nick might look the same, but I'd glimpsed a chilling stranger underneath. And I knew the danger in my dreams was real.

Reuben ran up, followed by Lola. "According to my watch, Nick's around here somewhere," he said breathlessly.

"Yeah," I said. "He is."

Lola caught sight of him. "Woo!" she said. "He *is* doing well!"

It struck me that Reuben was looking feverish. His eyes were too bright and his face was much too pale.

"Are you sure you're OK?"

"Let's make a deal," he said irritably. "When I'm not, you'll be the first person I tell."

Nick, Cat and Chance went off to a nearby tavern, with us following behind as close as shadows. They sat outside in the sunshine and Nick ordered ale and some kind of game pie.

"Now we can catch up on each other's news," he beamed. But before Cat and Chance could even open their mouths, Nick launched into this juicy scandal involving all these major court celebrities.

"And you must come and visit me in my new rooms," he said. "They are really very fine. As different to my old place as night from day."

"I liked your old place," Cat said quietly.

How's he *paying* for this? I thought. His family isn't *that* rich.

I didn't get the impression Nick actually worked for his living. Not in those sleeves.

I think Nick noticed that Cat wasn't as impressed as he'd hoped, because he suddenly said, "And how is life treating my lovely Catherine?"

"Very well," she said promptly and she totally couldn't prevent herself smiling at Chance. "But I don't know any lords and ladies, so I have no interesting news to tell."

Then her face lit up. "Oh, but I've heard my father will soon be home from sea! I wonder if he'll recognise me," she added anxiously. "He's been away so long."

"And you, Chance?" said Nick. "How are you liking the theatrical life?"

"Very much," said Chance eagerly. "I never know what I'll be doing from one day to the next. One moment I'm helping actors learn their lines, the next taking care of the properties."

"What are properties, exactly?" said Nick in a bored tone.

"Almost anything! For instance, if the heroine dies tragically of snake bite, I must make sure the snake is to hand!"

"Oh," said Nick. "A real dogsbody."

Cat looked annoyed. "He will be an actor one day. Only last month, he took the part of the fool, when Will Kemp had the fever."

Nick pulled a face. "He'd had plenty of practice, I'll be bound."

The entire angel contingent was squirming. It was like everything Nick said was designed to make Chance look like a total loser, compared to him.

"Chance, I must introduce you to this new friend of mine," he said loftily. "He could get you work as an actor tomorrow if I asked him. You don't need to do all this ridiculous fetching and carrying."

Chance suddenly spotted a young actor from the playhouse. "I've just got to ask Kit something," he mumbled. I got the feeling Kit owed him money.

Cat looked distinctly dismayed at the idea of being alone with Nick. I think she knew he'd try to chat her up. Didn't take him long either.

"Ah, Cat," he sighed, giving her that special smile of his. "When I think how you cared for me once."

"Yes, I did, when I was a little girl," Cat said pointedly. "But I am grown up now, so I prefer a man who is not afraid of his own heart."

Nick looked scornful. "They say that love is blind. But how you can prefer this nobody—"

"Chance is not nobody!" she blazed.

"He doesn't even know his own name!" Nick sneered. "What do you call someone who has neither wealth, power or influence?"

"I'm talking about hearts, Nick! And his heart is like a twin to mine."

"Ah, I see! You are twin souls!" His voice was mocking.

"Yes. We are!"

She calmly held Nick's gaze, letting him know that his attempt to put Chance down had basically boomeranged.

He quickly pulled himself together. "Then you must marry," he said in his lordly way. "Luckily I've put an excellent financial opportunity Chance's way."

"I heard." And suddenly Cat leaned over and put her lips really close to Nick's ear. "Don't hurt him, Nick Ducket," she said softly. "Don't you dare."

Chance reappeared, looking dejected. The actor had obviously fobbed him off.

Nick pushed back his chair. "Come to my rooms tonight, Chance, and we'll talk business. Sorry to rush off. I've arranged to meet someone."

Reuben got ready to leave too. For some reason this made me deeply uneasy.

"Maybe you should stay with us," I said. "I'm not sure you—"

"Melanie!" he warned. "Nick's my human now. Agency policy, remember? I have to go."

"He's right," said Lola. "He has to." But she didn't look happy about it either.

I watched them walk away across the green. I thought Reuben looked terrifyingly fragile.

Cat and Chance were leaving as well. Cat's aunt needed her to help in the tavern.

I noticed that Lola seemed unusually depressed. "I've really gone off Nick," she blurted suddenly.

"Don't feel bad about it," I told her. "People change."

"But you were right, Mel. He's not the glitch. Or if he is, he's only a little *part* of it. I'm so confused."

I slipped my arm through hers. "We're confused *now*," I said. "But when we see the light, we'll go, 'Wow! Was that ALL?'"

She giggled. "You're such an idiot."

We'd almost reached the Feathers when Cat said, "Chance, I do wish you'd turn Nick's offer down. I don't trust him."

Chance looked shocked. "You're wrong. When I had nothing, Nick saved my life. He's a wonderful friend."

"So he keeps telling you." Cat's voice was pure acid. She took a breath. "Nick did say one true thing. He says you don't know your name."

For the first time since our return, I saw Chance's eyes grow foggy with hurt. "He's wrong," he said.

"But your name's not Chance?" she said softly.

He didn't answer. She put her arms around him. "Are you ever going to tell me?"

I was quite interested to know this myself, so I deliberately tried to pick up on Chance's thought vibes. But they were totally confused. Even with my angel senses, I couldn't figure out what was going on. I could just see this agonizing struggle going on inside him.

"I promise," he said carefully, "that if I tell my name to anyone, it will be to you."

She laughed. "You'll have to tell me when we get married!"

As we reached the Feathers, a grubby white labrador bounded out.

"Promise me one thing?" Cat pleaded, as she tried to stop the dog licking her face. "Be careful of Nick's new friend."

"That's very dramatic," he teased her. "Why do you say that?"

"I told you, he came to the tavern with Nick.

Nettie said Snowball took one look and went streaking out of the house, with his tail between his legs. She says he's the devil in disguise."

Chance laughed. "Nettie thinks all men are devils in disguise!"

Like a song from a distant car radio, Reuben's tune floated into my head. *"You're not alone, you're not alone…"*

With a prickle of fear, I saw Lola mouthing the same words.

I grabbed my angel tags. They were burning hot as the Angel Link kicked in.

"Reuben, are you OK?"

His voice was hardly audible. "Mel, we got it wrong."

"What? What are you saying?"

"A trap… a cosmic trap!"

"You're not making sense, Sweetpea," said Lola urgently. "Someone trapped you?"

There was a long terrible pause.

"Not me," he got out. "Chance… for Chance."

"Reuben," I pleaded. "Are you hurt?"

But I could just hear the words "been so stupid" and "fight".

"Omigosh!" I said. "He's really hurt, Lollie! That means…"

"Reuben, try to hold on," Lola told him. "We're coming to get you."

"… careful," Reuben gasped. "Edward…"

"Who the heck's Edward?" said Lola.

There was another long rasping pause.

"… Nick's friend. He's with the PODS."

CHAPTER NINE

We found Reuben slumped in Nick's rooms. He tried to raise his head, but he was too weak. "Sorry," he muttered. "Such a wuss."

"You're going to be OK, Sweetpea," Lola told him. "We'll get you home." But I heard her voice wobble.

Reuben's visible injuries were truly terrible, but the worst PODS damage is always deep down. It was like he'd been totally drained of all his beautiful angelic energy, like he was hardly Reuben any more.

It seemed as if we stayed like that for an eternity – Lola cradling Reuben's head in her lap, me softly stroking his hand. Then a white light strobed down and two heavenly paramedics appeared.

"Len, it's just a bunch of kids!" one exclaimed. "How'd they get here?"

His mate immediately bent over Reuben. What he saw really shocked him. "What on earth did they attack him with?" he muttered.

And suddenly I remembered those jewelled knuckledusters. The way I couldn't take my eyes off them.

I swallowed. "There was only one agent. And I think it was his rings."

The paramedic was mystified. "This happened on a *research* trip?"

"Had to be," his mate muttered back. "No other cosmic personnel are allowed in."

"So who attacked the kid?"

"Beats me. Let's just get them back home. Come on, girls."

They were all ready to beam us all up. Lola and I exchanged panic-stricken looks.

"Thanks but we're staying." I tried to sound crisp and professional.

"We can't allow that, miss. This is officially an angel no-go area."

"Check it out with the Agency if you want," said Lola fiercely. "All I know is Michael gave us a job to do. Take care of our friend, OK?"

It felt incredibly lonely after they'd gone, and we both had a bit of a cry.

I was trying desperately to understand what was happening. Nothing seemed to make sense.

"Lollie," I said tearfully. "Have you ever heard of an angel-free zone?"

She shook her head. "It's not just our lot that can't come in. All cosmic personnel, he said."

"So how come that PODS guy is here?"

"Good question," she sighed.

"So are we violating some cosmic treaty, just by being here?"

"I don't think so, Boo. Remember how Michael kept insisting it wasn't a mission? Officially we're kids on an educational trip. That way we don't pose a threat to the big guys."

"Why didn't Michael explain?"

She frowned. "I don't know. But he never does anything without a reason. You know that."

"I know it in Heaven," I admitted. "Down here, you start to wonder."

Lola gave me a searching look. "Think you'll be OK by yourself? We really should check on Cat and Chance."

The prospect of Lola going anywhere without

me filled me with terror. I grabbed her hand. "Lollie, can we actually do this?"

She pulled her hand away and jammed her thumbs in her belt loops. "We're the cosmic musketeers," she said fiercely. "We don't give in and we don't give up. Got it?"

I swallowed hard. "Got it."

Lola touched her angel tags. "Later." And she vanished.

I was just about to beam myself to Chance when I heard someone cautiously lift the latch.

I practically went into orbit. *He's back! The PODS came back!*

Chance peered around the door. "Nick? Oh, nobody here."

I clutched my pounding heart. "That's right, nobody here," I said frantically. "So let's get out of here while we still can."

But Chance just ambled about, admiring Nick's pad. After he'd had a good nose round, he poured himself some ale, hacked a crust off a loaf he'd found under a cloth, then sat riffling through Nick's books, calmly chomping away.

"For Pete's sake!" I wailed.

But you can only panic for so long. An hour or so later, Chance was still riffling and I was nodding off.

Then for the second time I heard the metallic clunk of the latch. I totally broke out into goosebumps. And Nick walked in with his new best friend.

I could feel the PODS agent deliberately not looking at me.

"Ah, Chance, made yourself comfortable, I see!" said Nick in a forced tone. "I don't think you've met my friend, Edward Brice."

Chance jumped up, scattering crumbs, and went to shake hands.

Brice gave a frosty nod. "It's a pleasure to make your acquaintance, sir. I'll make myself scarce," he murmured to Nick. "You two have business to discuss."

I had to hand it to him. Brice had really done his homework. His speech, his Elizabethan manners, were perfect. The bleached hair, however, was pure twenty-first century. That's because he'd borrowed it from my old school crush, along with his gorgeous face and the bad-boy walk.

He waited until Nick was explaining Chance's go-between duties to him, then he strolled over. "Hi, Mel. How's it going?" he said softly.

Sometimes there's so much you want to say, it all gets jammed up inside, and absolutely nothing comes out.

Then I caught sight of those manicured fingers with their glittering rings, and what came out was pure rage.

"I'm so relieved you didn't damage your jewellery," I said icily.

Brice laughed. His eyes were totally dead, just like I'd remembered. "Admit it, Mel, you're out of your depth."

"So are you going to bash me too?" I said. "Or do you have some quaint PODS code about not hitting girls?"

"Oh, I've got other plans for you, Mel. Long-term plans." Brice stretched himself out on a wooden settle. "These are great times, aren't they?" he sighed. "I am in my element!"

Fortunately I didn't have to lose any brain cells guessing what this element was, because he couldn't wait to tell me.

"Chaos!" he explained gleefully. "You really should hang out at court some time, Mel. All those shadowy stone corridors! All those convenient tapestries for traitors to eavesdrop behind! It's a plotters' paradise – I love it!"

I remembered how Lola thought we'd beamed down in the middle of a wedding because everyone was so happy.

"You just see ugly things," I said. "You make me sick."

"I see what's real, sweetheart. Oh, did you know Golden Boy over there sold Chance's soul to pay his debts? Of course, Nick doesn't know that's what I'm after."

Listening to Brice has this numbing effect. After a while you want to give up, the way people fall asleep in the snow.

"You know what's tragic?" he said. "Chance can't believe Nick would hurt him. That's his fatal flaw." He shook with laughter.

On the other side of the room, Chance and Nick were coming to the end of their talk.

"Funny," Brice mused. "Chance would be dead if it wasn't for you. And by the time this is over, he'll wish he was."

"Why are you doing this?" I said angrily "If he's such a nobody, why go to all this trouble to destroy him?"

His eyes glittered. "Sweetheart, you'll never know!"

And his laughter followed us out into the night. I knew I should be thankful I was still in one piece. Brice could have finished me, if he'd wanted to. He appeared to be saving that treat for later. As if

Chance and I were his sad little pawns, so he could do what he liked with us.

Yikes! I suddenly realised that I hadn't been listening to Nick and Chance "discussing business"! I'd been too busy listening to that toe rag, Brice. What was going to happen now? A fine guardian angel you're turning out to be, Mel Beeby, I thought glumly.

I followed Chance down dark smelly side streets, until we reached the river. He was off on some evil little mission for Nick, I realised with a lurch.

"The palace, Greenwich," he muttered to a passing ferryman, who took him on board.

The palace! This was getting fishier by the minute!

It was pitch black out on the river, except for little glints and flashes where the ripples caught the moonlight, and the orangey flicker of the boatman's torch.

Sometimes a ferryboat slid past like a ghost. Most carried only one passenger, shadowy shapes in cloaks. I found myself shivering, and wondered if these were the evil conspirators Brice was talking about.

When we reached the other side, Chance gave the ferryman some coins. "Wait for me, and you'll have the rest when I return," he promised.

As soon as we left the river, he went zooming off

into the undergrowth, making his way through the trees until we came out in some kind of park. Finally, we arrived at the rear of a huge building, which I assumed was the royal palace. Like everything else, it was in total darkness.

Chance tapped softly at a side-door. It opened slightly and he handed a crackly roll of parchment to whoever was on the other side. I saw a green silk-gloved hand give him another in exchange.

The instant the door closed, Chance went racing back through the park. His thoughts jumped out at me. *So much money for so little work! I'll just take this to Don Rodriguez and I'll get my first payment!*

As we sped back across the Thames in the dark, I could feel Chance smiling beside me. It made me want to cry.

"Wake up!" I whispered. "I don't know why Brice has it in for you, but you've got to be ready for him, Chance. You've got to fight back."

The next few days were the most stressful of my angel career.

Chance was leading a double life, and unfortunately I had to lead it with him. Lola and I mostly had to catch up via Angel Link.

"So when am I going to see you?" she said in

despair one afternoon, her voice bouncing back at me like a bad mobile connection.

"I wish I knew."

I was talking from the playhouse. Two actors in holey tights were leaping on and off boxes, practising sword fighting skills.

"I'm not saying Chance has like, criminal tendencies," Lola was saying. "But I do think he gets a buzz out of this cloak-and-dagger stuff."

I felt despairing. "Lollie, I don't think I'm the right person to help him. Maybe we should swap."

Lola's voice crackled over the Link. "You're doing fine. Oops, gotta go!" And she'd gone.

"I am SO not doing fine, Lollie," I whispered miserably.

The trap was closing in. I knew it.

I sensed it as Chance went snaking between the trees in the dark. I knew it from the way I leapt out of my skin at the slightest twig crack. Details jumped out at me, like clues in a thriller. I didn't know what they meant, but I passed them on to Chance just the same.

"Don't you think it's suspicious, how they always wear the same gloves?" I told Chance one night. "It might be just the one glove, actually. You only see one hand after all. Don Rodriguez's is wine-coloured.

Though you'd think a Spanish nobleman could afford nicer leather. Hers is icky green silk. In my century we associate that colour with poison, hint hint."

The brainwashing was Lola's idea. "It's the dripping tap technique," she explained during one of our chats. "Repeat the same thing over and over and it's got to get through eventually."

So I badgered Chance non-stop. "How come such a noble lady only owns one pair of gloves? Come on, Cupid, how likely is that? She's probably just a maid. I bet Nick and Brice are paying her to pose as a lady in waiting. If you ask me, this lovesick lady thing is pure fiction."

By this time, we were at the house with the grand gates where Don Rodriguez lived.

"Chance, would you please stop being Robin Hood for one minute and check out the gloves!" I pestered. "Because if the Don is wearing wine-coloured leather tonight, I think you should open that letter and see what's inside. Wake up and open your eyes, Chance. Open your eyes!"

I can't say for sure that Lola's technique worked. I can only tell you what happened.

At first it was business as usual. Chance went through a little side-gate, and tapped at a leaded window. I hated that window. It always stuck. And tonight it seemed to grate open with an especially edgy sound. As usual, a leather-gloved hand appeared.

And suddenly Chance's expression changed. He looked, *really* looked at the glove, as if he was seeing it in huge cinematic close-up.

Then he and Don Rodriguez exchanged crackly letters in the usual way, and Chance set off through the dark. I heard him muttering. "Those gloves. Always the same colour and the leather is such poor quality..."

"Oh, *finally*!" I said.

But once again Chance was arguing with himself. "I ferry their letters from one side of the river to the other, and I have no idea what is in them. But Nick would never betray me. Would he?"

A solitary linkman passed by. London streets were dangerous after dark, so people hired linkmen, big tough blokes with lamps, to make sure they got home safely. Chance called out, "May I borrow your lamp?" followed by the usual chink of coins. "Could you hold it up?" he asked. "I have to read this important letter."

The linkman grinned. "A love letter, no doubt."

Chance broke the seal on the parchment and scanned the letter frantically. "It can't be true," he whispered.

The linkman looked sympathetic. "Given you the

cold shoulder, has she? Oh, steady now, young sir, steady, lean on me!"

But I'd snooped over Chance's shoulder. And I knew the message in this letter was far deadlier than some teenage brush-off.

When Chance and I finally reached the Feathers, it was almost dawn. He stood throwing stones up at Cat's window for ages, but I think she must have been in a really deep sleep. In the end I called Lola up on the Link and told her to wake Cat up. Finally Cat appeared at the door, dazed and blinking in her nightshift, a stump of candle flickering in her hand.

"They have betrayed me!" Chance gasped. "This letter says I am involved in a Spanish plot to kill the queen!"

Lola peeped out from behind Cat. "Mel, what's going on?"

"The dripping tap," I said feebly. "I think it worked." Lola threw her arms around me and we gave each other a big hug.

A burly, weatherbeaten man joined us in the doorway.

His beard had sprouted a few more grey hairs since I last saw him. Otherwise Cat's dad looked exactly the same, even down to the pearl earring.

He gave Chance a shrewd and very thorough looking-over.

"Catherine," he said. "This boy needs a shot of rum."

I don't condone piracy obviously, but there are definite advantages to having a pirate in the family. Assuming they're on your side, that is. Once Cat's dad had heard Chance's story, he was totally on his side. Plus he came up with some v. colourful suggestions for getting Nick back, mostly involving gizzards and slitting of various kinds.

In a funny way, I think it helped Chance come to terms with what had just happened. It showed him that even though his best friend had betrayed him, there were people who really cared about him.

And though his eyes were still shocked, they weren't vague or foggy. Actually, I got the definite sense that old foggy Chance had gone for good.

And all at once he said in a totally steady voice, "Cat, could you fetch me some paper and ink? I'm going to write a letter."

CHAPTER TEN

"This is the most long-winded, luke-warm, lily-livered revenge in the entire history of revenges!" Cat's father fumed. "You've been sitting at that table for hours, like a mouse scratching at a wainscot."

"Hush," said Cat. "Or he'll smudge the ink and have to start again."

Me and Lola edged forward invisibly to get a better look. That boy was constantly surprising us. Now it turned out he had a talent for forgery too!

"Why not just run the booby through with a cutlass and have done?" Cat's dad sighed.

Chance sounded exhausted. "Because I want

him to have a taste of his own medicine. And because I am sick and tired of being Nick Ducket's fool."

Cat's dad shook his head. "You think too much, boy, that's your trouble. Forget this treacherous knave. Go to sea, get some salt air into your lungs. That's a real life for a man."

Chance looked startled. "I'd never considered going to sea."

"You should," said the pirate. "It's a golden time for English seamen. And if you should happen to sink a Spanish galleon or two, you could make yourself filthy rich, and become the master of your own ship like me."

And then he dropped a total bombshell. "Cat's coming with me this time, aren't you?" He smiled fondly at his daughter.

Chance blinked. "I – I didn't know."

"I'm only thinking about it," Cat said. "I haven't decided."

"She *has* decided," her dad said calmly. "I know my daughter and the sea is in her blood. Who knows, you might take to it too. You make a handsome couple, to my mind," he added slyly.

Chance had finished forging his letter. Now he held the original in the candle flame, watching its edges slowly blacken and crumble. His eyes grew dreamy.

"Maybe I could do it," he murmured. "Maybe I could leave England and start a new life."

His face hardened. "I can't think about that now. I have a letter to deliver to Greenwich. But this time I'll do it in broad daylight."

"I'm coming with you," said Cat at once.

He shook his head. "No, I've got to go alone."

Lola smiled mischievously at me and hummed a bar of Reuben's little tune. I knew what she was saying. *You're not alone, Chance. Not now. Not ever.*

Chance had explained his plan to Cat and her pirate dad, which of course meant that me and Lola were also in the know. It was simple but stunningly brilliant.

The old letter named Chance as a conspirator. The new one, also signed by "Don Rodriguez", named Nick instead, stating that Chance was an innocent pawn, who had no idea what he'd got himself into.

But he was still taking a terrible risk. It was still possible Chance might not be believed. Which meant he'd be arrested for conspiracy and probably hung, drawn and quartered. Like Michael said, the Tudors were into revenge in a big way. Merely *hanging* criminals was far too tame for them. They preferred to split their wrong-doers down the middle and expose their internal organs as well.

Poor Chance looked so scared as the ferryman rowed us upriver to Greenwich, I truly thought he might be sick. I didn't feel too good myself.

At least this time we didn't have snake through the trees like commandos. Chance walked right up to the palace guards, where he stood peering anxiously from face to face, as if he didn't know which one of these poker-faced heavies to address. He really was a brilliant actor.

"Excuse me, sirs," he said in a timid little voice. "Don Rodriguez gave me a purse of gold to deliver this letter to a lady at the queen's court. At first I wanted his gold, but now I'm scared I might be doing wrong. What if he's plotting to harm our queen? Should we open the letter, do you think?"

As it turned out, that was the easiest part.

The hardest part was when they made Chance take them to Nick's lodgings, then having to watch as they marched his ex-best friend away to the Tower, and hearing their boots tramp away over the cobbles. "I fear your recklessness will kill you," Cat had said. And she was right.

I'll never forget Nick's face when he realised

Chance had turned the tables. He crumpled like a little kid.

"I thought you were my friend," he said. "And all the time you hated me."

Chance's voice shook. "I never hated you. But when I was with you, I sometimes hated myself."

"And now I'm condemned to a traitor's death," Nick said bitterly. "How do you feel now, old friend?"

Chance's eyes filled with sorrow. "Very sad." He hesitated. "But also free."

On the way back in the ferry, he dozed, totally exhausted. I was knackered too. All the emotion of the past few hours had totally drained my angel strength.

And suddenly Brice was there in skintight jeans and a T-shirt.

Sharing a small boat with a furious PODS agent is not an experience I'd wish on anyone. But I kept my voice steady.

"I guess this is goodbye. Since you've dropped the Elizabethan disguise, you must be heading back to Slime City or wherever you lot hang out."

His anger came pulsing at me in shock waves. "Don't try to kid yourself you've made a difference, sweetheart," he sneered. "You haven't changed a thing. The Agency must be insane giving this mission to a bunch of angel brats."

"That's your opinion. Thanks to us, Chance won't die a traitor's death. Now he and Cat can go off together and start a new life. Game over."

His lips twisted into a cold smile. "Melanie, please! You should get a job writing daytime soaps! You really think I went to all this trouble to thwart true love? You're even more clueless than I thought."

But I was looking at Brice's face, borrowed from that beautiful boy I'd fancied in the days when I was just another airhead with attitude – in the days before I died and got a life. And it occurred to me that Brice was wrong. I had changed something. Me.

"Brice," I said. "How come the Opposition sent you here, when this is a no-go zone for agents?"

He laughed. "They didn't."

I was bewildered. "Then who...? I mean, who else *is* there?"

"Oh, the Opposition like to call me in when anything interesting comes along. This little project for example," he added with one of his chilling smiles. "But I prefer to work alone."

I felt my skin starting to creep. Suddenly the

cosmos seemed weirder and scarier than I had ever imagined.

"Then what *are* you?" I almost whispered the words.

Brice stood up in the boat so that he was grinning down at me, and delivered his best-ever exit line.

"Oh, didn't you know, Melanie? I'm an angel. I'm an angel, just like you."

And like a vampire in a bad movie, he vanished into thin air.

"A fallen angel?" I said to Lola that night. "So did Brice like, go to our school and hang out at Guru?" I shuddered. The idea was too deeply disturbing for words.

Lola shook her head. "I think the last time the Agency made that kind of mistake, it was when angels still wore long white robes. And fought with swords," she added comfortingly.

"All the same."

We were in Cat's bare little attic. Cat was sorting through her few possessions. Chance was flicking through a book of Elizabethan travellers' tales, occasionally reading the more bizarre excerpts out loud.

It was a sweet scene, but somehow I wasn't

convinced.

"Lollie, this is our second shot at a happy ending," I said anxiously. "And I'm scared we're going to blow it."

"But this is so perfect," Lola assured me. "Chance and Cat are going to have a new life in a new world."

"But Brice seemed so sure this wasn't a love thing, and he had no reason to lie. We're missing something. Something he thinks I'm too bimbo-ish to see."

Chance gave an amazed chuckle. "Cat, according to this fellow, there is one island where all the people have only one foot each! One very *large* foot. He says they move around surprisingly quickly!"

If only Orlando was here to give us some advice, I thought wistfully. Even a passing Earth angel would do.

But for cosmic reasons which I totally didn't understand, me and Lola were the only angels available.

I sighed. "Lola, we had doubts before and we were right. This time we've got to try to help Chance do the right thing."

"I know," Lola admitted. "I feel the same way."

"But how? We can't materialise." I pulled a face. "And I don't think I really ought to whack anyone again!"

"There's only one thing we can do. We totally bomb them with vibes. And trust them to find their true destinies," my soul-mate added poetically.

I puffed out my cheeks. "Lollie, I'm trusting so hard, my trust muscles are like old knicker elastic."

So we did what Lola said. We bombed Cat's little attic until the air felt like tingly champagne.

After half an hour or so, Cat suddenly found her old shell necklace at the back of a drawer. She sat back on her heels, looking wistful.

"My mother gave me this," she said. "It's all I have of her. What a wild little girl I was. I loved the sea even then."

She darted a troubled look at Chance. "But you get seasick just watching the ships bob up and down in the dock."

He looked startled. "I'll soon get used to it."

"But your job at the theatre—" she began.

"I'm a dogsbody, fetching and carrying, that's all I do."

"But one day you'll be an actor! It's what you wanted! Why throw it all away?"

Chance shut his book with a snap. "Pretending

to be someone else," he said with contempt. "What life is that for a man? No, Cat, there is no future for me here." He looked anxious. "Don't you want me to come?"

"Of course, but—"

"Because you are my life, Catherine," he said passionately. "When I wake you are the first thing I think of."

Lola and I hastily looked away. Eavesdropping is one thing, spying on couples kissing is something else.

"Keep going," I hissed. "We've got to keep going."

And we went on beaming angelic vibes at them until gold sparkles fell like rain.

Cat went on sifting through her things. A comb, a brush, a hand mirror, a lumpy-looking sampler she'd been forced to sew when she was a little girl, some scuffed leather boots.

Then she sat fiddling with her necklace again, and I realised she'd made up her mind to tell her sweetheart some painful home truths.

"Chance, you say acting is no life for a man, yet that's exactly what you've been doing ever since we met."

He looked stricken. "Don't say that. I never

pretended with you, not when it mattered."

"No," she agreed softly. "Not with me, that's true."

"With some people, with Nick, it seemed to make things simpler. With you it's the opposite. You're the star I steer by, my compass! Together, we can start again. We can be whoever we want to be."

She stroked his hair. "I don't want to be someone else," she said quietly. "I want to be me. You're always starting again. You have no roots, no past, Chance. I know absolutely nothing about you. It's time for you to stop running away from everything and stay put for a change."

I felt a tiny twinge of recognition. I hate to admit it, but I used to be a total escape artist. Then I died and finally found something I wanted to do. But Cat was right. Chance was still all over the place.

"It's all right for you to run away," he said angrily. "But not for me, is that right?"

"I'm not running away. I'm following my dream. You must follow yours."

He buried his face in his hands. "Cat, you don't know what it's like! There's all these different characters inside me. All these voices. How can I tell which is me?"

Her eyes filled with tears. "You are a wonderful

person, Chance, and it truly breaks my heart to – to –"

Lola and me were trying hard not to cry.

"Will it make a difference if I tell you about my past?" Chance said eagerly. And all at once he was talking at top speed.

"My father was a glover and my brothers followed his trade, curing the skins, and turning them into gloves. Great troughs of animal skins soaking in salted water. They stank the house out."

The air was electric. Cat was utterly still and Lola and me hardly dared to breathe.

"A few months before I left home, my father's business began to fail. We never really got on. I disappointed him. He said I'd never amount to anything."

Chance's breath was coming in gasps. It was like, now he'd started to open up, he totally couldn't stop.

"Then my little sister died, her name was Ann. She was eight years old. She had five freckles on the bridge of her nose and she died."

"Shsh," Cat said, putting her finger to his lips. "Don't."

But he kept talking desperately. "Money was short. We could barely afford to put food on the table, I went poaching the local squire's deer, and got caught. If I'd stayed I'd have brought shame on my family, so I ran away to London. I thought I'd find my fortune. Then I could go home again, only this time I'd make my father proud of me. But instead I found you, Cat, and you are my home, my heart and now I'll lose you..."

Lola and I exchanged agonized looks. And without a word, we softly tiptoed out and left them alone.

I totally couldn't understand Chance. Barely an hour before he was due to see Cat off, he was at the playhouse, scribbling furiously in a notebook.

Suddenly he ripped out the page. "Eyes full of fire. Hair like black wire," he said contemptuously. "An ape could do better." And he scrumpled up the paper and tossed it disgustedly into a corner.

He only just made it in the end, arriving at the docks as Cat's father was about to help her down into the dinghy which was to row them out to her father's ship.

Cat gave a little cry of anguish and ran to Chance, pressing something into his hand. "My shell necklace," she said. "It's the most precious thing I own."

"I tried to write you a poem," he said into her

hair. "But I tore it up."

They clung to each other, but Cat's father gently detached her and helped her down into the boat.

Lola's eyes were red from crying. "I don't care if it's unprofessional. I can't stand to see Cat so miserable," she snivelled. "Some happy ending this is."

The boatman pulled on his oars and the dinghy began to move away from the jetty.

If he reached out now, he could still touch her, I thought. It was like I totally didn't want to believe it was over. But Chance didn't move.

Then I heard him draw a sharp breath. "I do have a farewell gift," he shouted suddenly. "My name! I want to tell you my name!"

But the wind snatched his words away and the water was widening between them and Cat couldn't hear.

In his desperation, he jumped on to a barrel. "Can you hear me, Catherine Darcy? I want to tell you my name!"

People were staring. Was this boy out of his mind?

Chance flung out his arms, the wind whipping at his hair and doublet.

"My name is Will Shakespeare!" he yelled. "I am

Will Shakespeare and I love you. I'll love you till I die!"

My mouth totally fell open.

Chance was laughing and crying. Something huge had happened to him. He'd said his real name aloud. He'd lost his one true love. He looked trembly and new, like something which had just emerged from a chrysalis.

His eyes! I thought. All of him is there behind his eyes!

OK, it's just possible I started something that rainy night, with my slightly unprofessional cosmic whack. But the important thing is that Chance finished it. He woke up all by himself, exactly like he was supposed to.

But right now the poor boy was in such a state, he didn't know what he was doing.

He jumped down from the barrel and stumbled away. And before I knew what was happening, he'd walked right through me, like some sort of angel car wash. Then suddenly he stopped, looking around in bewilderment, almost as if he knew I was there.

I was in total bits. Every atom in my body was fizzing with the delicious shock of mingling molecules with the greatest writer who ever lived.

And at that moment, some invisible gate between Heaven and Earth was unlocked, and there was a great whoosh of light.

People actually looked up in awe. They couldn't see what was happening. But they could feel it. It was like an invisible wedding, it was like the May day celebrations, only a billion times better.

All over the city of London, the angels were coming back.

CHAPTER ELEVEN

Days later, Lola and I were in our school library. No, really!

It's actually my favourite building on the campus. It's a bit like a lighthouse, but made from truly magical glass which gives the effect of clouds floating across the outer walls.

Inside it's even better. The ceiling is actually a planetarium. You can look up from your studies and see all the stars and planets doing their awesome cosmic thing.

Reuben was meant to be joining us later. Something had come up at his dojo, so we'd bagged him a seat. The comfy ones on the top floor are in big demand.

Anyway, there we were curled up with a huge stack of books. Lola had her cute spectacles on and looked v. intellectual.

All this book-wormery wasn't entirely our idea. The Agency had asked us to write a report, and we thought we should have at least some idea what we were talking about.

"I can't believe we missed all those signs," I told Lola. "I mean, it was staring us in the face. Like the way Chance really perked up when he was writing those love letters, or spinning some incredible yarn. He actually persuaded those crooks that Cat was an elf princess! He wasn't a liar. He was a storyteller galloping out of a control. He was..."

"He was a poet who didn't know it," Lola finished with a grin. She took off her specs and rubbed her nose. "Hey, wasn't Sweetpea hilarious about that scar!"

Thanks to the brilliant staff at the Sanctuary, Reuben was almost back to normal and his injuries were healing fast. A bit *too* fast for Reuben. He'd actually asked if he could keep one particular scar on his chest. It's shaped like a starburst and is quite stylish in a bizarre sort of way. "Battle scars," he'd explained. "So everyone knows I'm hard."

"You *are* hard," I told him. "You were a total

hero. You fought for your life, even though you were really ill." Reuben's strange symptoms had turned out to be the effects of severe angelic shock. Human violence really takes it out of pure angels at first. The bear business must have been the final straw.

"That's why I want the scar, Mel," he'd said fiercely. "To remind me. I'm never letting some PODS creep up on me again."

I leaned back in my chair with a deep sigh, and gazed up at the library ceiling, where the planets were doing their stately glittery dance. "Boys are so weird," I sighed.

"Hey," said Lola. "We've still got work to do, remember?"

We were gradually piecing things together. For instance we now knew that the no-go zone was all the Opposition's idea. Chance was an important Agency project which they were determined to sabotage. This may surprise you, but the PODS Agency has to abide by cosmic laws just like we do. So their lawyers went through the law books with a fine toothcomb, to find something they could use to their advantage.

Finally they found some totally forgotten statute, saying that in the unlikely situation that Earth's light levels ever reached 50/50, all cosmic personnel should be withdrawn, to let the levels settle naturally.

This law was originally intended as a safeguard for Earth. But one of the three 50/50s ever seen in the cosmos, just happened to coincide (yeah, right) with the particular years Chance was at his lowest ebb. In the books, these are referred to as "Shakespeare's Lost Years".

The Opposition made it look as if they'd totally tied their own hands, by agreeing with the Agency that they'd only try to influence Chance from a distance. But as soon as the Agency was out of the picture, the Opposition instantly hired Brice to do their dirty work for them. Cosmic laws don't mean a thing to him, apparently. He's the original cosmic outlaw.

Lola was frowning at her notes. "I hate to seem thick, but what's the big deal about Shakespeare exactly? I mean, how come both agencies were fighting over his soul?"

"I asked Michael about that," I said. "He said the Opposition does everything in its power to make humans forget who they are and what they came to do. But Chance, erm, Shakespeare, actually remembered, and Michael says it shows in every line he wrote."

Lola looked awed. "Boy," she said. "That was some thump you gave him, Mel."

"You know what's weird?" I said. "I've been flipping through his plays since we got back, and I keep seeing all this stuff Nick said. Remember that crack about 'Exit pursued by a bear'? That's in *The Winter's Tale*. And that line about a rose smelling sweet by any other name – that's *Romeo and Juliet*. As for Romeo, he is pure Nick! Before he fell for Juliet, he had a different girlfriend every day of the week."

Lola looked slightly sad. "I thought exactly the same thing. He's like the sweet Nick, before he listened to Brice and forgot who he really was."

I suddenly realised I was fiddling with my hair, something I do when I'm upset. "Tell you what," I admitted. "I'm really disappointed with Chance."

"I know what you mean," sighed Lola. "All that stuff about 'you are my guiding star and I'll love you till I die'."

"Yeah, then he writes a whole bunch of plays which totally wouldn't exist if it wasn't for his childhood sweetheart, and doesn't give her so much as a tiny mention. Huh!"

"Hmmn," said Lola. "He's an Elizabethan love-rat, definitely."

Someone coughed.

I looked up and turned bright scarlet.

Orlando was standing like, two inches from my chair. He must have heard every word we'd just said.

Did I mention that Orlando looks like one of those dark-eyed angels in an old Italian painting? Did I also mention that he's a total genius? Well, he is. And in two minutes he totally set us straight.

"So what did Shakespeare's childhood sweetheart look like?" Orlando seemed genuinely interested. Actually, he seemed slightly excited, and he is usually Mister Calm and Collected, believe me.

So I described Cat's green eyes and golden skin and her springy dark fuse-wire hair and suddenly Orlando broke into this big grin.

"Congratulations," he said. "You just solved the mystery of the dark lady." And he whipped a book off the shelves, *Shakespeare's Sonnets*.

Apparently Shakespeare wrote these poems which constantly refer to a beautiful dark lady, but no-one could ever figure out who she was. It's been driving scholars crazy for centuries!

Orlando gave me one of his heart-melting smiles. "I think you owe Chance an apology," he said. "He didn't forget her. He remembered Cat for ever, just like he promised he would."

And suddenly there was this embarrassing silence, which I knew I should fill with something intelligent, only I just went incredibly shy and tongue-tied instead.

Then I heard scuffly little footsteps and a muffled giggle. A small bossy voice said, "Ssh, Maudie – you're not allowed to talk in the library!"

A bunch of breathless nursery-school angels appeared at the top of the stairs. They beckoned frantically.

"Mel! Mel! Reuben says come outside!"

"Well, go and tell him to come up here," I grinned.

"No! Because he *can't*," said the tiniest angel hoarsely.

"Why can't he come, Maudie?"

"You've got to come downstairs and see!" She was practically jumping up and down with excitement.

So me, Lola, and Orlando went dashing round and round the spiral staircase and flew out of the door. Then we stopped dead with pure astonishment.

The library building is surrounded by this big green park and several nursery-school children had been busy picking daisies. Now, with great determination, they were arranging their giant daisy chain around the neck of a puzzled, but not completely unhappy-looking bear. Lola and I peered at him, hardly believing our eyes.

"Sackerson?" we said simultaneously.

Reuben beamed at us. "He just got here. He looks great, doesn't he? Doesn't he look *great*!"

flying
high

To Sally Beets, and to Gemma and Madeline of
Westborough Community School, all undercover angels

CHAPTER ONE

Last week I went back to Earth to visit my family.

OK, so it was just a dream, but it was totally true to life.

It was Christmas and my little sister was helping Mum to decorate the tree. I was amazed how much Jade had grown. She's getting to be a proper daddy long legs like me, I thought.

Apart from my sister's gangly legs, everything was exactly the way I remembered; the tomato-coloured throw on the sofa, the daft DJ rabbiting away on the radio, spicy chicken smells floating from the kitchen. Even the Christmas decorations were the same, right down to the painted wooden angel with glittery wings.

Perhaps Jade read my thoughts, because she took the little angel out of the box and suddenly she went all tearful. "Melanie's an angel now, isn't she, Mum?" she sniffled.

They glanced towards a framed photograph on top of the TV. It was one I'd never seen till now, which isn't that surprising. Des, my step-dad, took it on my thirteenth birthday, only hours before a speeding joyrider booted me out of the twenty-first century and into the next world.

Then I took another look at the photo and came out in major goosebumps. It was that look in my eyes. So dreamy and far away. Almost, well – wise. As if I *knew* what was going to happen. I felt a flicker of awe. Was it possible that as Des shouted, "Say Cheese!" and clicked the shutter, that I was actually secretly preparing to leave Earth?

Jade tugged anxiously at Mum. "My sister's an angel in Heaven, isn't she?"

Mum tried to smile. "Of course she is, pet."

My throat ached in sympathy. My mum thought she'd lost me for ever. She thought I'd vanished into a meaningless black hole called Death. I was suddenly desperate to tell her that dying wasn't like she thought. "Don't be sad," I whispered. "This might be hard to believe, but I really am an angel! I go to this special angel school and I've got angel ID. And I've made these brilliant friends..."

At least, that's what I tried to say. But the instant I heard my own voice – POP! My old home vanished like a soap bubble.

My ears filled with a vast mysterious throbbing, like a cosmic humming top. And all at once I was whooshing through space, past glittering stars and planets – and woke, gasping, in my room at the Angel Academy.

I felt genuinely shocked, like a castaway washed on to some far distant shore.

It's weird the things I miss, now that they've gone for ever. The way my little sister smells of warm wax crayons. The sound of Mum's voice. The taste of her cooking.

I sat up and took a few deep breaths. Heavenly air has this incredibly sweet, delicate scent. It reminds me ever so slightly of lilacs, but there's nothing on Earth quite like it. I was feeling better already.

Then I looked out of my window and saw the soaring skyscrapers of the Heavenly City, all sparkling and shimmering in the celestial light, and the last traces of homesickness melted away. I felt a blissful smile spread across my face. "*This* is your home now, Melanie," I whispered.

Yippee! It's the weekend, I remembered suddenly. No school for two days!

I wiggled my toes, admiring my glittery toenails. Lola had let me use some of her precious twenty-second century nail polish.

Omigosh, Lola!!

I hunted frantically for my clock. Yikes! I'd really overslept!

I grabbed the phone and tapped in Reuben's number. "Are you awake, Reubs?" I asked breathlessly.

I heard a familiar chuckle. "Pure angels don't need to sleep, remember? Unlike some people I could mention."

"Yeah, yeah, don't rub it in," I wailed. "Look, I'll have her down at the beach in two ticks, I swear."

"Wait!" Reuben sounded slightly panicky. "What's that thing I say to her again? Happy many returns? It sounds slightly bizarre."

Unlike me and Lola, our angel buddy has never lived on Earth, so concepts like birthdays leave him seriously confused.

But while we were chatting, I caught sight of my reflection in my crumpled PJs, and practically freaked! I was organising a top secret party and I wasn't even dressed yet! I totally did not have time to coach

Reuben in human birthday etiquette. "If it worries you, don't say it," I gabbled. "Just give her a flower or something. Later, OK?" And flinging down the phone, I sprinted for the bathroom.

Sorry, you're probably totally confused by this time. Isn't this girl Melanie like, dead? you're thinking. That means she's gone to live in Heaven, right? So how come she's still nattering about nail varnish and parties? Isn't that just a teeny bit, well, shallow? I know, I know! I've been at the Angel Academy for almost three terms now, and I still have NO idea why I was picked to be a trainee angel. It's not like I showed signs of unnatural saintliness in my former life. My teacher, Miss Rowntree, thought I was a total bimbo.

Of course, I prefer to think she was mistaken. I like to picture some celestial talent scout passing through my hell-hole comprehensive (bravely trying not to inhale the pong of school chips and cheesy gymshoes), when suddenly she sees me, Melanie Beeby. And it's like, "YESS! She's the one!!" Don't ask what I'm up to at this crucial moment. Probably in the back of the class, texting a mate, or in the girls' toilets, agonising over my latest pimple.

But whatever stupid thing I'm doing, this scout is totally not fooled. With her angelic super-sight, she zooms in on me in massive celestial close-up. Closer, closer, until BINGO! She sees clear through to the real, the essential, Melanie, with all her unusual and unused abilities. Qualities just like, *wasted* on someone like Miss Rowntree.

Ah well, I'll probably never know how it happened. The great thing is I LOVE my incredible new life. And like Lola says, who said angels can't have fun! (Lola is just her human name by the way. We only use our angel names for like, official purposes. Mine's Helix if you're interested.)

I met Lola Sanchez, otherwise known as Lollie, on my first day at the Academy and we clicked just like that. It was like we'd each found that special best friend we'd been missing, ever since the universe began, if that makes sense?

We even have almost identical taste in clothes. (Though being from the twenty-second century, Lola is that *tiny* bit more outrageous.) We're genuine soul-mates. Sometimes we actually read each other's minds.

Can you imagine what a nightmare it was, trying to keep my telepathic soul-mate's party under wraps!!

I'd been planning it for weeks. Reuben was in charge of the music. Thanks to me and Lola, he's shaping up to be a fantastic DJ, creating fabulous fusions of heavenly and terrestrial sounds, like you would *not* believe.

I'd managed to persuade Mo to do the catering. Mo runs Guru, one of our favourite after-school hang-outs. They do gorgeous party food there and I wanted to celebrate my soul-mate's birthday in style!

After the fastest shower in the entire history of showers, I threw on my bikini and matching sarong, fastened a gold chain around my midriff, tied a funky pirate bandana over my hair and beamed at myself in the mirror. I looked delicious, even if I did say so myself!

Grabbing my beach bag, I raced down the corridor to knock on Lola's door.

Lola opened it instantly, looking so hopeful that I felt like a real traitor. But I just said "Hi" and all the birthday sparkle went out of her eyes.

"Oh, hi," she said in a gloomy voice. "Did you want to borrow something?"

I *hate* keeping things from Lola. I sternly reminded myself that I only had to string my best mate along for a teensy bit longer, and gave her my brightest smile. "Sorry to bother you, babe, but I was hoping you'd help me out with this project?"

Lola looked more depressed than ever. "Oh, right."

"I won't blame you if you say no," I wittered. "It's going to be really boring. Mr Allbright wants me to do this stupid survey for Science."

She shrugged. "It's not like I've got anything better to do."

"You're a star! Erm, maybe you should change into some beach clothes first," I suggested cunningly.

Lola frowned. "What kind of survey is this?"

"Oh, who knows!" I babbled. "Mr Allbright said I had to find a rock pool. I'm meant to observe the microscopic lifeforms and take notes."

I was on safe ground here. Mr Allbright is always saying stuff like that.

"Oh, all right." Lola vanished and came back wearing a bikini top, hipster shorts and a stylish cowboy hat. She struck a cover-girl pose. "Will the teeny-tiny lifeforms approve, do you think?" she said in a bored voice.

"They'll go green with envy," I said truthfully.

But underneath I was panicking. We were running *really* late.

By the time we reached the sea shore, Reuben was slumped on the jetty, twiddling his tiny dreads. He sprang to his feet. "Finally!"

"What are you doing here, Sweetpea?" Lola demanded.

"Me?" he said innocently. "Oh, I came to help Mel."

As a pure angel, Reuben is physically incapable of

telling lies. But he's getting quite good at kind of *editing* the truth.

He jumped down into a little glass boat which was tugging gently at its moorings. "Are you girls coming or what?"

Lola looked puzzled. "You never said anything about boats, Boo!"

"Oh, duh!" I put an imaginary pistol to my head and did my best airhead giggle. "Yeah, Mr Allbright said I had to check out this special rock pool which you can only get to by boat." I secretly crossed my fingers, adding brightly, "Don't come if you don't want to, Lollie."

"Oh, for Heaven's sake," she sighed. "Let's all go and observe the thrilling rock-pool creatures."

Phew! Phase One of Operation Lollie was successfully completed. But I didn't know how much longer we'd be able to keep this up...

CHAPTER TWO

Reuben is a real water baby, always messing about with boats and surfer gear. So he did all the technical steering stuff, which left us free to do the film-star bit, trailing our hands in the spray and admiring the tiny fish darting in and out of the coral.

But I couldn't exactly enjoy myself, could I? Not with Lola being in such a huff. Several times I came close to cracking, but that would have ruined my big surprise.

Ever since I arrived at the Academy, Lola had been going on about this totally luminous beauty spot and how she couldn't wait to see it for herself. But as we sailed closer to the shore, I started to lose my nerve. When you get down to it, it's just sand and water, I thought. Can sand and water really be that special?

Actually, yes.

As we dragged the boat up out of the water, Lola suddenly went silent.

Lacy little waves lapped at the edges of sand so pure and glittery white that it looked as if the beach was strewn with powdered diamonds. Palm trees waved lazy green fronds in the sweet-scented breeze. Tiny parakeets zoomed to and fro, shrieking to each other as if they owned the place, which I suppose they kind of did. There was no doubt about it, Treasure Beach was the tropical paradise of your wildest dreams.

Lola gazed around her with a dazed expression. "This is Treasure Beach, isn't it?" she said at last.

I tried to sound offhand. "I've no idea. It's just where Mr Allbright said to go."

Her brow crinkled. "But why? There aren't any rock pools!"

"You noticed that too!" I said at once. "Darn! Mr Allbright must have meant us to check out the other side of the island!"

I saw Lola's expression change. "Does anybody live here?" She was staring at the sand.

Reuben and I shook our heads energetically. "Uh-uh."

"So how come there are all these footprints?"

I did a double take. "You're right! How weird!"

Lola started moving stealthily towards the trees, concentrating so hard on her big mystery, she totally didn't see what was right in front of her.

"Any minute now," Reuben whispered.

We heard Lola gasp. And when I saw what Mo had done, I gasped too, even though the whole thing was originally my idea!

In an airy shelter, thatched with palm leaves, was a little desert island café. Everything was beautiful: the snowy tablecloths, the exquisite place settings decorated with tropical blossoms. And overhead, in the shadowy branches, I caught the faintest glimmer of fairy lights.

"Ohh," I breathed. "This is just so sublime!"

I mentally fast-forwarded to the end of the party, with everyone dancing in a twinkly fairy-light haze. If only Orlando could be here, I thought wistfully. Then it really would be perfect.

But I didn't have time to feel sorry for myself, because just then all our mates jumped out of the shadows yelling, "Surprise, surprise!" They unrolled a massive banner with, "HAPPY BIRTHDAY LOLLIE!" in rainbow-coloured lettering, and people started throwing glittery confetti.

"I don't believe it!" Lola shrieked. "You monsters!"

I heard a chink of ice and there was Mo, his bald head gleaming, wearing a dazzling white apron over Bermuda shorts. He was holding a tray of drinks. He handed one to Lola and she went into fits of giggles.

Mo's special birthday cocktails were WAY over the top! Shocking pink fruit juice, crammed with fruit and flowers and topped with a cheesy paper parasol.

"Happy birthday, Ms Sanchez," he said calmly, and began unpacking goodies from a huge cool box.

Reuben had obviously taken my advice literally, because he totally skipped Lola's birthday greeting. Instead he seized a huge pink blossom from one of Mo's place settings and stuck it in her cowboy hat. "Have a lovely time!" he said shyly.

He ran off to do something to the sound system and Lola's favourite song came floating through the air.

I suddenly heard myself say, "He's looking so much better, isn't he?"

"Yeah! If it wasn't for the scar, you'd never know."

Not too long ago, Reuben came with us on his first ever trouble-shooting mission to Earth. Unfortunately he ran into an old enemy of mine, who gave him a really savage beating. Luckily we found our angel buddy in the nick of time, and the Sanctuary staff did a great job of patching him up.

"I still can't believe Brice used to be an angel." I had to close my eyes. Just saying his name made me feel as if I was dropping dizzily through space. "I mean, how does a total sleazeball like that make it into the Angel Academy? It doesn't make sense."

"I keep telling you, Brice left the Academy *aeons* before our time. Just forget about him because you're never going to have to see him again."

I shuddered. "He acts like we've got this bizarre cosmic connection."

"In his dreams! Just remember, you got the better of him, not the other way round." Lola pulled a face. "Anyway, what kind of angel are you, girl! Plotting parties behind my back! And why didn't you invite that beautiful boy Orlando?" she added, giggling.

I sighed. "He's gone missing again. No-one seems to know where he is. Anyway, I'm completely over him."

"Yeah, right!"

"I mean it this time." I took Lola's drink and handed her a carefully gift-wrapped box. "Happy birthday, babe!"

Her face lit up. "Boo, you shouldn't have!" (I have no idea why Lola calls me Boo. She invents mad nicknames for everyone.)

But before she could even tear off the paper, there was an outbreak of earsplitting bird calls. All the local parakeets left the trees in a huge screeching flock.

Everyone looked blank, then our mates started groping in bags and pockets. One by one we found our pagers and switched them off.

"Hey, Dino!" Reuben called. "Take over the decks, will ya?"

Lola handed her parcel to Mo. "Mind keeping this till I get back?"

"No problem. Perhaps you'd like to grab a snack?" Mo's eyes twinkled. "Who knows when you kids will eat again!"

We hastily helped ourselves to various goodies.

"Ever consider a change of profession, girlfriend?" I teased.

Lola took a last slurp of her cocktail. "No way!" she protested. "Enjoy my party, you guys!" she yelled to her remaining guests, and we raced down to the shore.

Minutes later, a flotilla of glass boats went skimming back across the water. That's how it is in the angel business. When you get the call, you drop what you're doing and just take off. No-one minds, in fact it's just the opposite. You know that someone somewhere needs you and let me tell you, that is an incredibly cool feeling!

CHAPTER THREE

When I first arrived at the Academy, I just could not understand why Lola was so desperate to get into the history club. I mean, who in her right mind would *choose* to memorise diagrams of the medieval strip field system?

But studying history at the Angel Academy is totally not like that.

Still not convinced? OK, then check this. At *my* school, we get to travel in time!

I know, I know, I couldn't believe it at first either. But now I'm completely into it. Last term, Lola, Reuben and I actually signed up to do history as our special subject, which got us on to the Agency's books. I am now totally convinced that being a time-travelling trouble shooter is what I was created for!

That's the thing I love about this school. On Earth they make you wait until you're grown up before you can do anything interesting. But here, you constantly get dropped in the deep end, which is scary but also incredibly exhilarating!

So even though we'd had to bale out of our own party, I was wildly happy. And I could tell the other trainees felt an identical mix of nerves, excitement and jittery pride. From the shore, the sight must be totally magic, I thought.

The Agency had called us and we had answered and now we were leaping from wave to wave like dolphins, in our tiny glass boats filled with light...

"Wonder what this is all about," said Lola, bringing me out of my dream.

"Must be serious for them to page us on our day off," said Reuben.

Simultaneously Lola and I looked down and wailed, "Omigosh!"

Neither of us had thought to bring a change of clothes!

"Great," I groaned, "I've got to go time-travelling in a silk sarong and sparkly flip-flops!"

"Oh, and hipster shorts and cowboy hats are so much more suitable," quipped my soul-mate.

Reuben gave us a pitying look. He wore his usual tragic tie-dyed top and cut-offs. Style is yet another Earth concept which baffles our angel buddy. But like Lola says, "Sweetpea is so chilled on the inside, he can totally get away with it!"

We'd barely set foot on dry land when a sleek limo purred over the sand towards us. We jumped in breathlessly. The driver executed a stylish U-turn and went bombing back downtown to the Agency.

When I first got here, that word really used to bother me, making me think of poker-faced men in suits, masterminding huge cosmic conspiracies. It's true some agents are a teensy bit poker-faced. And they do wear gorgeous suits! They also move in deeply mysterious ways. But hey, they're angels. What do you expect?

Officially we're known as "celestial agents" these days. But most people still affectionately refer to the Agency building as Angel HQ. It's the tallest skyscraper I have ever seen incidentally. And every few seconds you see brilliant bursts of light overhead as agents zoom back and forth.

I slid out of the limo, and snatched a moment to admire the Agency tower. It's made of some special celestial-type glass which constantly changes colour.

Two more limos drew up, letting out a stream of angel trainees. They hurried in through the revolving doors, waved their IDs at the day staff and sprinted for the lifts. Reuben spotted our friend, Amber, on the other side of the doors, and instantly went in to join her. I could see her hopping on the spot, desperately trying to put on her trainers. Like everyone else, she'd sensibly changed her outfit on the way over.

"I can't go in like this!" I moaned to Lola. "I look like a refugee from a cheesy package tour!"

She looked shocked. "Melanie, we're off to save planet Earth. Who cares what we wear?"

My jaw dropped. "You really think it's *that* huge?"

She laughed. "No, you dope, I was kidding! It's probably yet another boring drill to keep us lazy trainees on our toes."

I tried to decide if this would be deeply disappointing or a major relief. Before I could make up my mind, Lola disappeared through the Agency doors, cowboy hat, hipster shorts and all. This didn't leave me much choice. Adjusting my slipping sarong, I sashayed into the cathedral-sized foyer, flashed my ID, and followed my mates into an unusually crowded lift.

"Anyone know what's up?" I asked, as we went humming up to the top of the building.

Amber was carefully braiding her hair into a perfect fish-tail plait. That girl is *so* organised it's not true. "I heard they'd got a problem in ancient Egypt," she said through a mouthful of grips.

"Egypt? No way!" scoffed a boy from our history class. "First World War, someone told me."

The lift doors slid open and we hurried down gleaming corridors to the hall I remembered from our Dark Study training. Michael was there already, conferring with someone on an invisible ear-piece. As well as being our headmaster, Michael is a major big cheese at the Agency. He's so gentle and approachable, it's really easy to forget he's an archangel. Then he fixes you with those terrifying archangel eyes, and it's like he sees right into your soul.

He stepped up to the mike and we all fell silent.

"Sorry for calling on you at such short notice," he said. "As you know, the primary function of the Academy is to train the celestial agents of the future. Normally we only send trainees into the field for educational purposes. But in times of extreme cosmic necessity, we have to call on trainees to provide support for an existing task force."

Woo! I thought. Maybe they need us to save the planet after all!

"A unique situation is unfolding in thirteenth-century France," Michael went on.

Lola waggled her eyebrows at me. Trainees know that "unique" is well-known Agency-speak for "dangerous".

"Normally, when we identify a trouble spot, we send in divine personnel to liaise with local angels. On this occasion, we sent in a small team of highly experienced senior trainees. I'm sorry to say, we underestimated the scale of the problem."

Michael paused, scanning the rows of silent trainees. "Our young workers are in danger of being completely overwhelmed by local conditions and urgently need back-up. Unfortunately, all our trained operatives are tied up elsewhere, which is why I called you here today."

A ripple of excitement went around the hall.

"You'll be leaving shortly. The maintenance crew is just running last-minute checks on the time portals." Michael paused. "It's only fair to warn you that this crisis could go on for days. I know some of you have exams."

The seniors gave theatrical groans.

He smiled. "We'll try not to disrupt your studies too much, but until this situation is resolved, you'll just have to catch up on your school work between shifts. Is that clear?"

Everyone nodded eagerly.

"Of course, this is an excellent opportunity for those of you who haven't previously visited Earth, to experience the, erm, realities of earthly existence," Michael added mischievously.

All the regulars exchanged world-weary grins. Our headmaster was teasing us about the down-side of time-travel, which is basically mud and poo!

Like everyone else, I complain madly about time field trips, but apart from the icky smells, I secretly adore them and I learn *heaps* more than I ever learned from history books. OK, it's not all corsets and castles, not to mention I invariably ruin my best trainers. Plus when we get back, Mr Allbright makes us write a humungous report! But boy, do we write fabulous essays!

"Anyone here know anything about the Children's Crusade?" Michael asked in a casual voice.

Now try not to die of shock, but it just so happens that I knew heaps about this bizarre historical episode. We'd just finished studying it with Mr Allbright. But naturally I had no intention of saying so. I have a complete phobia about speaking in public. Anyway, at my old school, only sad try-hards like Venetia Rossetti spoke up in class. But Michael just gave me one of his humorous all-seeing looks, and said, "Melanie, perhaps you'd like to fill us in?"

I stood up gulping with nerves. Everyone stared at me expectantly.

"Erm," I said. "Well, it all started with this shepherd boy. Oh, did I mention he was French?" I quavered. "I didn't? Well he was, he was French. And he had a vision. At least, that was his story!" I added darkly. Everyone laughed. Hey, this isn't so bad, I thought.

I ploughed on bravely. "News of this vision, or whatever, spread like wildfire, and suddenly thousands of other kids were leaving their families, their ploughs, their herds of goats and whatever, to follow Stephen."

I noticed a new trainee studying her nails and deliberately pitched my voice a little louder.

"Maybe that doesn't sound like a big deal," I said. "But what you have to realise is that in those days, kids had absolutely no freedom. Even rich kids were like their parents' *chattels*, their property in other words. As for peasant kids, they were put to work practically as soon as they could toddle. So they never had one spare moment to stop and think like, 'is this all there is?' OK, so Stephen's project was completely insane, but the fact that the kids got as far as they did makes it an incredible achievement."

"What was this project exactly?" someone asked.

"They planned to march all the way to Jerusalem where a big holy war was going on."

All the pure angels looked amazed. "A holy war?" said one. "Are you kidding?"

I sighed. I hated to admit that humans were still murdering each other in my own time, on the grounds of religion. So I just said, "No, I'm not kidding. These holy wars were known as the Crusades. Now, like you guys, Stephen thought all this killing was wrong. He believed a kids' crusade could win their enemies over with love, a really radical idea back then. Unfortunately," I told my audience dramatically, "the whole thing went totally pear-shaped."

"Thank you, Melanie," said Michael in a firm voice. "That was most informative."

Ow, I thought. I was just getting into it!

He launched into the usual pep talk. We were not to attempt to be heroes. We were members of a team, links in a divine chain, blah blah blah.

Then we all had to zoom off to Departures, where we collected our Agency insignia. They're like little platinum tags you wear round your neck, to show you're on official business. Tags also help us stay in touch with the Agency, via the Link (that's sort of like the angel internet).

To my relief, I managed to squeeze into the same portal as Reuben and Lola. I always get massive butterflies before take-off. My worst moment is when that glass door slides shut. Like, EEK! The point of no return!

Then I heard Reuben humming our private theme song. "You're not alone," it goes. "You're not alone…" And I instantly felt myself relax. I was going time-travelling with my best mates. What could be better?

"Can you believe we're going to medieval France!" Lola burbled.

"I can't believe we're going to France full stop," I said truthfully.

She looked shocked. "You've never been to France? But it's so close to England."

"I know, but Mum never had any money, did she?"

At that moment our portal lit up like a royal firework display and we were blasted into history.

Time-travel, Agency style, is incredibly smooth and speedy. Just a few minutes after take-off, or several centuries earlier, depending on which time system you're using, I stepped out on to my favourite planet.

We were in a river valley somewhere in the south of France, totally surrounded by rolling hills, making me feel as if I was at the bottom of a massive misty blue bowl.

To judge from the position of the sun, it was somewhere around midday. The heat was phenomenal and the air was filled with the busy ticking and scraping sounds of zillions of little insects.

It probably sounds really sad, but I was totally over-excited at being in a foreign country! And even though this was Earth, not Heaven, the air smelled fabulous. I think the heat was bringing out the scent of all the wild lavender and rosemary growing everywhere.

Lola frowned. "Have you seen that river? It's way too low."

"Looks like a major drought," Amber agreed. "See all the cracks in the dirt?"

I'm a city girl myself, so I don't pretend to know about stuff like dirt or average rainfalls or whatever. But I did notice that the valley had a bleached, stone-washed look, as if all its bones were getting a bit too near the surface.

I'd gradually become aware of faint surges of noise drifting down the hillside. Soon, I was able to make out individual sounds. The dumty-dumty rhythm of drums, the toot of flutes and wave upon wave of sweet young voices singing some medieval hymn.

I felt a shiver of excitement go down my spine. My mates and I exchanged awed glances.

They're coming! I thought excitedly.

Tiny figures appeared over the rise – first a trickle, then a stream and finally a flood of marching children.

We stood totally stunned as the child crusaders straggled over the hill and down into the valley. Tattered blue and gold banners fluttered over their heads, their bright colours wavering in the intense heat.

"Omigosh," Lola breathed. "I had no idea there were so many."

Some of them were just little tots and had to be carried by the older ones. None of them appeared to own a pair of shoes. Their feet were in a terrible state. Yet they limped along, singing with heart-rending beauty.

The first kids into the valley instantly spotted the glint of water. Everyone broke ranks and went rushing down to the river to drink, bathe their feet, or simply cool off.

I found the scene really disturbing, to be honest. It reminded me too much of refugee camps I'd seen on the news in my own times. Michael's right, I thought. This situation is way out of control.

Reuben nudged me. "Uh-oh! Lollie's run into some local personnel."

I saw Lola chatting away with an Earth angel in medieval dress.

Eek, I thought. Don't think wimples will make a comeback!

I think the Earth angel was equally startled by Lola's outfit, because I heard Lola say, *"Oh pardon, madame!"* And she started explaining how we'd had to leave Heaven in a hurry.

This is *so* cool, I thought. They were speaking in medieval French, yet I understood every word! It's one of the perks of being an angel, and it still gives me a major buzz. If Miss Rowntree could only see me now, I grinned to myself.

Then my heart almost stopped beating.

A dreamy-eyed boy was making his way towards us through the crowd. His T-shirt and jeans were so faded by the sun that I could only just make out the familiar angel logo. It had been too long since he'd had a haircut and he looked completely shattered. But I'd have recognised him anywhere.

It was Orlando.

Chapter Four

Now I'm not, repeat *not*, one of those tragic girls who go yearning after boys who don't even know they exist. But you can't tell a heart what to feel, and my heart was secretly hoping for a teeny tiny sign that Orlando was pleased to see me.

But he didn't even smile. "What happened to you, Mel?" he demanded rudely. "Get lost on your way to the beach?"

"Erm, actually we're your back-up," I mumbled. "The Agency paged us in the middle of Lollie's birthday party."

I was genuinely shocked. It is SO not like Orlando to make hurtful personal remarks. He is usually on this totally higher plane.

Did I mention that Orlando actually looks like an angel? Well he does; a soulful dark-eyed angel in an Italian painting. Officially he's still at school. But he's such a genius that the Agency is constantly sending him off on major missions. Unfortunately I only tend to run into him when I'm flouting a major cosmic rule or generally acting like a ditz.

I think Orlando guessed he'd upset me because his expression changed. "Sorry if I overreacted," he said awkwardly. "It's great to see you guys, honestly. It's just that we're a bit overstretched as you can see."

"Tell us what you want us to do," said Lola.

I don't think I've ever seen Orlando look so depressed. "It's a nightmare," he sighed. "Stephen's totally convinced these kids they're going to witness a miracle. When they reach Marseilles, the sea will part and they'll walk across dry land all the way to Jerusalem."

"It isn't going to happen, is it?" Reuben said softly.

"No. And I'm not sure how they'll handle the disappointment. So I'd appreciate it if you guys could keep your eyes and ears open. That way we can nip any trouble in the bud. Apart from that, just do what you can for them. The little ones especially."

We set to work. The children were in such bad shape that they soaked up healing angelic vibes like blotting paper. The pure angels, in particular, couldn't get their heads round what they were seeing. "Why would a little kid put himself through so much suffering?" one said in horror.

"Most of them probably didn't get much TLC at home, remember?" I pointed out.

Reuben whistled through his teeth. "I don't believe it. They're on the move again."

All around the valley, exhausted children were gathering up their pitiful possessions, getting ready to go back on the road. It seemed like we'd given them just enough strength to press on to Marseilles. Of course, without food and rest, the effects of their angelic energy transfusion would soon wear off. But even if the kids had understood this, I don't think they'd have cared.

Reaching Jerusalem, that's all they cared about.

We marched on through the simmering heat. An old man came out of a tumble-down hovel to watch. He shielded his eyes as the never-ending procession tramped past. The sight seemed to upset him. "Go home and help your fathers," he called.

"We have but one Father," a girl replied through parched lips. "And he is in Heaven."

I tried to imagine my mates on Earth getting all steamed up over some weird holy crusade. Queuing for tickets for a pop concert maybe, or even doing some hilarious fund-raising stunt. But these kids were putting themselves through hell for an *idea*. Some of them were literally dying on their feet. Forget going to Jerusalem. They'd be lucky to make it to the docks. And it really upset me.

"Give me five minutes alone with this Stephen," I muttered. "I'd give him a vision he wouldn't forget in a hurry."

Orlando gave a tired laugh. "Be my guest!" He pointed back up the track. A covered cart was rattling in our direction, stirring up swirling clouds of dust. The cart was painted in the same vivid blue and gold as the banners and hung with fluttering blue and gold pennants.

Three kids shared the driver's seat, taking it in turns to sip from a leather flask. A posse of teenagers on horseback rode alongside. They had the wary expressions of professional bodyguards.

From the way the other kids cheered and tossed their dusty caps in the air, it was obvious this mysterious Stephen was the medieval equivalent of some big rock star.

Suddenly someone yelled, "Tomorrow in Jerusalem!"

The cry was taken up in a great roar. "Tomorrow in Jerusalem! Tomorrow in Jerusalem!" Once it had started, the cry went on and on, wave upon wave of sound crashing on my ears.

"Tomorrow in the cemetery, more like," said Lola grimly.

I puffed out my cheeks. I'd only been here a few hours but it felt like a lifetime. Poor Orlando had been coping with it for weeks. There and then I made a secret vow to do everything I could to help him. I'll be totally professional, I thought. Then Orlando would see me in a completely different light.

We were getting closer to the port. The air had acquired a fishy smell, along with the familiar olden-times pong of sewage and rotting garbage. Except for an occasional horse-drawn cart rumbling along on clunky wooden wheels, there wasn't much traffic. It was too hot for sensible folk to be out. But the children went marching on.

We had left the countryside behind by this time, and the dirt track had turned into narrow cobbled streets. Medieval tenements loomed up on either side of us, like gloomy great canyons, blocking out the sunlight. A sleepy murmuring came from behind closed shutters. It seemed like the locals were waking from their afternoon siesta. But as they heard the kids approaching, doors and shutters flew open.

Everyone wanted to see this extraordinary procession.

Orlando caught us up. "This is where things could get ugly." I could hear his tired voice going up the line, keeping the overworked trainees on their toes.

It was obvious he was expecting major trouble. But the people were really sweet, clapping and calling out encouragingly, as if the kids were athletes at the end of a marathon.

A girl leaned out of an upstairs window and started throwing flowers. The idea quickly caught on and suddenly rose and jasmine petals were raining down. The children marched on through falling blossoms, their eyes feverish with excitement.

The cart with its outriders had moved to the front by this time, the bright flags and the sound of drums and flutes all adding to the party atmosphere. Some kids actually found the energy to turn cartwheels and somersaults. The childish singing echoed eerily around the walls of the medieval tenements. The whole thing was dreamlike and deeply disturbing. Then I realised why.

"Omigosh, this is like that story!" I whispered to my mates. "The Pied Piper or whatever."

Reuben didn't know the fairytale, and by the time I'd reached the part where the spellbound children followed the mysterious piper into the countryside, never to be seen again, the cobblestones ran out. And there in front of us was the hot dazzling blue of the Mediterranean.

Ships, like elaborately carved wooden castles, rode at anchor, their sails tightly furled. Sailors climbed up the rigging as nimbly as if they were just going upstairs. Others were unloading sacks and barrels, or ferrying small rowboats back and forth across the harbour.

Marseilles is only just across the water from Morocco, and the dockside smells of rope and tar were deliciously mingled with exotic spices and the scent of foreign perfumes.

I had no *idea* the Middle Ages was so multicultural! The whole world was there: black, white and golden-skinned seamen, all cheerfully fraternising with local tarts and gangsters, not to mention Arabs and Africans in dazzling ethnic clothes.

This is *so* cool, I thought. Just in time I remembered I was supposed to be on duty. Stop being a time tourist, Melanie, I scolded myself. You're supposed to be looking out for trouble.

I didn't have far to look.

A boy emerged from inside the cart, shielding his eyes from the glare. He was dressed in what was once a white tunic, with an extra bit of grubby white drapery trailing over his shoulder. His wispy gold hair badly needed a wash.

Now personally, I would never recommend the guru look, unless you've got a brilliant suntan. And after months of travelling through sweltering heat, in a cart with no springs, this boy was the colour of sweaty cheese.

But style wasn't nearly such a biggie then, and the instant he appeared, I heard excited whispering, like wind blowing through grass. "It's him, it's Stephen!"

Adults had joined the crowd by this time: sailors, fishwives, priests and local tradespeople, all dying to see this famous youth for themselves.

Stephen made his way to the front of the crowd, where his minders had improvised a stage from a plank and a couple of barrels.

He sprang lightly on to the platform, and gazed peacefully down at the crowd with eyes that were just that little bit too blue. Later Lola said it was almost like his eyes had literally been dazzled by his glimpse of Heaven. Like he saw how the world could be, not how it actually was.

He started to speak and everyone hushed at once. Speeches all sound the same really, don't they, but I think the gist of it was that the medieval adults had screwed up big time and now it was up to the kids to put it right.

Then he stopped talking and it went electrifyingly quiet. Stephen gazed dreamily down at the crowd with those disturbing Heaven-dazzled eyes and thousands of awed sweaty faces gazed back. Well, it's not every day you see a kid with his own hotline to Heaven, right?

Suddenly Stephen swung to face the ocean, whirling his arms like wings, yelling, "LET THE WATERS PART!" And at that moment, with his gold hair and drapery, he did look alarmingly holy.

"He believes it, doesn't he?" I whispered to Orlando.

"That's what's so scary," he whispered back.

The crowd held its breath, waiting for their miracle.

And absolutely nothing happened.

No thunderclap, no bolt of lightning, no waves scrolling back like curtains. Nothing.

First his followers just seemed bewildered, but as the moments ticked past, they looked totally panic-stricken. Several started weeping and tearing at their clothes. Some even fainted. I saw Stephen's minders muttering to each other, probably feeling like dopes for believing him in the first place.

Poor Stephen just looked as if he wanted to crawl away and die.

Two richly-dressed merchants were watching all these goings-on with close interest. One had a thick shock of silvery hair and a smile which never quite reached his eyes. He slung a fatherly arm around Stephen's shoulders.

"Don't lose heart, boy," he told him encouragingly. "My name is Gervase de Winter, and if you are willing, my friend and I may be able to help you. Miracles come in many shapes and disguises."

The men explained that they owned several ships. By a strange coincidence, two were sailing to Jerusalem in just three days' time.

When Stephen finally grasped that they were offering to take them to the Holy Land for free, I truly thought he was going to burst into tears.

I wanted to be pleased for him, but I couldn't help feeling suspicious. The merchants didn't strike me as the holy type somehow. I mean, what was in it for them?

In all the confusion I'd lost sight of Reuben. Suddenly he came flying out of the crowd looking terrible. He spotted Lola and they had an agitated conversation, then next minute Reuben went flying off again.

I ran over to Lola. "What's up?"

"Mel, Reuben heard those guys talking. Those ships aren't going to Jerusalem. They're planning to sell the kids as slaves."

"No way!" I gasped. "Someone's got to tell Orlando!"

"Reuben's gone to tell him now."

And then, as if there wasn't enough going on, a cosmic fire alarm went off in my head. I'm sorry, it's the only way I can describe it. Angels constantly pick up vibes which humans don't even register. But I'd never experienced this particular horrible silent jangling before.

I saw Lola clutch at her ears, almost losing her balance.

"What's going on?" I hissed.

She shuddered. "It has to be the PODS. A juicy slavery scam would be just up their street."

The official Agency term for the Powers of Darkness is the Opposition. My mates and I call them the PODS, private shorthand for the gruesome beings who constantly try to sabotage our work on Earth. Unlike angels, PODS have no actual shape of their own, which unfortunately means they can disguise themselves as pretty much anything or anyone they fancy.

Luckily a routine scan revealed absolutely no evil cosmic personnel in the vicinity. Then I clocked some children standing slightly apart from the crowd.

"Lollie, bet you anything it's those kids!" I hissed.

We moved in for a closer look and the jangles immediately doubled in intensity.

"Well, that's weird!" I said. "I mean, they're not PODS, so they've got to be for real, right?"

Lola frowned. "I'm not sure. Don't they look just a teensy bit too clean to you?"

She was right. They looked more like child actors in a movie set in the thirteenth century. Nice shiny hair. No sores, fleas, or pockmarks. Costumes miraculously free from grease and grime.

But it was the humans themselves who really baffled me. They had a quality I've only seen in angel kids. Nothing to do with being good or saintly, but a kind of lovely inner glow.

The kids *definitely* weren't behaving like angels, however.

"If we don't get a question about this in the exam, I want a full refund, de Winters," one boy complained.

"Yeah, Dominic," his mate chipped in. "I can't be doing with this religious garbage. To think I paid money for this."

From the way everyone was glaring at him, I decided that Dominic must be the intelligent-looking kid in the stylish medieval cap.

"Come on, you guys!" he said despairingly. "I'm giving you a unique experience. Real live history is happening right in front of your eyes. So stop moaning and give it a chance!"

Lola and I exchanged puzzled glances. What was going on?

"Admit it, Dom," said one of the girls. "Stephen's a total nut."

Dominic sighed. "Agreed. But give him some credit. Before Stephen came along, these kids were like dumb animals, blindly following orders, half asleep. But Stephen woke them up. He made them see things could change for the better." There was real excitement in Dom's voice.

"Oh, who cares," another boy whinged. "This place stinks."

A girl with freckles turned on him. "Of course it stinks, you bozo. History's supposed to stink. Anyway, that Roman arena stank to high heaven and I didn't hear anyone complain."

"Yeah, but the gladiators were lush!" one of the girls giggled.

I'm only giving you the gist of what they said. They were talking really rapidly in a weird slang which is quite tricky to translate.

"Come on, Dom," said his freckled sidekick in disgust. "Take these losers back to school."

Dom fumbled inside his jerkin, fishing out

something that looked like a miniature mobile phone and hit several tiny keypads.

The air started to flicker. Scribbles of colour appeared, weirdly superimposed over thirteenth-century Marseilles; colours so wild and futuristic, I couldn't even tell you their names.

At that moment Reuben came to find us. His eyes grew huge with awe. "Is this actually happening?"

"You tell us!" I squeaked.

The scribbles formed into ropes of light, all twirling at different speeds. As they twirled they emitted confused crackles and bleeps, like someone tuning an old-fashioned radio.

Dom watched tensely, as the ropes twirled faster and faster. He seemed to be counting under his breath. "NOW!" he yelled suddenly.

And as if they were playing some bizarre skipping game, the children dived through the ropes – and vanished!

CHAPTER FIVE

I finally found Orlando in the middle of some big meeting with the local angels. I have to say, he didn't seem too thrilled to see us.

"This had better be important, Melanie."

"Oh, it is! We've come to report a major time anomaly!" I burbled.

I felt quite proud of myself. Mr Allbright had explained all about anomalies last term. But of course brain-box Orlando had to go one better.

"What kind?" he said at once.

I sighed with irritation. "Duh! Some kids who totally shouldn't be in this century, that's what kind. Like, they belong to another time?"

"They were from the future, definitely," said Lola.

"I'd say some time around the twenty-third century."

Orlando shook his head, "You're mistaken. The Agency put a ban on human time-travel until at least the twenty-fifth century."

"So?" I said. "Someone's obviously broken the ban."

"You did say to tell you if we saw something unusual," Reuben pointed out.

"Unusual!" I snorted. "That's the understatement of the year!"

Orlando darted a nervous glance at the Earth angels, who weren't looking too impressed at having their meeting interrupted by three over-excited trainees in beach wear. "What exactly do you think you saw?" he asked in a low voice.

I was practically jumping up and down. "We don't just *think* we saw something, OK? We registered a major cosmic disturbance, which we traced to a bunch of time-travelling kids in medieval outfits."

"Suspiciously pristine outfits," Lola chipped in.

"Way too pristine," I agreed. "One boy activated some kind of device and he and his mates jumped through some kind of worm hole or something and vanished."

Orlando looked desperately stressed out. "Look, I can't deal with this right now. As you can see, I've kind of got my hands full as it is."

Don't think I wasn't sorry for him, but we'd stumbled across something potentially huge and I knew it. "So, you're going to just like, pretend it never happened, is that it?" I demanded.

Orlando shut his eyes and took several deep breaths, while I tried really hard not to admire his incredibly lovely eyelids. And when he opened them again it was like our conversation had never taken place.

He called cheerfully to a passing Earth angel: "Lucius, meet Melanie and Lola! Think you can put them to work?"

If Lucius thought our clothes were weird, he had the good manners to keep it to himself. "But of course," he smiled. "It will be my *plaisir*."

Orlando shifted swiftly into trouble-shooting mode. "The slavers won't dare to kidnap these kids in public," he explained. "And the ships don't sail for another three days. If we all pull our weight, there's a chance some of the kids will change their minds about going to Jerusalem."

"Will you please follow me," Lucius asked politely.

I flashed him my most professional smile. "Sure!"

But inside I was seething. Why, oh why, wouldn't Orlando take me seriously? I've made a few mistakes in my angel career, I admit. That time I materialised to a human without permission, for example. Oh, and I once sort of *whacked* an Elizabethan human, accidentally activating his hidden angel powers. OK, so it was William Shakespeare, but it all worked out brilliantly in the end. Yet Orlando insisted on treating me like this major fluff-wit.

But in the angel business, as you know, your private life totally has to take a back seat. Actually it was quite a relief to throw myself into work. As well as the actual kids, we targeted local adults. Like Lucius said, some of them must know the slavers' true intentions. And a cosmic nudge from a celestial agent just might inspire them to tell the kids what was really going on. We even zapped the evil merchants themselves. Well, it was worth a try!

In the end, Lola and I got so blissed-out on cosmic energy, I think we could have happily gone on all night. Lucius had to tell us our shift was over.

"I don't know 'ow we would have manage wizout you," he said.

"He's *so* charming," Lola whispered.

Unlike some, I thought bitterly.

Orlando came to see us all off. "Thanks, guys! I'll see you tomorrow, yeah?"

I gave him the briefest possible nod. But he turned to talk to his colleagues, never even noticing he'd been blanked.

We blasted back to Heaven in a blaze of white light.

"I want to sleep for a week," I moaned. "Plus I want you to swear you'll never let me go on a field trip in flip-flops again."

Lola looked dazed. "Uh? Oh, sure."

"Are you OK?" I asked her.

She gave me a faraway smile. "Just trying to remember something."

Minutes later we were handing in our angel tags. We dragged ourselves through the Arrivals bay and out into the street, where a fleet of Agency limos waited in the heavenly twilight.

All the way back to school, I was longing to fall into bed. Yet after a long hot shower, my tiredness magically disappeared.

I looked at my nice clean PJs on my pillow and I thought, "Nah!"

And I went into a mad whirl of activity. I threw on jeans and a cropped T-shirt, splashed on my favourite fragrance (it's called Attitude, and comes in the cutest bottle) and grabbed my new beaded clutch bag.

I was just on my way to find Lola when she appeared in my doorway, wearing an almost identical outfit.

"The Babylon, right?" she grinned.

We slapped palms. "The Babylon!"

And giggling like idiots, we rushed downstairs and out of school.

These days, when we need to unwind, we head straight for the Ambrosia district and dance ourselves silly at the Babylon Café. It only opened a few weeks ago, and already it's the coolest club in town.

We'd just checked in our jackets when Reuben turned up.

"I don't suppose you're up to dancing," he teased Lola. "Now you're such an old lady!"

"Hey, buddy, I can dance you off your feet any time!" And Lola dragged him on to the dance floor.

I hadn't seen Reuben dance since his run-in with Brice, the cosmic outlaw. It was great to see him behaving like his old mad party-animal self.

After several dances, we went outside to cool off. The gardens at the Babylon are unbelievably lovely, designed so that they literally seem to float in mid-air.

We found a private little arbour, all overgrown with passion flowers, and sat sipping ice-cold fruit punch, gazing up at the glittering fields of stars overhead. For some reason I started thinking about Stephen. What was it Dominic had said? *Before Stephen came along these kids were like dumb animals, blindly following orders, half asleep...*

Suddenly Lola blew out her breath with relief. "Oh, finally!! I've been going nuts trying to think where I'd seen them!"

I shook my head. "I've no idea what you're on about, babe."

"Duh," she said. "Those weird FX. What did you think I meant?"

I gawped at her. "You've seen them before! Do you know where?"

"Sure, babe! On the news."

I couldn't believe my ears. "You mean in your time?"

"Six months before I got shot," said Lola calmly. "My grandmother was just about to dish up her famous *fajitas*. My brothers were fighting over the TV remote as usual. My grandmother said to cut it out. She wanted to watch a current affairs programme. She switched channels and there was Bernard de Winter talking about how time-travel was finally—"

"De Winter?" I interrupted. "That is *so* bizarre. I never even heard that name before today and now it's cropping up all over the place. That dodgy merchant was called something de Winter, and it's Dom's surname too."

Lola's eyes widened. "Are you sure?"

"One of the other kids definitely called him de Winter."

"So what was your de Winter saying, Lollie?" asked Reuben.

"That I can't tell you," she laughed. "I shared my house with five hungry brothers, remember. I was panicking I'd miss out on Gran's fajitas! I just remember glancing at the TV with my mouth full, and seeing those exact FX. And I remember my grandmother saying this guy was one scientist who actually cared about our planet's future."

"Did he?" asked Reuben.

Lola nodded vigorously. "He was definitely one of my century's good guys. Which is incredible considering the rest of his family."

"Don't get you," I said.

"Oh please," she said impatiently. "The de Winters have been creating mayhem since human history began. Of course, they don't always use that name," she added darkly.

"You make them sound like the PODS," I said.

Lola took a sip of her punch. "Trust me, the de Winters are like the PODS' special best friends on Earth. They're total gangsters. So when they got wind of this device, they went flat out to get the..." She frowned. "What's that thing which means an invention legally belongs to you?"

"The patent?" I suggested.

"Right, they wanted to get hold of the patent for themselves. There was this major court case. But finally the authorities ruled that the time device could lead to dangerous cosmic repercussions, so the court had it destroyed, plus all the relevant computer files were deleted."

"Yeah, but they weren't, were they!"

Our ice cubes tinkled madly as Reuben jumped up from the table.

His face blazed with excitement. "OK, maybe they destroyed the device, but someone obviously kept copies of the research."

Reuben's excitement was catching. "Omigosh," I gasped. "Someone's like, *reinvented* the device!"

"But however did those kids get hold of it?" breathed Lola.

"Good question," said Reuben. "But we'd better get down to the Agency ASAP and tell Michael."

But at that moment Amber appeared. "Sorry to interrupt, you guys," she said brightly. "Michael wants to see you. He says it's urgent!"

Chapter Six

"Maybe we should just move our beds down here," I complained as we flashed our IDs. "It would make things a whole lot simpler."

"This is my weirdest birthday ever," sighed Lola. "I never even got to open my present."

We jumped into the lift and went flashing up past various brilliantly lit floors with Lola still moaning on about her present. "Mo probably left it on the beach. I'll never get it now. Won't you just give me a tiny little clue what was inside?"

"No way," I told her.

We sped along the maze of gleaming corridors. Michael's door stood open. A blaze of diamond-white light poured out. This meant he had at least one archangel visitor.

Uh-oh, I thought. Not counting Michael, who is a total sweetie, I have this terrible mental block with archangels. I simply can't tell them apart. For one thing, they generate so much celestial radiance that apart from their eyes, it's hard to identify any actual features.

I squinted into the light and just made out two dazzling outlines.

"Er, hi!" I said shyly. "We got your message."

The light levels instantly grew more bearable, and Michael came sharply into focus. "Come in, come in!" he said warmly.

His visitor gave us a distant nod. Archangels aren't unfriendly exactly, it's more that they don't really do small talk.

We perched ourselves on uncomfortable office chairs, waiting for Michael to explain why we'd been summoned to the Agency for the second time that day. But his first words made my heart turn over.

"I just spoke to Orlando on the Link," he said.

I swallowed and said, "Oh, really?" about an octave higher than I intended. What *had* Orlando been telling him?

"As from tomorrow your Earth duties will change," Michael announced with a grave expression.

"Oh, right," I said bravely, picturing myself scrubbing a huge medieval lavvy with a very small toothbrush.

"Well, you were the only agents to witness the illicit time-travellers, which makes you the obvious choice for this mission."

I was stunned. "Orlando *told* you about them? But he said—"

Michael smiled. "He asked me to apologise for not giving you his full attention. When you reported the anomaly, he was having a rather sticky discussion with local personnel."

I was amazed. "So you actually believe us?"

"My dear child," sighed the mystery archangel. "Do you think we don't notice when humans go tinkering with cosmic laws?"

"As it happens, other agents detected similar anomalies." Michael checked his computer screen. "The latest was apparently in ancient Rome."

"That's right!" I turned excitedly to Lola. "Lollie, remember that girl saying the gladiators were lush?"

The archangel looked blank. "Lush?"

"It means really fit," I explained. "Presumably she was into big rippling muscles."

I could feel myself getting flustered and no wonder. I couldn't believe I was discussing sex with an archangel! Lola was trying desperately not to laugh.

Michael rescued us. "You may find these useful." He produced three pairs of sunglasses from a drawer and slid them across the desk.

"Oh, cool," I said.

The archangel sounded slightly tetchy. "These are not fashion accessories, Melanie. They are to help agents detect illicit emanations."

"Wow! How incredible," I breathed.

But I'm fairly sure Michael sussed I had no idea what his archangel colleague was on about, because he immediately explained about how each human energy system has to be specially customised, to fit his or her particular slot in time.

"Mr Allbright said something about that!" I said eagerly. "Except for geniuses, he said, who are like, ahead of their times."

"Correct," Michael agreed. "But even a genius has to share the same time band as her contemporaries. As you know, every time has different charms and challenges. Its own time 'weather' if you like. What you may not realise, is that this 'weather' leaves traces in the human energy field."

Lola perked up. "So these shades will help us to see auras, is that right?"

I was startled to hear Lola talking about auras as if they were like, a genuine scientific fact. I'd assumed they were invented by the same dodgy psychics who claim to get weird personal info from the dead.

"With practice you'll see energy emanations quite naturally," Michael explained. "But for the time being you'll probably find the glasses helpful."

Reuben seemed fascinated by his shades, tilting them back and forth, trying to figure out how they worked.

I cleared my throat. "Can I ask something?"

"Go ahead," said Michael.

"Well, humans have free will, right?"

He nodded. "That's correct."

"So why did the Agency ban time-travel? If humans have the brains to invent time-travel, why shouldn't they use it? If I'd had the chance to go time-travelling when I lived on Earth, I'd have gone like a shot, no question."

"'Banned' isn't quite the word I'd use," said Michael doubtfully. "But in more primitive eras, yes, time-travel is actively discouraged."

"But those kids didn't come from a primitive era," I objected. "They're from way in the future. They're almost, well, like angels."

"Mel's right," Lola chipped in. "It's like they're evolving into a new race or something."

"That's it exactly!" Michael sounded delighted that we'd figured this out for ourselves. "And one day, I promise you, humans will freely explore the fields of Time and Space. But not yet."

"Why not?" I argued. "I mean, Dom's just having a laugh. He's not doing anything like, *evil*."

"The child is playing with cosmic fire!" said a remote voice.

Archangels are incapable of losing their tempers. They're heaps too advanced. But his tone made me cringe.

"I don't think I understand," I said in a small voice.

He sighed. "Some humans will do anything for money. Sell fellow humans into slavery, rob the Earth of precious metals, poison the seas. For them Time is simply one more resource to pillage."

The archangel explained that humans could use the device to interfere with historical events, ensuring that certain people inherited lands or gold or oil wells.

"Not to mention scientific discoveries, priceless art treasures," Michael chipped in. "The list is endless..."

"I guess I wasn't thinking," I said humbly.

Reuben seemed doubtful. "What makes you think those kids will go back to medieval Marseilles anyway?"

Michael gave us one of his all-seeing smiles. "Let's just say I have a hunch."

I don't know about you, but I feel heaps more confident when I'm wearing the right clothes. So when I got back to the dorm, I forced myself to keep awake until I'd planned what I was going to wear next day. And like they say in the style magazines, that little bit of extra effort totally paid off. Because when my alarm went off all of two hours later, there was my trouble-shooting outfit all ready for me to jump into.

Actually my new look was pretty cool; Skechers trainers, boot-cut denim flares and a Triple 5 Soul hooded top in spicy orange. I quickly twisted the front of my hair into little Zulu knots, letting the rest cascade casually down my shoulders. Then I splashed on some Attitude, grabbed my tote bag and went to find Lola.

It was just getting light by the time we arrived back at the Agency, but I wasn't a bit tired. In fact I was buzzing with excitement.

Thanks to Orlando, we'd scored a cool new assignment detecting time misfits, and I was determined not to screw up. Here was my chance to prove I wasn't just some sad little airhead.

"Hey, Reubs," I said cheerfully, as we stepped into the time portal. "Was that Raphael or Japhiel in with Michael yesterday?"

Lola looked surprised. "Oh, I thought it was Gabriel."

"Uriel," said Reuben. "Definitely Uriel."

I giggled. "They should wear big gold initials on their chests like Superman."

Lola burst out laughing. "That is so wicked!"

But Reuben just said, "Who's Superman?"

And by the time we'd briefed our buddy on Earth's major superheroes, we were coming into land.

The instant we stepped on to solid ground, Lola and Reuben put on their Agency sunglasses. "Oh wow," they said simultaneously. "Mel, you've got to see this!"

So of course I put mine on too. "Oh wow," I breathed.

To think I'd walked around for thirteen years never knowing I had my own gorgeous wraparound rainbow.

I peered down at myself through my shades. "So where's mine?" I said disappointedly. "I mean angels must have massive auras, right?"

"The shades were invented to detect time anomalies," Reuben reminded me. "Not so vain little angels can play 'My energy field's bigger than your energy field'."

Lola laughed. "Ooooh! He really told you, Boo!"

We had a brilliant time, patrolling medieval Marseilles in our Agency shades going, "Oh wow, that one is totally luminous," and "Check that guy! Is his aura sinister or what!"

But after a while I noticed something disturbing. Everyone seemed to be talking about the same thing, a huge Crusader victory in the Holy Land. People were really over-excited, almost hysterical.

"Hey, there's Lucius!" said Lola. "Maybe he knows what's going on."

But there was no charming twinkle this morning. The Earth angel seemed deeply depressed. "The slavers start zis rumour deliberately," he sighed. "They think news of a crusader victory will make zese poor children even more desperate to board ze ships."

"Omigosh," I gasped. "Did it work?"

Lucius gave a shrug. "*Voilà.*"

I took off my shades and without any auras to distract me, immediately noticed what I'd failed to see earlier; kids practically climbing over each other to get to the little rowing boats bobbing alongside the jetty.

A boatman fended them off with an oar. "Go home! Forget about the crusades!" he yelled. "The ships are leaky as sieves. You will drown before you reach Jerusalem."

He obviously wanted to warn the kids off, but daren't name the slavers openly. But it was useless.

Hyped-up by the false rumours and terrified of missing their one chance of getting to the Holy Land, kids started diving off the dockside and swimming out towards the ships.

I caught sight of the older merchant, shaking his sleek silver hair, as if he didn't know what today's youngsters were coming to.

I was so upset that I put my shades back on without thinking. And then I saw them. Seven pulsating energy fields.

"Omigosh, they came back!" I shrieked. "Michael's right! Their auras are completely different!"

I whipped my glasses off again and the pulsing lights vanished.

In their place were Dom, his freckled friend and a new bunch of wide-eyed time tourists. "Isn't this cool?" I heard Dom say. "Isn't this worth every single penny?"

"So what do we do again?" asked a boy nervously.

Dom broke into an infectious grin. "Mingle with the natives of course! And try not to draw too much attention to yourself."

But it was too late for that. I saw the silver-haired merchant clock these new healthy specimens. And it was like, "Kerching!"

Then something really weird happened. Dom caught the merchant watching and I saw a flicker of horrified recognition in his eyes. He hastily pulled himself together. "Don't look round," he hissed. "Act like you've got somewhere to go and follow me!"

All seven kids sprinted down the nearest alleyway.

The merchant snapped his fingers. Four medieval heavies detached themselves from the crowd and went charging after them.

This was getting serious. "I'll watch the kids," I gabbled. "You guys get Orlando."

And I went hurtling after them.

This had to be the ultimate cosmic chase scene. Medieval heavies chasing illegal time-travellers, hotly pursued by an angel in Zulu knots!

The kids and I quickly put an impressive distance between ourselves and the thugs. Dom produced the time device, and breathlessly zapped its tiny keypads. The familiar time FX scribbles appeared. Dom waited with an agonised expression, counting to himself, as the luminous ropes became a twirling technicolour blur.

The thugs panted into view.

"NOW!" screamed Dom,

The kids dived simultaneously

I must have been a bit overexcited, because I didn't think twice. It seemed so obvious that I had to go after them. Behind me someone yelled, "Melanie, no!" But I totally ignored Orlando's warning. Taking a big breath, I jumped feet first into the future.

CHAPTER SEVEN

I was in rushing darkness, lit by fierce stabs of lightning, and crackling with ancient sounds. Confused snatches of conversation, ferocious battle cries, muffled sobbing, long-lost love songs.

If I'd known Dom's device was so primitive, I'd never have risked it. Compared to that bone-rattling helter-skelter ride, angelic time-travel is a walk in the park.

At one point I was convinced I was turning inside out. That was just before all my limbs went dead. I couldn't actually tell if my body was still in one piece, or if I even had a body. I was totally numb.

And as I hurtled towards some unknown future century, deafening new sounds erupted around me. Explosions, wailing sirens, crazily mixed up with TV laughter and dog-food commercials and raw pounding hiphop. And I'd thought MY century was insane!

Then everything stopped, dead.

There was a silence so total I genuinely thought I'd gone deaf. Then I realised I could hear my own scared breathing in the dark. "Omigosh!" I whimpered. "Is it over?"

Had I been fast-forwarded to the end of the world by mistake? Had some hideous future war finally exterminated everyone on Earth? Was this the silence of total nothingness?

Actually, no. Because all at once I heard something. The tiny liquid sound of a bird singing. A bird and a soft whisper of wind through leaves and somewhere in the distance, a small child laughing its socks off.

I felt my eyes fill with tears. The human race had pulled through! This wasn't an ominous hush. It was world peace, how about that!

And suddenly all the feeling flooded back into my body. It was agony, the worst pins and needles ever. And with a terrifying whoosh, I landed on solid ground. Seconds later, Reuben and Lola crashed down on top of me.

"OW!! What are you doing here, you morons?" I hissed.

"You didn't think we'd let you swan off to the future on your own!" Reuben gasped out.

Lola just lay whimpering softly. "Tell me we don't have to do that again," she moaned.

We lay in a tangled heap, trying to get our breath back.

It was almost evening and I could smell a sweet fresh smell, like the smell you get in really expensive flower shops. We'd crash-landed in someone's old summerhouse. From where I was lying, I could see bright blue trumpet-shaped flowers and a glossy orange tree complete with perfect baby oranges. I felt pangs of jealousy. I've got a v. small orange tree in my room. I grew it in ten minutes flat, when I helped in Miss Dove's nursery class one time. But though I water it faithfully every day, it still hasn't produced a single orange.

I dimly registered Dom's school mates melting out of sight between some pillars. I knew we should follow them, but I couldn't seem to move. Then Lola gave a tiny gasp, so naturally I looked up. Staring down at us with stunned expressions were Dom and his little freckled girlfriend.

I was so shocked that I actually stopped breathing. We were visible!

The device must have messed up our angel molecules, causing us to materialise.

The girl pulled off her medieval head dress and all this frizzy red hair sprang out. With her looks she could totally have gone on as orphan Annie without a rehearsal. (If it wasn't for the scowl, obviously.) She jerked her thumb in our direction. "What are they?"

"I have no idea," Dom admitted. "But if a teacher sees them, we're history."

I almost shrieked with laughter. I know it's not cool for an angel to have hysterics. But I was in shock. Thanks to me, my angel buddies were totally exposed to human view, and I had no idea what to do.

Then I heard the creak of the summerhouse door and the sound of approaching footsteps. "Dom, Lily! Do I have to come and get you?" said a friendly voice.

Dom froze. "It's Mr Lamb."

Lily looked appalled. "Oh no! We totally forgot about Metaphysics."

They started frantically changing into their normal clothes, not space suits with slanting zips as you might think, but the twenty-third century equivalent of smart casuals.

"Is metaphysics like metalwork?" I whispered.

"More like philosophy," Reuben whispered back.

Ooer, I thought. Talk about high fliers.

"I tried to tell you," Lily was moaning. "Twice in two days is pushing it, I said. Someone's going to rumble us, I said, but oh no—"

"Will you just shut up, Lil! No-one's going to rumble anyone. Let me do the talking, OK?"

"Yeah, and how d'you plan to explain the time stowaways?"

Time stowaways? I sagged with relief. They obviously had no idea that we were angels.

Leaves rustled madly. "I know you're in here!" the teacher called. Any minute now he was going to find our hiding place.

Lola smiled at the kids. "Don't worry," she said in perfect future slang. "We won't grass. Just tell us what you want us to say."

Dom looked panic-stricken. "Don't say anything," he pleaded. "You have no idea what you're getting into."

All the tiny oranges trembled on their stalks as a man came pushing through the foliage. He had one of those bland harmless faces, like a kids' TV presenter. "There you are! Everyone's waiting."

I saw the teacher suppress his surprise. "And who's this?" he said in a joky voice.

"It's OK, Mr Lamb, I can explain—" Dom began.

"Don't worry, we're just leaving!" I interrupted airily. "Our parents are thinking of sending us to your brilliant school, so Dom and Lily kindly offered to show us round." I dug Reuben in the ribs.

"Oh, yeah," he said solemnly. "Great school."

"Wow, is that the time!" said Lola. "We'd better get moving."

But somehow nice harmless Mr Lamb had got between us and the door. "Sorry kids," he said in his child-friendly voice. "You know the rules. No-one enters or leaves a Phoenix School unless we've checked your ID. You'll have to come with me."

I saw genuine terror flicker across Dom's face. What could possibly be scaring him so badly? I wondered. We obediently trailed after the teacher.

Lola pulled a face at me. "I feel totally naked."

"You feel naked," Reuben muttered. "I've got major stage fright. I can't believe humans can actually *see* me!"

I wondered if materialising without permission was still a cosmic offence, if you did it by mistake. I mean, we hadn't actually blown our divine cover or anything.

Then we went through the door into the school grounds, and everything else went clean out of my head as Lola went, "Ohhh."

The sun was setting, bathing everything in its warm peachy light. Kids in stylish casuals flitted about the campus, chatting, laughing and generally being kids.

Lovely music drifted from windows. Several pupils were practising martial arts under the trees. Every child had that special glow I'd noticed in Dom and his mates.

I think Reuben had forgotten about his stage fright because his eyes shone with excitement. "Lollie's right! These humans are *way* more evolved. They've totally grown out of that primitive war stage. Now they're producing beautiful genius kids. It's literally Heaven on Earth!"

It all sounded so tempting, and you have *no* idea how much I wanted to believe him. But like Mr Allbright says, we should always listen to our angel intuition, and mine just wasn't convinced. Look closer, Mel, it insisted. What's wrong with this picture?

Take the teacher. He knew what Dom had been up to, I was sure of it. OK, he hadn't actually sussed we were angels, but he'd definitely twigged we weren't from their time-zone. So why was he stringing us along, as if he'd genuinely swallowed our story?

Mr Lamb took us into a building so perfect that I could not believe it was a school. There was the sweetest indoor garden with a little Zen fountain and shells and coloured gravel, plus they'd hung the kids' artwork everywhere, not Blutacked any old how, but beautifully framed, as if the teachers actually valued it. The school even *smelled* lovely.

I was wrong about this place, I thought dreamily. This really is Heaven on Earth.

Then I saw the retina scanner and my heart dropped into my trainers. As you probably guessed, we don't do retina scans in Heaven.

We had to take turns to stand in front of the machine, trying not to blink, while eerie blue lights sizzled and flashed, like those evil flykiller thingies they have in chip shops.

Not surprisingly the scan showed that my mates and I had no official existence in the twenty-third century.

The teacher vanished into an office and I heard him talking softly on the phone. "Definitely not from this era. Of course. Yes, I'll hold on to them until the authorities get here."

And like a tiny candle flame, my vision of a peaceful harmonious future gave a last sad little flicker and blew out.

Mr Lamb reappeared. "Sorry about this kids," he said in his jolly TV presenter voice. "But until we sort out this little mix-up, we'll have to keep you here, I'm afraid."

He wagged his finger at Dom and Lily. "And you two have a class to go to!"

Dom looked desperately strained. "Bye, you guys," he said feebly.

But the Mr Nice Guy act was obviously for Dom and Lily's beneft, because the minute the kids disappeared, he hustled us upstairs and shoved us into an empty classroom. "I don't know who you are," he snapped. "But believe me, I'm going to find out!" And his tone was pure menace.

The door slammed and I heard an ominous clunk as he locked us in.

I looked miserably around the room. With its pastel pink walls and teeny tiny furniture it looked almost exactly like Miss Dove's angel nursery class. But somehow that only made our situation more depressing.

"Still think it's Heaven on Earth?" I said in a sour voice.

"Sorry," Reuben said humbly. "I got a bit starry-eyed, didn't I."

He looked so forlorn that I felt really ashamed of myself.

"It's OK, Reubs," I said quickly. "You'll get the hang of it."

"Yeah, don't beat yourself up, Sweetpea," said Lola. "I lived on this gorgeous planet for thirteen years and I have NO idea what's going on at this school."

"Me neither," I admitted. "It looks perfect. But something's just that little bit off."

"Totally," said Reuben. "But what? None of this makes sense."

Lola sighed. "It looks like the cosmic musketeers are seriously out of their depth this time."

"We'd better call up the Agency," said Reuben gloomily. "Get them to beam us home."

We fished out our angel tags, centred ourselves and tried to connect with the Link. We waited patiently. But nothing happened. No cosmic tingles. No answering heavenly vibe. Nothing.

"I hate to depress you," said Reuben, "but I think that device demagnetised our tags."

My stomach gave a lurch. "You're kidding!"

Lola sounded scared. "But we can still get out of here? We can still dematerialise?"

"Sure we can," I said bravely. "We're angels, right?"

But a quarter of an hour later, we were still 100% visible.

I slumped on to a tiny chair. This nightmare was all my fault.

At the Academy, our teachers are constantly telling us we shouldn't try to be heroes. But had I listened? No, as usual I'd just gone ahead and done my own sweet thing without once thinking of the consequences.

I could tell that Lola was trying to keep calm. She wandered around the classroom, inspecting the work on the walls. "Hey, these babies are doing really cool stuff."

Reuben started doing martial-art stretching exercises. He said it helped him to think. "What did that guy call this school again?" he called over his shoulder.

I wasn't in the mood for giving Earth lessons to be honest. "A Phoenix School," I said wearily. "A phoenix is a mythical bird. When it's old and ready to die, it sets fire to its nest, and a little baby phoenix chick is reborn from the ashes—"

He instantly straightened up. "That's so beautiful!" he breathed. "It's like these genius schools are the new hope born from the destruction of the past."

"Pity about their teacher training," Lola said sarcastically.

"We only met one teacher," Reuben pointed out. "The others might be total saints."

"So why are we getting these weird vibes—" I began.

But just then we heard something scrape against the window.

A ladder appeared. Its top rungs waved about wildly, then came to rest against the glass.

Voices drifted up from below. "They came out of nowhere!" Dom was explaining excitedly, and Lily grumbled something I couldn't catch. "I told you, I'll sort it," said a male voice.

I stiffened. I'd heard that voice before.

The ladder grated against the glass as someone started climbing up. "You'll have to open it from inside," called the voice.

I felt myself go dizzy. *It can't be.*

It was like a bad dream. I tried to scream a warning, but my vocal cords were paralysed. I couldn't even move, just watched helplessly as Reuben ran to flip the catch.

The glass slid back and a boy appeared outside the window.

His eyes were as beautiful as I remembered. Beautiful and totally empty. "Hi, Melanie, how's it going?" he said smoothly.

It was Brice.

Chapter Eight

Reuben instantly went into a defensive martial-arts stance, but Brice totally didn't take any notice. He jumped down into the room, his face carefully blank like a gymnast bringing off a tricky dismount.

"The ladder seems OK, so you shouldn't have any problems," he said. "I'm not saying it's great or anything. It's probably better not to make any sudden moves."

Apart from his twenty-third century casuals, my deadly enemy looked just the same, the exact double of a boy I once had this hopeless crush on. The PODS adore having this kind of humiliating info about people. It gives them a major power rush.

I realised he was avoiding my eyes. In fact if it

was anyone but Brice I'd have said he was nervous, rabbiting on like he was our special best friend.

"Hope you don't mind heights, Sanchez," he said.

"I'm an angel, moron," Lola snapped. "Air is my natural element."

"How are you with heights incidentally?" I asked sarkily. "Now that you're a – oh, what is the correct term for a fallen angel these days?" I asked my mates. "A former angel? An ex-angel?"

For the first time I saw a flash of the old Brice. "Cut this angel garbage," he snarled. "Just climb down the ladder and get out of my life."

No-one moved. It wasn't that we were defying him, more that this whole situation was too weird. None of us knew how to handle it.

He flung up his hands. "Fine! Stay here! But I don't think you're going to like what happens next. Future science labs, weird tests."

Lola looked disgusted. "Oh, please! Like you'd actually care. I can't believe you're daring to show your face after what you did."

"Yeah, why would you help us?" I said disbelievingly.

He gave his cold laugh. "I don't give a monkey's about you, darling. It's Dom I care about."

"Yeah right!" I snorted. The idea of Brice caring for someone was just bizarre.

"Will you guys just get a move on?" Dom called hoarsely.

To my astonishment Reuben shrugged. "Well, we obviously can't stay here. I say we take a chance."

Lola was scandalised. "Are you nuts? How do we know he hasn't got some gruesome little PODS posse down there?"

Brice gave her a nasty grin. "I guess you'll just have to trust me!"

But when we reached the ground, we only found Dom and Lily waiting. Dom was still agitated about something. I heard him whispering to Brice.

"I'll look after it, mate, if you're worried," Brice offered.

Omigosh, I thought. Things were getting worse by the second. My mates and I gave each other helpless glances, as Dom handed the time device to our cosmic enemy.

"Now let's see if you can keep the school rules till bedtime, eh Dom?" Brice gave Dom's arm an affectionate biff.

"Dave's always getting me out of trouble," Dom explained bashfully. "He's like my guardian angel."

There was a stunned silence.

Reuben recovered first. "That's erm, great," he said a little too brightly "Everyone needs a guardian angel. Right, *Dave*?"

"Right," said Brice, looking incredibly uncomfortable.

When Dom and Lily had gone, Brice let out a sigh of relief. "It's cool. He has no idea who you are."

"He certainly doesn't know who *you* are!" I snorted. "So what's a bright kid like Dom doing mixed up with a jerk like you?"

Lola's lip curled. "Maybe Brice is like, grooming him to be his evil successor."

The air practically crackled with tension. I genuinely thought Brice was going to hit her. Reuben quickly put himself between them.

Brice was so furious he could hardly get the words out. "You kids are all so freaking morally superior! Even when you have *no* idea what you're talking about."

She shrugged. "Oh, please, put us right, *hombre*. We're hanging on your every word."

"It will be my pleasure," he spat.

We didn't exactly have a choice. Normally nothing would induce us to hang out with Brice. But as you know, he had the time device, so where he went, we had to follow.

He led us through the beautifully kept grounds to one of the dorms. A little kid spotted us. "Hey who are you?" he yelled.

"Oh, we're ange—" Reuben began eagerly.

"Shut up!" Brice shoved him roughly through the door.

We followed him up a flight of stairs to a large open-plan kitchen. It was a really homey space with sofas and a massive blackboard. I suppose that was in case a young genius felt the need to solve a mathematical equation while he was heating his baked beans.

Someone was practicing a cello in one of the upstairs rooms. It sounded beautiful yet tragic, you know how they do. All at once I felt horribly depressed. It had just dawned on me that I had screwed up a major celestial mission.

I found myself compulsively listing my latest cosmic boo-boos, and there were quite a few. Materialising without permission, stranding my mates in the distant future, damaging Agency property (our platinum tags); damaging them so badly in fact, that we couldn't even let the Agency know where we were.

Worst of all, we'd just watched like lemons as Dom handed a dangerous time device to the PODS' favourite messenger boy.

Miss Rowntree was right, I thought bleakly. I'm just an airhead with attitude.

I didn't know what else to do, so I went to gaze out of the window.

A set of tail-lights were moving slowly along a tree-lined avenue. In the distance I could see a gorgeous house, ghostly pale in the twilight. The kind of house I'd once dreamed of buying my mum, when I was rich and famous. Though of course, as it turned out, I didn't live long enough to be either.

A jeering voice cut through my thoughts. "Well, kiddiwinks, are you ready to be shocked out of your tiny angel minds?"

I could see Brice's reflection in the glass. He was doing his cosmic outlaw pose; thumbs in belt-loops, mean expression.

A terrible tiredness came over me. "You can always try," I said wearily.

"Then sit down," he said. "This could take a while."

And Brice started to tell us a story so horrifying, that it might almost be true.

CHAPTER NINE

"Once upon a time I was a human being." Brice sounded coldly chatty, like nothing he was saying actually mattered. "And sorry, Mel, I didn't live in the distant past, as you'd like to believe."

"You lived in this century, didn't you?" said Reuben softly.

"Correct, angel boy. This was my little personal slot in time. This school was also my school. And Dominic de Winter, amateur time-tours operator – well, he was my little brother."

I think I actually gasped. But Brice was still talking.

"Dom was just three when I died. And before you ask, he has no idea we're related. He doesn't remember he even had a brother. A little magic trick of mine."

I was horrified. "Didn't your parents tell him?"

Brice's eyes glittered. "Dad was out of the picture by this time. As for Mum, well, better not get me started on her."

The cello was still sobbing away overhead and frankly I wished whoever was playing would just knock it off. Things were already tense enough.

Brice took a breath. "Everyone uses that word 'family', like we're all talking about the same thing. But my family is truly unique. Oh, on the surface, we're incredibly civilised, darlings. But underneath – oh man, it's like swimming with crocodiles."

He laughed. "Yeah, crocodiles is about right. In the days before war was banned, you'd always find a de Winter lurking at the bottom of the pond, making a stonking profit. No matter which country lost or won, the de Winters made a killing. They'd buy and sell anything. Guns, bombs, planes, medicines, artificial limbs, human beings..."

Brice watched dreamily as several sets of tail-lights went glimmering slowly up the avenue towards the house. I counted five – no, six vehicles. They must be having a party, I thought vaguely.

"Isn't it funny how each kid always thinks he'll be different?" Brice said. "They see their parents screw up and they say, 'Uh-uh, not me! I'm better than that. I'm going to change the world.'"

"Some of them do," Lola pointed out.

"Oh spare me," he said. "Aren't you guys ever off duty?"

Lola's eyes were steely. "I don't know. Are you?"

"Just let the guy talk," Reuben told her.

Brice was still watching the cars. "But Dom really was different," he said softly. "I saw that right from the start. The kind of kid Phoenix schools were invented for. Bright, sensitive, totally magic."

The cello stopped abruptly. A door banged overhead and a small boy came flying down the stairs, lugging an instrument case practically twice his size.

Brice waited until the baby cellist was out of earshot.

"Don't laugh, but when Dom was born, I actually thought I was getting a chance to make up for all the bad stuff I'd done. I made this ridiculous promise to myself. I was going to save my little baby bro from our evil reptile rellies." Brice laughed. "But like I said, I died.

"But here's the really hilarious part, you guys. It turned out I'd been talent-spotted by someone at the Agency who decided I'd make an absolutely super angel!"

He blew out his breath. "Woo! Talk about culture shock! No blackmail, no lies, no undercover thuggery. Just never-ending bliss."

Brice's voice grew softly intimate. "It feels so safe in the Heavenly City, doesn't it, Mel? Like nothing could ever hurt you?"

I felt my skin begin to creep. I hated the thought of Brice going anywhere near my favourite heavenly hang-outs.

He was talking as if it was just the two of us alone together. "At nights I'd lie in my narrow little bed in the Academy dorm, listening to that cosmic lullaby you like so much, Melanie. The humming-top music?"

I went bright red. Brice loves to make out that he has this private window into my mind.

"It's OK, sweetheart," he jeered. "Your lullaby never did it for me. I was far too worried imagining what my family was doing to Dom."

He started pacing. "Oh, Michael gave me all the usual guff about how no-one's ever really alone on Earth. And I'm thinking, well I was on Earth for fifteen freaking years and you never helped me. And I'm supposed to trust you with my baby brother!"

He was back at the window now, staring out at the house. "Anyway, why would the Agency help a de Winter kid, a bad seed? It didn't make sense."

Something about Brice's life story must have really got under my skin, because to my annoyance my eyes went all blurry with tears.

Will you get a grip, Melanie, I snuffled to myself. You're supposed to be thinking up a plan to get the time device away from this creep, not sympathising with his lousy childhood.

Luckily my soul-mate is made of sterner stuff. "OK, we've heard your tragic story," she said in a bored voice. "What's your point?"

Brice whirled round. "What's my *point*! To educate you, Sanchez. I'm giving you brats a free reality lesson."

"Yeah, right," Lola snorted. "Like you're the only person who ever suffered."

"Stop it," said Reuben. "Stop it right now. Can't you see this is just what they want?"

Our angel buddy didn't even raise his voice, yet it went right through me like a bell. Everyone shut up, even Brice.

"Better," said Reuben calmly, and he nodded towards the window. "Now Brice can tell us what's going on up at the house."

"Oh, that," Brice said in a careless voice. "My evil rellies are having a get-together."

"Like a party, you mean?" I said.

"You have no idea how big my family is, have you? No, I'm not boasting, Sanchez," he added, seeing Lola's scathing expression. "I'm trying to explain that this is not some small local nightmare you've stumbled into. Oh, no. It's global, baby. The cars you saw just now? They're just the latecomers. Guests have been arriving from all over the world for days."

"OK, so your family has flash parties," Lola began but he totally ignored her.

"That house with its oh-so-distressing vibes belongs to my uncle, Jonas de Winter. Didn't you realise? He's the Phoenix school headmaster."

My mouth completely turned to cotton wool. *What's wrong with this picture*, I'd asked. Now I knew.

Omigosh, I thought. It wasn't the school which was radiating confusing signals. It was my lovely dream house.

Brice gave a terrible laugh. "You've got to hand it to the de Winters. We're adaptable. War is out. Peace is in. Hey, let's take over a Phoenix school and use it as cover for our less respectable activities."

Lola frowned. "So why the party?"

He looked surprised. "To celebrate Dom's achievement, of course."

"Huh?" Lola and I stared at him.

"Oh, do try to keep up, you guys!" said Reuben impatiently. "Dom reinvented the time device. Didn't you figure that out yet?"

I stared at him. "But he's just a kid."

"A Phoenix kid," he said. "A boy genius."

It seemed that de Winter scientists had been trying to reconstruct the device for decades. Finally they were almost there, but there was one tiny detail they simply couldn't figure out.

Then Dom won a major science prize and the Family were over the moon. Maybe little Dom could succeed where the scientists had failed. Someone "accidentally" left the relevant research material at Dom's mum's place, where he was bound to find it in the holidays. Then they sat back and waited. They didn't have to wait long.

"Dom knocks a prototype together in like, a weekend, but my little brother is this total innocent. He has absolutely *no* idea what he's got himself into! So what does he do with this world-shattering invention?" Brice looked as if he didn't know whether to laugh or cry.

"He runs a time-tour scam for his mates?" I suggested.

Brice made an impatient gesture. "The little idiot could have got himself killed, but do you think Mum and the rest of them care? No, they just want to know if the thing actually works. So they simply look the other way and *let* him take all these stupid risks."

"Can't someone stop them?" I asked.

"No-one stops the de Winters, believe me. Oh, sure they're human. Just. If you stick pins in them, they bleed. When their hearts stop, they snuff it. But there's always another de Winter to take their place."

"But the government—" I objected feebly.

He shook his head. "The government has no idea they're there. The de Winters are masters at camouflaging their activities. It's an art form, how they operate. They suck people in so gradually they don't even notice it happening. A well-timed reward here, a little painful pressure there, until they own you body and soul."

"They'll never own Dom," I said fiercely.

"They'll never own Dom," he mimicked. 'Don't make me laugh. They'd have got him years ago, if it wasn't for me."

"So how come you were allowed back to these times to keep an eye on your brother?" said Reuben.

There was an electric pause, then Brice said lightly, "Oh, the er, usual deal."

"You made a deal with the Agency?" I was shocked.

Lola shook her head. "He sold his soul, Boo. To the PODS."

Brice shrugged. "You know the great thing about the Dark Powers. They keep things simple. They don't give a monkey's about your morals or motives. It's a straightforward trade. I do them favours. They let me keep an eye on Dom."

"Now tell us the bad thing about the PODS," Reuben said softly.

The question seemed to take Brice by surprise. I saw a tiny muscle move in his cheek. "I told you, they're cool. Anyway, I'm a big boy. I can handle it."

We just waited. Eventually he said, "The worst thing is when they won't let me see Dom. Last time they didn't let me near him for months. You saw what he got up to then."

"That's when he re-invented the time device, right?" I said.

"Do you blame him?" said Brice angrily. "He was in our mother's house for a whole summer. He was lonely as hell."

"How do we know this isn't one of your sick little games?" Lola said suddenly. "Like, 'Oh I'll make the angels believe my sad story, then catch them off-guard and totally trash them'."

"I don't really care what you think, darling," drawled Brice. "I know why I'm here, that's all that matters."

Reuben's voice was quiet. "I believe him."

Lola was horrified. "After what he did to you in London!"

"Like I said," he repeated firmly, "I believe him."

Sometimes pure angels take your breath away. After all Brice had done to him, our buddy was still willing to give him another chance.

But the weird thing is, I thought Reuben was right.

For the first time Brice made a warped kind of sense. He wasn't just some evil cosmic joker delighting in chaos. He actually loved someone. He loved his brother like I loved my sister Jade. But unlike me, he didn't trust anyone else to keep his brother safe.

Brice only trusted one person. Brice.

The atmosphere in the room had totally morphed. I think even Lola was on the verge of giving our old enemy the benefit of the doubt. And perhaps our expressions had changed or something, because Brice's face suddenly shut like a trap.

"OK, the freak show's over. Now flutter off back to Heaven where everything is pretty and nothing hurts."

"But I thought you—" My voice trailed off.

"You thought I wanted your help!" Brice's face twisted. "Don't make me laugh! I've taken care of Dom all his life and I don't need a bunch of little angels getting in my hair. You've got him into enough trouble as it is. So just shove off."

A door slammed and a desperate voice yelled, "Dave? Dave, are you there?"

Dave? I thought dimly. Who's he? Then I remembered that bad-boy Brice was currently posing as good-guy Dave.

Lily came charging upstairs. She'd gone so white that all her freckles were standing out like braille. She could hardly get the words out for crying. "I'm so scared," she gasped at last. "They've got Dom."

Brice looked as if he might be sick with shock. "What do you mean?"

"They know what he's been up to..." Lily babbled.

I knew instantly who she meant by "they". The de Winters.

"... about the device and everything. They said he had to hand it over. Dom said he had no idea what they were on about. I totally lost it, Dave. I said I saw him give it to you, so they sent me to find you. I've been looking everywhere!"

In other circumstances I'd have been sorry for her, but I'd gone completely cold inside. I backed away from Brice in horror. We'd been such *idiots*. Brice didn't love Dom. He didn't give a stuff about anyone and he never had. He'd been working for the PODS all along.

"You evil jerk!" I was in tears of fury. "I can't believe even you would stoop so low. You actually betrayed your own brother!"

Chapter Ten

To my astonishment, Brice just stood there, taking all my contempt and hatred like he thought he totally deserved it. It was weirdly dignified somehow, and I have to admit it kind of took the wind out of my sails.

He waited until I'd finally run out of abuse, then said, "Go back to the house, Lily. Tell them I'll bring the device."

"You hate me, don't you?" she said miserably. "I don't blame you. I really hate myself. But they said they'd hurt him and they meant it too. I've never seen Mr de Winter like that before. He always seemed so—"

"You don't need to explain, believe me," Brice interrupted. "You did the right thing. Now run back to Mr de Winter, and give him my message, OK?"

But Lily hovered, looking anxious. "Dave," she blurted out, "why did she say you were Dom's brother?"

"Oh, Mel's just a bit confused," Brice said smoothly. "Time-travel scrambles people's brain cells sometimes."

I glowered at him. But Lily seemed reassured by this explanation. She rushed downstairs and a few seconds later I saw a little figure go racing through the dusk.

"You can't do this, Brice," said Reuben in a low voice. "These people have been feeding off human misery for centuries."

I clenched my fists. "Yeah, and now he's going to hand them history on a plate, so they can rip off everyone they missed first time around."

"You don't know that for certain," Lola said softly.

I shot her a betrayed look. I couldn't believe she was standing up for Brice. I was *so* upset. It wasn't just Brice. It was everything.

I remembered how I'd felt when I heard the bird singing outside the summerhouse. Humans had so nearly got their act together, but they just had to mess it up, didn't they?

I mean, what's the use of creating Heaven on Earth, if you don't take proper care of it? What's the use of schools for genius kids, if you let an evil family like the de Winters exploit them for their own sinister ends? They didn't ban war at all, I thought miserably. The suffering is still going on. Like Brice said, it's just out of sight.

I buried my face in my hands.

Brice's voice was unusually tender. "You're wrong about me, Mel," he said. "I might be a jerk and a creep, but I'd never betray Dominic. I'm trying to save him, and I will. He's got something they want, something they'll do anything to get, even if it means letting Dom leave the Family."

"You're crazy," I said in a muffled voice. "These guys bamboozle whole governments. They're not exactly going to play fair with a kid."

"They will. If you help me," he said hesitantly.

"Erm, excuse me," objected Lola. "'Buzz off,' you said. 'I can take care of Dom by myself,' you said. 'You angel brats are so freaking superior,' you said."

Brice rolled his eyes. "Give me a break, Sanchez. I can't be seen in that house. They'll know who I am."

"How come?" I said.

"My mum's there, isn't she? She may not be the best mum in the world but even she'd recognise her deceased eldest son."

I stared at him. "You mean that's your *real* face?" The words were out before I could stop them and I felt my face burn with embarrassment.

I'd naturally assumed that Brice had disguised himself as my bad-boy crush, purely to humiliate me. It never occurred to me this was how he actually *looked* in his lifetime.

Suddenly Brice grabbed my arm. His energy felt weird, kind of comfortingly familiar and terrifyingly alien all at the same time. His eyes blazed. "Say you'll help me?"

"Hey," said Lola angrily. "Let her go, creep!"

I felt Brice press something into my hand. "Mel, your job is to look after humans, not save history," he said. "History's just an idea. My brother's real."

And he'd gone.

I uncurled my fingers and found a wafer-thin piece of plastic, about the size of a regular KitKat. Brice had given me the time device.

We looked at each other helplessly. I'm pretty sure we were all thinking the same thing. If we'd been human, all our troubles would be over. Unfortunately we were angels on a cosmic mission.

"I can't *believe* he did that," Lola wailed. "That was so sneaky. It's our one chance to get back home, and he knows we can't use it."

For once, I disagreed with Lola. I had the feeling Brice had acted completely spontaneously. It was like he'd trusted us to do the right thing.

"So now what?" said Lola.

Reuben gave her a serene smile. "I guess we do what he says."

Lola looked appalled. "Give the device to the evil de Winters! Are you crazy!"

A strange calm flowed into me, a welcome sign that my angel intuition had totally kicked in. "He's right," I said. "Come on guys, we're going to a party!"

We crept down the drive to the headmaster's house, carefully keeping in the shadows.

But as we got closer to the house, a terrible tiredness came over me. Like, what *is* the point. There was no way we could do this alone – and no matter what anyone said, we were *totally* alone. With our tags out of action, we couldn't even call home for back-up. If the Agency really cared about us, they wouldn't put us through this, I thought miserably. It's simply too much responsibility. We're just kids. We're not even properly trained yet.

By this time, it was an effort just to keep walking. It felt as if I had invisible stones in my pockets weighing me down.

Suddenly Lola whispered, "Anyone else getting a PODS vibe?"

Reuben pulled a face. "Just a bit."

Lola gave a low chuckle. "Phew! What a relief! Thought I was having a major crack-up there for a while!"

Honestly, what would you do without your mates? My depression vanished like magic.

"I'm so embarrassed," I hissed. "I can't believe I fell for that old doom 'n despair routine!"

"Me neither. I suppose we should have expected it," whispered Lola. "The de Winters might be human, but they've been in cahoots with the PODS since history began. This place must be saturated with evil vibes."

"It is. You can feel it." Reuben tapped his solar plexus. "But it's so pretty, you think you're imagining it."

We had almost reached the house. The atmosphere was incredibly foul. Lola said it was like wading through evil cosmic treacle, but frankly I don't think there are any words to describe it. Normally in a situation like this, we'd use our tags to access extra angelic protection through the Link. Unfortunately this was not an option.

The house was ablaze with light. No-one had drawn the curtains, so we could see right into the downstairs rooms. It was the most luxurious place I have ever seen, like a celebrity's house from a twenty-third century *Hello!*.

We slipped through a side entrance and crept stealthily up a velvety carpeted corridor. I heard soft chinks of crockery and a subdued murmur of voices.

Passing an open door, I saw staff in uniforms bustling around a vast dining room, smoothing crisp tablecloths, buffing up silver and twitching at gorgeous flower arrangements, making everything perfect for the big party.

It was all so beautiful, yet I just wanted to bolt out of that house and never come back.

My mates obviously felt the same way, because at the same moment they grabbed hold of my hands.

"Oh that is *so* touching," said a mocking voice in my ear. "Excuse me while I puke."

Brice hadn't gone away after all. He'd just made himself invisible.

"Are you trying to give me heart failure?" I snapped. "What are you doing here, anyway?"

"You don't seriously think I'd trust my brother to a bunch of little halo polishers?" Brice inquired.

I was completely confused. "But you said your family would see you."

"Get a grip, Melanie. I said I couldn't let myself be *seen*. Hey, my people might run with the PODS, but they don't interact with the dead, sweetheart."

"So if you're here, why do you need us?" hissed Lola.

"I told you, Sanchez. We're going to save Dom. My way."

You can't exactly glare at someone who's invisible, so I had to resort to sarcasm. "You ooze charm, don't you," I said in disgust.

"Oh, he definitely oozes," said Lola. "But charm? I don't think so."

"Will you just give the guy a break?" sighed Reuben.

"Hey, buddy, I can stand up for myself, you know!" objected Brice's disembodied voice.

This was definitely the weirdest situation of my short angel career.

OK, so I still haven't quite finished reading *The Angel Handbook*, but I'll bet good money it doesn't say anything about the forces of light actively like, co-operating with the forces of darkness! But what choice did we have?

Exactly!

So following Brice's whispered directions, we found our way to the foot of a seriously majestic staircase. It was just like the ones people dance down in old musicals and my mum would have totally adored it.

Crouching on the bottom stair, looking more like orphan Annie than ever, was Lily. She sprang up in a panic. "Where's Dave?"

"He got held up," I said hastily. "Don't worry, we've got the device."

Poor Lily almost fainted with relief.

We followed her up the stairs.

As we reached the first floor, some beautifully dressed little kids went scampering happily across the landing and out of sight.

Peals of laughter came from one of the rooms. I could hear a hum of cultured voices as the international de Winters made small talk in all the major European languages.

Brice prodded me unpleasantly in the ribs.

"Hey, no physical contact, OK?" I hissed.

"Stop being coy, darling, and look through that door," he hissed back. "There's someone I want you to see."

A woman sat with her back to us. I could see her upswept hair, long suntanned legs and an elegant hand gesturing as she talked. Wafts of expensive perfume drifted my way.

She looked amazingly stylish, yet even without my agency shades, I knew there was something alarmingly wrong with this woman's energy field. She's like this house, I thought. Lovely to look at. Totally deadly inside.

Brice sounded amused. "That's Laura de Winter," he said. "She's my mother."

I had the horrible feeling he'd just read my mind. "Oh," I said, "She's erm, really…"

"Toxic?" he suggested. "Dad certainly thought so."

"Oh yeah, and what was he like?" I burbled, desperately trying to cover my embarrassment.

"I have no idea. I hardly knew him. He was a scientist. A brilliant one apparently. The Family hired him to solve the time-device problem. They wanted to keep him keen, so they married him to Mum."

"You're kidding," I breathed.

"Time goes by, Dad earns the Family's trust, blah blah blah. They leak vital info about their dodgier activities. Dad doesn't like what he hears and unwisely makes no attempt to hide his feelings. The de Winters decide he's failed the Family loyalty test, so obviously he has to go."

I gasped. "They *killed* him?"

"Good as. They faked a big scandal and Dad mysteriously disappeared. It happened just before I died. Dom doesn't know a thing about it."

"Well, I think your dad sounds great," I said. "He totally stood up for his principles."

"And a lot of good it did him," Brice said bitterly.

I started spinning romantic fantasies of reuniting Dom with his scientist dad. "Do you know where he is?" I asked.

"Will you just drop it?" Brice snapped. "The guy's a loser. He works nights in some freaking laundry or something. Only the evil survive, haven't you figured that out by now?"

I felt a flicker of pity. So that's why Brice has such a warped attitude, I thought. He's scared to join the good guys, in case he ends up like his dad.

I saw my mates waiting at the end of the corridor and hurried to catch them up.

"Where did you get to?" Reuben complained.

"She's fraternising with the enemy," said Brice.

"You wish," I told him under my breath.

Lily was tapping at an ornate panelled door.

A cultured voice called, "Come!"

We followed Lily into an imposing boardroom.

I vaguely noticed drapy curtains with ties of floppy gold rope, and a long table of dark wood, polished so brightly it looked exactly like glass. Around it sat maybe fifteen or twenty people, presumably key members of the de Winter family.

They were all of different ages and races, but their hungry expressions were identical. Like they were just about to get what they wanted most for Christmas.

"Well, now," said the same beautifully cultured voice. "This is a delightful surprise."

"My uncle Jonas," Brice hissed in my ear.

"Do you have to stand so close?" I muttered.

Then I saw Jonas de Winter and almost fainted. No wonder Dom had been so gobsmacked when he saw that medieval slave merchant. Jonas was like the medieval guy's total twin! It was just like Lola said – these gangsters had been causing mayhem since the dawn of history.

Dom stood beside his uncle, looking defiant.

The door opened again and his mother swept in, in a gale of lovely perfume. "Oh, these must be Dom's little time-travellers!" she gushed. "What time do they come from again, Dominic?"

"You tell me, Mother," he muttered. "Since you know so much."

I felt Brice's breath tickle my ear. "OK, darling, you're on. This is your big moment. Just say exactly what I tell you."

I felt unpleasantly like a PODS glove puppet, but I obediently said my lines: "We've brought the device, but we're not handing it over until we're convinced that Dominic is free to go."

Unfortunately, I don't think I was very impressive because all the de Winters broke into tolerant smiles, like I was a little kid just playing at being grown-up.

"Free to go," repeated Dom's mother in a wondering tone. "But of course Dominic is free to go. What do you think we are, dear? Monsters?"

Jonas de Winter smiled. "Dom is free to leave this house any time he likes." He slung a casual arm around his nephew, and it was like a creepy action replay of the merchant with Stephen. "Just out of curiousity, dear boy," he said casually. "Where *will* you go?"

Dom's next words blew everyone away, including Brice.

"I'd like to go and live with my dad," he said stiffly.

The atmosphere instantly dropped way below zero.

Laura de Winter's beautiful face tightened like a mask. "Dominic, dear, I'm afraid you're a little confused," she said coldly. "Your father is dead, you know that."

He looked disgusted. "You people are unbelievable. Did you seriously think I'd never find out about Dad?"

Omigosh, I thought. Maybe little Dom isn't quite so helpless as everyone thought.

There was a stunned silence.

"Well," said Jonas de Winter. "If that's the case, of course you must go to be with your father. We understand perfectly, don't we, Laura?" And he totally released Dom from his embrace. He actually held his hands in the air so we could see he wasn't holding Dom against his will.

Dom strolled casually over to our side of the table. He was acting dead cool, but I could see he was trembling with strain.

Jonas beamed at us. "You see! All very civilised. But civilisation works both ways, my dears, so now you must keep your side of the bargain."

"Give them the device and get Dom out of here," Brice hissed.

I stared wildly round the room, trying to think of something, anything, which would get us out of this nightmare.

"Just *do* it, Melanie!" Brice threatened in my ear. "You're supposed to be saving Dom, remember?"

I will, I will, I thought. Just as soon as I figure out how.

Because no matter what Brice said, I knew I couldn't do it his way.

Just think about it. Generations of evil de Winters snaking in and out of eternity, buying and selling human lives, wrecking my lovely blue-green planet. And I'm supposed to trust these characters with the sacred keys of history? I don't *think* so!

If only our tags were still working, I thought desperately. We could send for Agency back-up, then we'd get these people sorted, no problem.

Then clear as day, I heard a voice inside my head.

It wasn't Michael or Mr Allbright. It wasn't anyone celestial, funnily enough. It was Des, my down-to-earth step-dad. I could actually see him, in my mind's eye. He was sitting in his favourite armchair and he was smiling at me. "Melanie," he said earnestly. "If you can't make it, then you've just got to fake it, girl."

I felt a prickle of excitement. My step-dad could have a point. Wasn't Mr Allbright always saying that imagination was a genuine angelic power? Then why not use it? If I tried to *imagine* I still had my personal hotline to the Agency, maybe it would come true?

Well, it was worth a shot. I felt furtively for my damaged tags.

"Excuse me you guys, if you're listening," I said silently. "We're trapped somewhere in the twenty-third century and we have a major problem. We've got to stop the de Winters wrecking history but we totally don't want to sacrifice this really great kid, Dominic. Please help us ASAP."

Did I feel a genuine tingle of angel electricity then, or was I just so desperate I wanted to believe it?

Jonas de Winter's voice was as soft as ever. "The device, if you please."

I made a major production out of it, slowly groping inside the wrong pocket of my jacket, then exploring the pockets of my jeans.

"Don't screw up now, sweetheart," Brice warned. "My brother's life is on the line here."

"So no pressure then," I muttered.

The headmaster's smile was becoming a little fixed. "I hope you aren't playing games with me, young lady."

My heart sank. I knew we'd finally run out of time. And not knowing what else to do, I miserably held out the device.

"Just push it across the table," he coaxed. "That's it, nice and easy. No sudden moves."

In agonising slow-mo I laid it on the table, and felt a collective quiver of excitement go through the de Winters.

My mates and I watched, hypnotised, as Jonas de Winter reached out.

I felt numb with horror. By the time this evil family had finished ransacking the past, Earth's future would be totally in their hands.

And it very nearly was. But then, unbelievably, Dom's mother broke the spell.

"You silly boy," she snapped. "You could have had everything, yet you gave it all up to be with that fool."

Dom went white with rage. Before anyone could stop him, he snatched up the device, frantically pressing keypads.

I heard Brice give a hiss of pure surprise.

Scribbles of neon light appeared in mid air.

The de Winters looked oddly fascinated. But under their studied calm, it was obvious they were terrified.

"NOW!" yelled Reuben.

Angel martial-arts teachers say that when you're in tune with the cosmos, you don't have to think about your moves, you just spring effortlessly into action. And that's exactly what we did.

For the first time in our training, my mates and I used angelic martial-arts skills on humans. Brice invisibly lent a helping hand. Dom and Lily pitched in. There was a brief, incredibly dramatic struggle which I'm happy to say we won.

Just minutes later we had them all neatly tied up with the pretty golden curtain ropes.

I almost cried with relief. Against all the odds and with absolutely *no* back-up, unless you count that inspired advice from my lovely step-dad, we had done it. Impossible as it seemed, we'd saved Dom *and* history!!

Reuben clapped Dom on the back. "Nice work, mate. Now give us that device, before someone really gets hurt."

Dom shook his head. "No way! This is payback time."

Uh-oh, I thought. My mates and I exchanged startled glances.

Dom had a weird sleepwalking expression, as if he couldn't believe this was finally happening.

"You know what I hate about you people?" he said. I saw that he had tears glittering in his eyes. "Your kids are just like cute little pets to you. You buy us expensive clothes, send us to be educated in your special Phoenix schools. And all the time, you're filling our heads with your disgusting lies. I've been on to you for years, Uncle Jonas. And you, Mum. You think you've been watching me, when all the time I've been watching you."

"Dom," I said gently.

"Oh, don't worry, I'm not going to kill them," Dom said earnestly. "I just want them to suffer, the way they've made people suffer for centuries. And now I've come up with the perfect punishment."

He laughed. "You thought it was hilarious, didn't you? Funny little Dom, so naïve, he'd actually use a powerful cosmic device to run some sad little time scam for pocket money. Yeah, right!"

"You little toad!" said Jonas in a startled voice. "You were running scientific trials all along!"

"Correct, Uncle Jonas! I was also getting an excellent education. I saw a boy succeed where the grown-ups had screwed up. In thirteenth-century France I saw a boy inspire thousands of other kids to follow him, not out of fear or for money or because the de Winters yanked their strings. But out of pure love."

"That's highly commendable, dear—" his mother interrupted.

"Just shut up and listen!" Dom yelled. He drew a shaky breath, then went on in a quieter voice, "So I figured, hey, I get it! We really can have Heaven on Earth like everyone says. Except that Stephen made one big mistake. He forgot about the dark side. But I won't do that. I've been watching them operate my whole life. That's why I had to perfect the device, so I can get rid of my family."

"Dom," said Lola. "Maybe, this isn't—"

But Dom wasn't listening. "The only thing is where to send you," he pondered. "Personally I'd love to zap you all back to Marseilles and put you on your own ancestors' slave ships. Poetic justice, don't you think?"

He laughed.

"But then it might be even more fun to zap you forwards, to one of those experimental space colonies they're planning to build in our future. That way, you wouldn't even be contaminating the same planet as the rest of the human race."

I was getting a wee bit concerned at this point, to be honest. Don't get me wrong. I totally sympathised with Dominic's feelings. But as you know, the Agency doesn't exactly encourage violent acts of revenge.

But like all de Winters, once Dom got going, he seemed kind of unstoppable. He pointed to the madly twirling time FX. "See that, you guys? In twenty seconds max, you'll be gone for ever."

"He won't do it," his mother said scornfully. "He's all talk like his father."

Dom's face twisted. I'm not exaggerating, he looked totally desperate. He swung round, deliberately aiming the device at the captives. All the relatives ducked, whimpering with fright. I think that's when we all realised that Dom wasn't playing around. He really meant to do it.

"He's completely out of control," Lola whispered.

Reuben's voice rang out like a bell. "This won't work, Dom! You can't create Paradise by just *deleting* all your enemies, man."

But I knew it had all gone too far. It was like Dom didn't *dare* to stop now. His fingers flickered to the keypad and with no expression whatsoever, he activated the device.

There was a collective flinch of horror. I felt totally helpless. But there was nothing we could do except wait to see what happened next.

Apparently Dom had decided to zap the de Winters to that space station after all, because when they appeared, the new time FX were lovelier and more futuristic than ever. Unbelievably beautiful colours filled the room, but at their core was a light so pure and unearthly, that my eyes filled with tears.

My step-dad's advice had worked. Our Agency back-up had arrived in the nick of time.

The light levels adjusted and Michael stepped into the room, closely followed by several other agents.

He calmly took the device from Dom.

"Reuben's right. This is not the way," he told Dom. "The power to judge and punish does not belong to you. If you really want to change the world, you have to understand that."

Dom looked completely awed. I don't think he had any idea his uncle's boardroom was full of angels. I think he just took them for humans from some wonderful far distant future.

Forgetting that we'd ever been enemies, I whispered eagerly to the invisible Brice, "Isn't this brilliant? You finally kept your promise! You saved Dom!"

At least that's what I was going to say.

But he had silently slipped away. Later it occurred to me that he totally couldn't face Michael.

I noticed Michael watching me with his lovely all-seeing eyes. "Actually, you all saved Dom," he said gravely. "His father is a good influence and now Dom will have his true guardian angel to watch over him. Though the truth is, we never stopped watching over him, you know, Melanie. Not even for a moment."

He seemed to think we could leave it at that, but my mind swirled with unanswered questions. OK, so Dom was safe. But what about Brice? I wanted to ask. Where's *his* happy ending? Is anyone watching over him? Can he break his bargain with the PODS and come back home now that Dom's safe? Or has he just blown it with you guys for all Eternity?

Michael passed his hand lightly over my hair, and I felt about a zillion archangel volts sizzle down my spine. "Go home," he repeated softly. "We'll take care of this from now on."

CHAPTER ELEVEN

A few days later my phone jolted me out of a really deep sleep.

"Melanie speaking," I mumbled.

"Sorry if I woke you," said Michael's amused voice.

I shot up in bed like a rocket. "No problem, I'll be down at the Agency in two ticks," I promised groggily.

I caught sight of myself in the mirror. With my bed hair sticking up all over the place, I looked exactly like a cockatoo.

"Oh, didn't I say? I'm at Guru," he said cheerfully. "I've been at the Agency all night. I thought we could have a chat over breakfast."

I carefully replaced the phone.

Then I registered what he'd said and practically went into orbit, madly throwing on the first clothes which tumbled out of my wardrobe.

"Omigosh, omigosh," I moaned. "I can't believe he wants to see me by myself."

There could only be one explanation for this exclusive invitation.

My cosmic crimes had caught up with me at last. I was going to be reprimanded big-time.

As I walked into Guru, Michael waved from a booth.

"I ordered some rather delicious looking pastries. Hope that's OK?" he said.

But when our food came, I couldn't manage a mouthful, just sat fiddling nervously with my cutlery. My heart was thumping so hard, I was sure Michael must be able to hear it. Why didn't he get it over with and put me out of my misery?

"If it's about the tags, maybe I could just pay the Agency back or something," I blurted out.

Michael looked blank. "The tags?"

"We didn't plan to materialise," I said desperately. "It was an accident."

Michael poured me some freshly squeezed orange juice. "A very useful accident as it turned out," he said serenely.

I was totally bewildered. When was I going to get my ticking off?

"Oh, did you hear the good news?" he added. "Orlando's team saved about fifty of those brave young Crusaders."

I felt a pang of distress. OK, so it was better than nothing, but I'd wanted all the kids to be saved.

Michael gave me one of his looks. "At the Agency, we believe in evolution," he said gently. "So we try to take the long-term view."

I took a sip of juice. I got the definite feeling he was working up to something.

"That's the marvellous thing about Eternity," he said. "There's no need to rush. Forests turn into diamonds. Evil changes into good. Sometimes whole centuries go by before you even begin to see the big picture."

I had a funny feeling we'd moved on from evolution. In fact I thought Michael might actually be answering my questions about Brice, but I wasn't quite sure.

"Erm," I said, "did I do something wrong? Did I break another cosmic law, you know, by co-operating with a fallen…" I'd started playing nervously with my hair, a sure sign I'm stressed.

"No, Melanie," Michael said firmly. "You played your part perfectly."

I stared at him. "Really?"

I thought I might cry with relief.

"Really. So do you think you could help me out with these pastries now? There seem to be rather a lot." Michael sounded so plaintive, that I truly wanted to hug him. Imagine an archangel worrying about his waistline!

"I'd love to," I said truthfully. "It's just, this is a really busy day for me."

He gave me a delighted smile. "Of course, Lola's party."

I stood up to go. "I don't mean to be rude, but after last time, I want everything to be perfect," I explained shyly.

"Just one thing." My heart turned over. Michael sounded deadly serious. "Next time you see a worm hole, please don't feel you have to jump through it. Perhaps you might like to pass that message on to the others?"

Just in time, I saw that his eyes were twinkling. I went weak at the knees. Michael's such a tease sometimes.

Mo caught me up at the door. "Who knows, maybe she'll actually get to open it this time!" He gave me back my parcel.

I slapped his palm. "See you later, yeah?"

"Wouldn't miss it for the world," he beamed.

But as I hurried out into the early morning streets, I don't think I was completely awake. Because for the first time ever, I had this moment of pure clairvoyance, a vision almost, like I was being shown a movie preview of Lola's party.

Everything was going brilliantly. The DJ was cool. The music was hot. Fairy lights twinkled in the trees and I was dancing with my mates under a big fat moon. Any time now, Orlando would step out of the shadows, and tell me what a great job I'd done in the twenty-third century.

But at this moment my soul-mate was boogeying up to me, proudly wearing my present to her.

"Do you really like it, Lollie?" I asked anxiously. "I can take it back, you know."

"Are you kidding!" she said. "This isn't a T-shirt, babe. It's our cosmic mission statement!"

She leaped into the air, giving a cheeky cheerleader twirl as she came down, and for an instant I saw the message glittering on her T-shirt. Two words which for me and Lola, totally sum up what being an angel is all about.

Flying High

Don't miss Mel Beeby's fourth amazing
mission...

calling
the
shots

TIME: 20th Centruy

PLACE: Hollywood

MISSION: Get into showbiz!

REPORT: My first mission as a solo
Guardian Angel and I've got serious stage fright!
It may look exciting in the movies, but life is
dangerous in tinsel town, even for someone as
angelic as me...

www.agentangel.co.uk

Don't miss Mel Beeby's fifth amazing
mission...

fogging over

TIME: 19th Centruy

PLACE: Australia and London

MISSION: Take a trip Down Under!

REPORT: It's a new term, I get to choose our
next assignment and my soul-mate Lola is back in
town! But what's she doing holding hands with
bad boy Brice? And why Australia when I asked
for London?

www.agentangel.co.uk

Don't miss Mel Beeby's fifth amazing
mission...

fighting
fit

TIME: 1st Centruy AD

PLACE: Rome

MISSION: Get into the gladiator Groove!

REPORT: The boy of my dreams, Orlando,
wants a team of angel volunteers to go to
Ancient Rome, so guess who's first in the queue?
Of course I don't reckon on him falling for a cute
girl gladiator when we get there...

www.agentangel.co.uk